John G. Williams

The Adventures of a Seventeen-Year-Old Lad and The Fortunes He Might Have Won

John G. Williams

The Adventures of a Seventeen-Year-Old Lad and The Fortunes He Might Have Won

ISBN/EAN: 9783337266905

Printed in Europe, USA, Canada, Australia, Japan

Cover: Foto ©Andreas Hilbeck / pixelio.de

More available books at **www.hansebooks.com**

JOHN G. WILLIAMS.

THE ADVENTURES

OF

A Seventeen-Year-Old Lad

AND THE

Fortunes He Might Have Won.

By John G. Williams.

BOSTON:
Printed for the Author by The Collins Press.
1894.

TO ALL

My Countrymen

WHO HAVE FELT THE LONGING DESIRE TO VENTURE FORTH INTO THE
WORLD'S WILD PLACES, AND WHOSE HEARTS ARE THRILLED WITH IN-
TEREST AT THE NARRATION OF ADVENTUROUS EXPLOITS; TO
ALL THOSE WHOSE COURSING BLOOD IMPELS THEM EVER
ONWARD, BY PATHS TRODDEN OR BY WAYS
UNKNOWN,— TO SUCH, AND TO ALL
BRAVE SPIRITS, BOTH OLD
AND YOUNG,

THIS WORK IS RESPECTFULLY DEDICATED

BY THE

Author.

PREFACE.

The " Adventures of a Seventeen-Year-Old Lad" is the story of the experience of a young man, who spent the best seventeen years of his life in beating the bush, while others caught the bird. The first chapters relate the first seven years' experience as a sailor on board a whaler, and adventures while travelling in foreign lands and dwelling with cannibals and other savages. The later chapters contain the gold-mining experience of the author in California, Australia, and British Columbia, commencing in the early days of 1849 and continuing until 1858. The work contains several illustrations, showing scenes of interest, and some of the dangerous positions the author was placed in.

The story has been written from memory forty years after the events narrated took place; and in carefully reviewing the stirring experience of the youth, the author has seemed to live the life of his early days over again, and this fact has caused him to realize the importance of an unexaggerated tale of the times described and scenes visited.

It has been the intent to state facts as they happened ; and although some digressions have occurred, they have only been when apparently of interest as of similar character to events passed through, and the author trusts that all who may read his experiences will find material to amply reward them for their time and patience.

While the events narrated are but the adventures and experiences of a young fortune seeker, the pictures are drawn first of that wondrous section of our globe, which can never be so well known as to lose its romantic interest, the broad, mystic Pacific Ocean. With its innumerable islands, its half-clad races, its piratical crafts, its changing mood from terrific storm to protracted calm, this immeasurable expanse of water must ever excite the interest and imagination of the reader.

The mining experience of the author in California was at a time well remembered by older people,—a time when the country was aflame with excitement, every one lending eager attention to the story of fortunes being taken from the earth in California. It was a time which proved a great history-making period for the Pacific slope. To individuals in " the camps " it was a time of great efforts, of privations, and of great rewards. It was the day of the " forty-niner," a character in our history who must ever be surrounded with romance.

The narrative of the author's life in Australia gives insight into a period of early life in that great colony still less understood in this country, and it has been the author's aim to relate everything in such simple language that the reader may easily picture to himself all scenes described.

In his travels the author's motto was always, when applied to himself, " You can, if you will try." Some abler pen might have been employed, but the pen of the author has tried to add some new pictures of life as he has seen it, thus spreading knowledge and giving pleasure to many readers, and preserving pictures of scenes many phases of which have passed forever away.

J. G. W.

CONTENTS.

CHAPTER I.

CHAPTER II.

CHAPTER III.

CHAPTER IV.

CHAPTER V.

CHAPTER VI.

CHAPTER VII.

CHAPTER VIII.

CHAPTER IX.

CHAPTER X.

The Adventures of a Seventeen-Year-Old Lad.

CHAPTER I.

EARLY BOYHOOD — LEAVING THE FARM — THE JOURNEY TO
BOSTON ON HORSEBACK — NOVEL SIGHTS — AN UNPAID
HOTEL BILL — THE JOURNEY AFOOT — ARRIVAL IN BOS-
TON — BECOMES A BAKER'S BOY — SHIPS UPON A WHALER.

IT was in the year 1841 that I packed my gripsack at my father's house, a little hamlet in the backwoods of Canada. I was seventeen years old, and had lived on my father's farm up to that time. Getting enough of farming, chopping wood, clearing land, and such other work as is connected with farming, I concluded that I did not like the business. We had no exciting novels or story books at that time to fill the young heads with a desire to see the world, but I had three brothers in Boston; and to hear my father read their letters home convinced me that Boston was the place for me, instead of a farm in that wild locality in Canada.

With the consent of my father I packed my little bundle, and started afoot to seek my fortune. I had seen a bit of wood that one of my brothers had brought from Boston, which he said was a piece of a ship that had been around the world. I did not see why I could not go around the world the same way: but little did I think when leaving home that spring morning that before another year had passed over my young head I would be on the other side of the globe, among wild, nude savages.

Leaving the farm, I travelled alone and hopeful until reaching a place called Stanstead Plain, on the line be-

On Horseback.

tween Canada and Vermont. I had but little money, yet, with the lofty ideas of youth, I put up at a hotel. I met a man there who was going to Boston with a drove of horses to sell. He learned that I was on my way thither, and kindly offered me a chance to ride one of his horses, which offer was readily accepted.

In about three days we started. I carried a pillow-case, partly filled with clothing; the part unutilized I filled with crackers and cheese. Mounted upon the horse, I placed my outfit in front, where I could hold on to it with my hands. I wore a beaver hat which was about two sizes too large for me. I did not mind that, for I was going to Boston, and my mind was so fully occupied with bright anticipations that I did not care how my dress might appear, nor the inconvenience of ill-fitting clothing. Started on our journey, we were soon over the line into the States. One can imagine the comical appearance I made with a big white bundle in front, and a beaver hat either down over my eyes or perhaps tilted backward on my head at an angle of forty-five degrees. When the horse began to trot I would hold the hat on to keep it from getting too near my nose or entirely off my head. After a day or two out on our journey, as I got better acquainted with my companions, and there were eight or ten of them, I dis-covered that most of them were in the same fix as my-self, and were getting a free ride. The owner of the horses took this plan of giving free rides to men going his way, and getting his horses along much better than he otherwise would.

The others of the party had but little money, like myself, and we found that when we stopped at the differ-ent hotels we were charged pretty high for meals. None of us wanted to live on crackers and cheese through a journey which would last at least a week. Bread and

milk were only ten cents, while something more solid
cost from forty to fifty cents ; so we arranged that one
half of the party should call for bread and milk, and the
other half for meat and vegetables. As a matter of
course, all would be served on the same table, and we
would help ourselves to what we wanted. By that method
all fared pretty well, and at a much less cost than we
would had we not devised the scheme.

We arrived at Andover about a week later, where the
owner of the horses stopped over in order to recruit
his horses. My crackers, cheese, and money were all
gone, and I was unable to pay my expenses at the hotel
in Andover, which was one night and two meals.
Learning that Lowell was only eight miles away, which I
thought was the home of my brother, as, in one letter to
my father, he wrote that his store was at the corner of
Lowell and Minot Streets, and I thought Lowell Street
must be in Lowell. Leaving my little sack and my big
hat as security for my hotel fare, I started for Lowell
with a little cap on my head which I happened to have.
I arrived about two o'clock P. M., and began to inquire as
soon as I entered the city, of every person I met, if they
could direct me to Lowell Street, and if they knew my
brother. To my surprise, no one knew of either. Sick
and disgusted with hearing everybody say no to my inquiries, I sauntered down the street, and saw a gate open
which led to a small yard of a cotton factory. I went
through the gate and, as the door of the factory was
open, walked in. Never having seen a factory, I was
curious to look the place over, and did to my heart's
content.

On the street again I determined anew to find either
the one or the other of the objects of which I was in
search. I found myself near the depot, from which the
steam cars left every few hours for Boston. I made some

inquiries about the trains and Boston. I was told by a man that the track led to Boston, and to follow it; it would take me there; and after hearing my story, he said there was a Lowell Street at the end of that track in Boston. I had made a mistake and was hunting the wrong city for my friends, but it was too late in the day to think of starting for Boston afoot. A hotel stood not far ahead across the street. It was no use to think of applying there for anything to eat, or to get shelter for the night; yet I was sadly in need of something to eat, as I had eaten nothing since morning. With a choking lump in my throat I thought of my father's bounteously filled table; however, I silenced the rising thought of home, and braced myself to face the music, let the tune be what it might. I started down the street, when presently I heard beautiful music. It seemed to be in the air overhead. I looked about, but could see nothing except an open door with a long flight of stairs.

Desiring to investigate, I mounted the stairs. After passing three long flights I stopped to consider the propriety of proceeding farther on my pilgrimage; and while pondering the situation, a blast of music came down the flight of stairs above, too tempting for me to hesitate longer, for such music I had never before heard. At the top step a door stood ajar. From this door the music poured in waves of melodious tone. I pushed the door open and walked in. Some half-dozen men were blowing into as many long crooked brass things. Awe and admiration were no doubt depicted on my face. All stopped blowing. One pointed to the door and at the same time raised his foot and said, " Git." He meant business; the hint was very broad. I did not wait for further tokens of their pleasure of meeting me, but retreated with speed and energy. On the street again I looked myself over, and found myself none the worse for my venture, and congratulated myself to think that they did not extend their hospitality so far as to assist me to the street, as they seemed inclined to do.   Objectless mentally, I started for the factory gate which was open as before.   A man stood inside, but I paid no attention to him, but passed in.   I felt a grip on my arm, and was pulled back.   The man at the gate had me.

" What do you want in here?" said he.

" I don't know as I want anything."

" Well," said he, " you get out of this quick, or I will help you."

I told him that I had seen all that I cared to see, since I had been into that factory once before that day, and started up the street at a lively pace, and I soon came to the hotel and the little depot.   My experience during the day troubled me not a little.   To know where I should put up for the night was a serious question.   The prospects were rather slim: I had neither friends nor money ; was a stranger in a strange city and in a strange land.   I knew it would not do to weaken on my first adventure in a city.   As I approached the hotel I began to think that as I had come out without a scratch, and what I had passed through had not only sharpened my appetite but also a desire for further adventure, I soon made up my mind to continue my travels whether the road led me to Africa or west of Texas.   Little thought I at that time how soon the time would come when I would be sailing along the African coast, and yet a little later many thousands of miles west of Texas!

Putting on a bold face I made for the front door of the hotel.   I noticed many coming out picking their teeth.   I pushed on up the steps and entered the front room, which was the dining-room.   Here was a large table running down the room with a few men sitting at it

who had not yet finished their supper. Looking around
to see to whom I should apply for supper and lodging, I
saw a man behind a little counter looking through a
square hole above the counter. Thinking he was the man
in charge, I approached him rather briskly, as if I had
been there many times before, and spoke to him. I told
him that I wanted supper and a bed, perhaps breakfast
in the morning.

" Very well," said he.

I waited, expecting an invitation to the table at once.
Instead of asking me to dine, he said that they generally
required their pay in advance. For once my cunning
came to my rescue in good time. I ran my hand down
into my pocket as a man would if he expected to draw
forth a well-filled wallet. I knew full well there was
nothing there but a chew of gum that I found on the
trees by the roadside in Vermont. I pulled my hand out
empty and felt in my other pocket, where I knew there
was no pocketbook, yet I went through it with some
expression of alarm on my face. Finally I drew my hand
forth with the remark that I had left my wallet in my
trunk, which was in the car-house, and further, that I
intended taking the cars for Boston in the morning, and
thought the station shut up for the night.

" Well," said he, " the morning will do just as well,"
pointing to the table, which was the part of the drama that
I had long been looking for with hope deferred but now
realized. I seated myself, and was in capital condition
to do justice to anything they might set before me. One
dish which was brought on was strange to me. It
seemed neither fish, flesh, nor fowl. The waiter pushed
it nearer to me and told me to help myself.

I thanked him and told him I would. Finally, out
of deference to the waiter, who, by the way, was all
attention, I helped myself to a little piece; I tasted it,

but did not like it, but managed to get it down with an effort. The balance, small as it was, I desired to get rid of somehow, since I was afraid that the waiter might think me green and make some remarks, and I was too sensitive at that time to care to hear his comment. I wished to say as little as possible until I was out on the street in the morning, and then I should have the day before me, and Boston only about twenty-five miles ahead. That bit of strange food on my plate I could not eat. I did not think it would poison me, and to hide it mashed it up with some potato, and by that means got it out of sight. My desire was to get from the table without being interviewed by the waiter. After finishing my repast I seated myself in a comfortable place, with mind at rest. I felt there would be no more difficulty until morning, and I had high hopes of being the first one up in the morning.

At about eight o'clock I went to the man at the pigeon-hole and told him that I was tired, and would like to retire. He called a waiter, gave him a candle and told him to show me to room No. —, which he did, and after putting the candle on a stand retired. I began to investigate my new quarters, glancing around the room with increasing wonder and admiration mingled with apprehension. The man had surely made a mistake and put me into a room that might well have been reserved for the governor of the State. What if they should discover the mistake in the middle of the night and pull me out by the heels !

I was very still a half-hour, and not hearing any one approach my door finally went to bed with the satisfaction that the key was on my side of the door, and no one could enter without my knowledge. I placed the candle and matches near, that I might reach them if disturbed in the night, settled myself back in bed and began to study and ponder over the beauty of my room which was handsomely painted all over. The room was only covered with highly colored wall paper, but having never seen the like before, it was then to me both novel and beautiful. Nor had I ever seen lobster, which was the strange dish at the table.

I thought over my day's experience for the twentieth time, yet could settle on no definite plan for the morrow. Finally I came to the conclusion to trust to luck, and soon lost myself in slumber.

I slept soundly until daylight. Then arose immediately, as anxious to get out of the place then as I was to get into it the night before. I did not wait to consider the mode of my exit, but trusted to luck and circumstances to help me out of the dilemma. At the dining-room I glanced at the pigeonhole. I saw no one where I expected to see that fellow waiting for me. One of the servants was sweeping out the room. The front door was open; I sauntered toward it and looked out, then made some remark about the weather, and inquired at what hour I could have breakfast. The servant replied that the usual hour for that meal was seven o'clock; it was then about six. I told him that I guessed that I would have time to take a little walk before breakfast.

"Oh, yes," said he, "plenty of time."

I stepped out upon the street, and wondered if he knew how pleasing his parting words were what he would think. Going directly across the track, I passed around to the back side of the depot, which was hardly more than a shed, but a long one, the lower end of which was quite a distance from the hotel, and there I came out on to the track. With one farewell look at the hotel, I shaped my course for Boston, with square yards and a stiff breeze behind, under which I sailed away at the rate of two-forty. I was not long putting several miles between myself and my friends in Lowell, who no doubt were at that time wondering whether they had been accommodating a count or a *no-account*, instead of a country clam without as much as a shell, let alone pearls, to bestow upon them for their amiable hospitality. After travelling eight or ten miles toward Boston, I felt it safe to slacken speed a little, so shortened sail, lashed the helm, and took things a little easy. I had time to review the past with more deliberation than I had done before; and when I came to realize my duplicity felt guilty enough.

My father was very strict with his boys, teaching them to always tell the truth, and to be always faithful and true in all our dealings with every one. This was my first fall from grace; but thinking the matter over, I concluded that no one in Lowell knew my name or whence I came. I had no doubt but they had a lively realization that some one had occupied their best room that night, yet doubted whether or not they would recognize me should I return again.

I was going to Boston. Pushing on at a moderate pace, about ten o'clock I espied a little shanty not far ahead, which stood back a few rods from the road. Beginning to feel the want of food, I decided to call at that shanty and ask for something to eat. If I got only a crust, I should appreciate it. I found the door open. A comely motherly sort of a woman sat at the table. I bade her good morning; she returned the compliment. I told her that I was on my way to Boston, that I was out of money, and wanted something to eat, and would be very thankful if she would give me something.

She said that she could give me some bread and milk, and accordingly placed the food on the table, and requested me to be seated.

While eating my breakfast, dinner, or supper, — it

matters not which, since I did not know where the next
meal would come from, — I related some of my experience in Lowell, just enough to inform her that I was
from Canada and expected to find my brother there, and
that not finding him there was going to Boston where,
no doubt, I should meet him. I finished my dish of bread
and milk and thanked my hostess for her kindness.

Preparing to continue my journey, she requested me
to stop until her husband came home to dinner. He was
from Canada, and would no doubt like to talk with me.
I replied that I should be glad to do so, but was very
anxious to reach Boston that day. I thanked her again,
bade her " Good morning !" and began again my lonely
tramp.

I have given my first adventure somewhat in detail to
show the young, who have a desire to seek a fortune,
what trouble they may meet unless they have a well-filled
wallet, and thereby avoid the embarrassing predicament
I was placed in in the Lowell tavern. My experience
in Lowell proved of much benefit later on in life. It
taught me to state my case truthfully when in need, and
I always found that I fared better for so doing. I formed
my ideas in this respect after my experience with the
woman who lived in the humble shanty beside the railroad, remembering the dish of bread and milk with
which she so kindly served me.

Arriving near what seemed to be my journey's end,
I walked over what I thought a very long bridge, and
at the end found a long shed with both sides open. I
followed the track along the side of the shed, and at last
came to its end. I was in Boston, — the goal for
which I had searched was reached at last. I stepped
through the open gate and out upon the street. I saw
a store door standing open across the street, and began
my search by accosting a young man who, at that mo-

ment, came to the open door. He eyed me rather closely. I suppose it was my rural appearance that attracted his attention.

My first question was, if he knew a man by the name of ——, who kept a store on the corner of Minot and Lowell Streets.

He pointed to the sign over the door, and asked me if that was his name.

To my surprise and joy I was really at my brother's store. The young man told me that my brother was out, but would soon be in. I waited around for a half-hour or so, but he did not come. Feeling a bit rested, I went out upon the street.

I was now on Blossom Street, where they were driving piles, upon which they were to build a brick block. I had never seen anything like it. The great block of iron hoisted high in air came down with a crash and beat the posts down into the ground. When the piles were driven so far down that I could reach their top, I put little stones on them and watched the gravel fly under the hammer.

While engaged in this rather reckless sport I felt a grip on my arm.

I turned around sharply, expecting to hear the words, "What are you doing here?" It was my brother. He had returned to the store during my absence, and on learning that I had been there he started out to find me. I was gratified enough to meet him, and was contented to let the big hammer do its work without me.

I remained at my brother's that night, and learned through him that one of my uncles lived on —— Street, where he was running a bakery. The next morning after breakfast my brother went to the store and left me at the house with his family.

I waited around, and finally, when my brother's wife

was busy, slipped out to the street and began at once to inquire where —— Street was. After many inquiries, and turning of many corners, I found myself on —— Street, and began to inquire for my uncle, and soon succeeded in finding him.

My uncle was unmarried at that time, and my aunt, a maiden lady, kept house for him. I had never seen either, but that made little difference to me. Finding his bake shop, I walked in, and met a man whom I asked if Mr. —— was in. He said he was the man. I then made myself known to him. He was somewhat surprised to see me, since he supposed me in Canada. He did not appear to be overjoyed, but somewhat indifferent. His face had a scowl rather than a smile. However, I was going to see it through. I gave him to understand that I wished to see my aunt, so he showed me up-stairs to where she was. She seemed to be rather more pleased to see me. I liked her very much. She looked so much like my mother that I felt myself at home at once, and put aside all restraint. Spending half an hour with her, I went down to the bakery again. I had not been there long when who should come in but my brother, who had returned to his house and found me gone. He thought I might get lost, so started out on the chase after me, and had just run me to earth. He took me to his home, where I remained for a few days, but never for any time out of sight of him or some of his family. My brother and uncle soon began making plans for me.

My brother had nothing that I could do. He did not want me idling about his place, for he was a man who believed in keeping every one at work, whether they earned much or little. My uncle had all the help that he needed, and did not care to take an apprentice. It was agreed, however, that I should go to work in the bake shop until something better offered.

My first work there was chopping mince-meat. This was put into a hole dug out in the end of a log of wood, which made a very nice bowl to chop in, and quite profitable to its owner. Every time it was used it would wear down, thereby adding enough wood to the mess to make an extra pie. I had to use two knives, and the hole had been chopped down so deep that I had to reach down considerably to get at the meat. The result was what might be expected with a novice. I chopped my fingers about as much as the meat; in fact I did so much chopping in the wrong place, that I am very forcibly reminded of my early experience at the block whenever looking at my hands after the lapse of fifty years.

My uncle came to see how I was getting on. When he saw my hands, he wanted to know what I had been doing. I told him it was very easy to see. He directed me to be more careful in the future, as he was not in the habit of mixing live meat with his mince. Perhaps he preferred wood. I got through it though without losing any fingers. After that my uncle put another man at the block, for which I felt very grateful. I looked at the fellow's hands to see if he had any scars, but failed to see any.

The next work which my considerate uncle put before me was a pile of raisins to pick over. I had never seen so many together before. We seldom saw at my father's more than half a pound at one time, as they were quite scarce, and were regarded as expensive in that far-away land where we lived. I was always very fond of them, and what youngster was ever without a sweet tooth? I thought out of so many a few would not be missed. When I found a plump raisin, my hand instinctively sought my mouth. It was a fortunate thing that the fat ones were few, for my uncle had thrifty notions about what he put into his mince.

He did not care to give me that work very often.
However, it made but little difference what he found for
me to do; when he came to figure up, there was a short-
age somewhere which he could not account for. He
had a large number of customers whom he used to visit
daily with his team; also quite a number on streets ad-
jacent to the bakery, whom he served from a basket. He
set me serving his customers with the basket, perhaps to
locate the cause of the shortages of his accounts, thinking that if the basket customers did not get served on my
route he would know where to look for his leak. He
was never the wiser, however, on that point, through
any act of mine.

My kit consisted of pies and cakes; but I fed so boun-
tifully on cakes and broken pies which I found in the
cart on its return, which I had to clean out, that I cared
nothing for the cakes, neither did I care much for
the pies. He sent me one day to serve an old invalid
negress who lived on what I believe was called Nigger
Hill. I cannot locate the place now, for there have been
many changes in that locality. I had seen but one colored person before I came to Boston, — a travelling min-
strel who had strayed from his troupe, and who finally
got into that part of the country where I lived. All
looked alike to me in Boston, as I could see no difference, except in size and dress.

My uncle sent me around to that old lady with a lot
of pies and cakes. He showed me where to find her,
and I started out with some misgivings. I had passed
the alley where she lived once before, and both sides of
it were lined with colored people. I hardly knew what
my experience would be with them. I had to go, no
matter what happened; that must be an after consideration, so pushed into the alley. Both sides were lined
with black faces, old and young, male and female. I

hurried toward where the old lady lived, while these fellows began to guy me as I passed along, and looked wistfully at the basket. I divined their thoughts, and kept a sharp lookout, knowing that if anything was missing at the end of my route, the old lady would not pay for more than she received.

My uncle knew just what money I should bring back, and if I did not bring the full amount, or those black fellows stole any of my cakes, I doubted if he would believe my story. I gained the end of the alley safely, knocked gently at the colored woman's door, but no answer came. I rapped louder, still no answer. Another rap, with greater force, brought a howl which appeared from its wildness to come from the lips of a lost soul. The voice said, —

"Why don't you beat the house down at once?"

I opened the door and stepped in. The first sight I saw was about forty cats, of all colors and sizes; the floor appeared covered with them. The room was large, and from it a smaller one opened, from which came the admonition, —

"Come here, now, and don't step on my cats."

The cats didn't seem to mind whether they were stepped on or not, but I was more particular than they, since I had received ample warning from the little room. I entered the room, and there the old lady was well tucked up in bed.

Her face looked to me nine times blacker than any other face I had ever seen, and with a scowl on her face she snapped out, —

"What do you want here?"

"Mr. —— sent me with some pies and cakes."

"Oh, well!" said she, pointing to a little table on which was a wallet.

She then told me to hold the wallet before her, then

to open it and take what change the things came to, and to replace the wallet on the table. She was a hopeless cripple. I emptied the basket and was about to pick my way out among the cats, when a sudden storm of hail broke with much fury. As large as pigeons' eggs, the hailstones bounded off the roofs below. The old lady insisted upon my remaining with her snarling that I would be killed if I went out of the house.

It was hard to tell where the greatest danger was, between the cats and the storm outside. The cats had scented the food and began to gather around it. I was always a lover of cats from my childhood. If anything troubled me, I would catch Tabby by the tail and drag her into the old cradle, where I would rock myself to sleep.

But at this particular time, with the old lady's cats I thought there was such a thing as carrying a good thing too far. They were very bold, yet I dared not correct them. I was working myself into quite a fever, when the storm abated and I started. With another warning ringing in my ears about the cats, I hurried from the room. On my arrival at the alley I found that, like Daniel after he came out of the lions' den, I had escaped without a scratch. But the end was not yet, for there was a dark line both sides of the alley through which to make my exit before being out of danger; and the darkies, as I passed them, chaffed me a little: but I had nothing in the basket, and they seemed to think that what was outside was of no account to them. Out upon the street again, I started at a lively pace for my uncle's shop, nor did I ever visit that alley again, nor have I forgotten the place to this day.

I was kept pretty busy on little odd jobs around the shop, but my liveliest time was Sunday mornings, dealing out baked beans and brown bread, — Boston's favorite dish, brown bread and Beverly beans, with a slice of her next-door neighbor for seasoning.

On Sundays I liked to seek out new fields for study and recreation. My aunt soon stopped that, for she was a member of Park Street Church. She would take me by the hand and hold it until we were inside the church, when she would loosen her hold. I dared not leave her when inside, but outside would somehow get lost in the crowd and not get home for some time after she had returned.

Finally my uncle found me more plague than profit. He saw my brother and they arranged with my uncle's milkman that I should go to Squantum to work on his farm. I was told to get ready to go next morning. Had I been consulted, I should have hesitated. I left my father's farm to avoid farming, and hardly liked the idea of taking up the work again. I made no objections, however, but kept up a lively thinking. I had no clothing to speak of. My brother wrote to Andover to get what I left there at the hotel. The answer came that there was nothing there, and if anything had been left there it was either lost or stolen. I packed what few things I had, and the next morning was ready for a drive into the country. We arrived at the farm about noon. I was pleased with the appearance of the place, a nice large farm, well cultivated, and in sight of the harbor, where I could see the vessels sailing along. There was also a fine house, and what attracted my attention most was that the house was presided over by two beautiful young ladies; one about my age. I felt at once I should be contented for a while, and perhaps get to like farming well enough after all; but in a few days the newness was worn off, and I wanted to go back to the city again.

My short experience on that farm changed my mind.

I did not like farming as well as I thought, and notified my employer that I would not stay longer on the farm, but that I would go to the city next morning with the milk team, which I did.

My desire, when leaving home, was to devote half of my time to attending school until I was at least twenty-one. I had not so much schooling when I left home as the children get nowadays in the primary schools. I would have worked willingly for my food and clothes could I have attended school a part of the time, but no one seemed to care much what became of me, so that I was off their hands. Had my friends put me in school, with reasonable opportunities before me, it would have made a vast difference with my future life. The need of an education has been like a millstone hanging to my neck all my life. Therefore, let me say to the truant, attend school faithfully, since there is no other time like youthful years, when you have so many advantages, so many years in which to study and improve your mind before you are launched on your own resources. You will find few to extend a friendly hand, and unless you happen to have a "nest-egg" to start with, it will be an uphill road throughout life. If one has a good education, and push and vim, one can soon get on in business which will bring both honor and profits.

Without an education a man is at the mercy of others. Put aside those yellow-covered novels, for they will do you no good. If you want to read out of school, there is nothing so instructive, or that which will improve and elevate the young mind better than a good daily or weekly newspaper. Select those papers that will teach you the doings of men who are engaged in all manner of business, and from their experience and practice you can learn much which will be of use to you when you are ready to take up some branch of business.

Without such knowledge you might lose a deal of valuable time before deciding what business to follow. "To be forewarned is to be forearmed." You can learn many of these valuable lessons long before you need to put them into practice, and learn them much easier and cheaper in your young days than you can later in life. You are getting the actual experience of many an old and wise head by merely reading and heeding their management of business. You will find much in the daily papers concerning commonplace, every-day matters that will be of use to you later on, for such is the life, bustle, and business into which you must soon enter. You should prepare yourself as well as you can, because you will have to take your chances with the rest of humanity in the struggle for success, and you must consider what advantage those old heads of much experience have over you. It is a duty you owe to yourself to prepare for the work that is yet to come. Never put too much confidence in men until you have tried them and found them trustworthy. Never unfold your secrets or plans to others, for they are no longer secrets; neither are they yours, but public property. Weigh your words. Bear in mind that beautiful Chinese proverb, "That of a word unspoken, you are its master; when spoken, it is master of you." Another thing that you ought to bear in mind is this, the Good Book says, " All men are liars."

When I arrived in the city, I left the milk wagon before it reached my uncle's. I wanted to take in the sights as I went, so got out of the wagon. I started to find a Mr. Brown, who manufactured root beer. I had a brother who worked at that place then. I found the place readily, for everybody seemed to know where Brown, the beer man, lived. I watched the process of bottling beer awhile, took dinner with my brother, and finally left for my other brother's, who kept the store. He was surprised to see me again, but did not scold, as I expected. I now became a sort of hanger-on around the store.

One morning I started out to seek employment. About ten o'clock I found myself down at Quincy Market. There was a man near there who kept a little store, by the name of James Drake.

No doubt many Bostonians will recollect Mr. Drake as well as I do, for he not only sold dry goods but green goods as well. I happened to be just green enough to suit him; and he had a customer at that time who wanted just such goods, so he called me into his store. He was well posted in his line of business, for it did not take him long to discover that I was very verdant, and it did not take long for him to get my name on a ship's articles for a three years' cruise in a whaling ship.

He told me that I could go on a three years' voyage and come home with three or four hundred dollars, that I would have a fine time and see many different parts of the world. That pleased me much better than the fish part did. I booked myself for the voyage. My early ideas of going around the world were to be realized; and they certainly were. The bark was to sail from Duxbury. Mr. Drake told me it would take some three days to get all the crew, and when the full number was obtained we would all be sent to Duxbury. If I desired to remain with him until then, I could, and it would cost me nothing. That suited me, as I knew if my brother discovered my doings he would put a stop to my adventure, and perhaps find another farm for me. I had obtained all the experience on farms I wished, and preferred now to try the sea.

At Drake's my meals were served at the counter in the store, and at night I slept behind it. On one occasion I saw my brother near the store, and ran inside and hid behind the counter.

One morning all of the crew then ready went aboard a schooner lying off Long Wharf, which was to take us to Duxbury to the vessel that we had shipped to go in. Soon under way, we headed for Duxbury. That was my first voyage on salt water, and I thought it would be my last. I could neither eat, drink, nor sleep. Usually I was blessed with a good appetite, but somehow it had left me and taken with it my desire for further adventure on the ocean wave. If I could get on shore I would stay there; but alas! I found that my fondest hopes were to be long deferred.

At Duxbury, instead of landing as expected, we were all put on board of the bark, which was anchored some three miles off shore. I found that I could now stand up instead of getting down on all fours as on the schooner.

I gained my balance after a day or two, and could eat my regular allowance of salt beef and hard-tack quite as well as an old salt. We were now kept busy getting the vessel ready for sea and getting supplies on board, and in about three weeks were ready to sail, when we were all taken ashore and given a good dinner. My longing for the shore was forgotten by that time, for the vessel at anchor was quiet and without motion. I concluded that going to sea was not so bad, after all. My fears vanished. From the hotel I wrote to my brother that I was on shipboard, where I was going, and also who shipped me. I knew that he would not get the letter before the ship would be out to sea.

We went aboard and soon got under way and out of the harbor. As we moved farther from the land, and as prominent objects dropped from sight, the water began to get rough. The situation began to look more serious. A fishing boat ran alongside; I gazed over the rail into that boat, and would have given half of my life could I have jumped into her and gone ashore. The boat soon drifted away and left us to our voyage. The last point of land faded away, and with it went all hope of getting ashore again for a long time.

Night came, and the captain and mate chose their watches. I was the last one chosen, and fell to the mate, Mr. Holmes. The captain of our ship, Rufus Coffin, was one of the Nantucket family of that name. He proved the best, as he was also the first, captain with whom I ever sailed. Rufus Holmes, of Duxbury, was also one of the best mates that I ever found on shipboard. I had my first watch on deck that night, and in the morning was soon on deck.

I scanned the horizon, but could see nothing that I wanted to see, since it was nothing but sea all around, here, there, and everywhere. Finally I made up my mind to face the music, whatever it might be or where it might lead to. There was no use in rebelling at fate; so I swallowed my trouble, and banished from my mind all thought of home and friends, with a reservation, however, to run away at the first landing where white people lived.

The experience of one whaling voyage, in detail, covers many, since it is about the same over and over; therefore I will give only the most important of my experiences, which occurred mostly on land, in different ports of the world, with a little salt-water experience to season the story.

CHAPTER II.

THE VOYAGE OUTWARD — FIRST TRIUMPHS IN SEA-FARING LIFE — HABITS AND OCCUPATIONS OF SEAMEN — THE NATIVES OF THE ISLANDS — CRUISING FOR WHALES — ADVENTURES AND PERILS IN THEIR CAPTURE — DESCRIP-TION OF DIFFERENT SPECIES — A PARADE ON SHORE — A CHARACTER IN HISTORY — DESERTS THE WHALER.

THE first two weeks out I was very seasick and could not bear the sight of food. The mate would give me a lemon to suck, which did me more good than anything else, notwithstanding the lemon juice, I had to look over the ship's side quite often to see how deep the water was. Two weeks of that, and Richard was himself again. I soon learned the ropes and how to steer the vessel, yet I was the but-end of every joke, being the youngest on board and the greenest one. All the crew except myself had had some experience on shipboard, and they would play their tricks on me quite often. I stood their jokes without complaint, and tried to learn all that I could in order to lift myself above a novice, and to finally live down their jokes, which I soon did. I soon was able to do a sailor's duty on a whaleship, with the exception of pulling the boats after whales. I was not strong enough for that at that time, but a few months later they found that I was one of the best oarsmen they had on board.

After a few months' cruising and seeing nothing larger than a porpoise, we touched at Fayal, one of the Azore Islands, where we got a supply of vegetables. When we first sighted the islands we saw first the peak of Pikeo, which is an island near Fayal. It towered far above the clouds.   The reason that it looks so lofty is that it runs so steeply up from the water.

I have seen many mountains much loftier than the peak of Pikeo in Colorado, some that were sixteen thousand feet above sea level, yet only five or six thousand feet above the plains below them.   The impression of great height was lost in the foothills which lay between them and the sea.   Place one of those lofty Colorado peaks beside that of Pikeo, and its crest could not be seen even on a clear day.   The height would be something like three miles, while Pikeo is hardly a mile high.

Getting our supplies, we set sail again, and for a month or two more saw nothing.   We finally ran for an island called Brah-vo, as we wanted two or three more hands on board.   At that time I could take my turn at the masthead to look out for whales.   I was at the forward masthead the day that we expected to sight the island.   I had never raised land myself, and did not know how the first appearance of land would look; however, I was told to keep a sharp lookout.   After a while I observed a hair-line, which appeared to run a little above the water.   It would rise and then run down, and so on, up and down, and finally lose itself in the water.   It did not change its form, so it could not be a cloud.   I sang out at the top of my voice, "Land 'o."

The captain wanted to know where away.

"Two points on the lee bow."

He called to the boat-steerer, who was at the topgallant crosstrees, to know if he could see the land, and he answered that he could not.

I sang out again.

The captain sent an old man up to where I was.   I tried to point the land out to him, but he could not see it.

He went down and told the captain that there was no land in sight, but I knew better; so I sang out again, " Land 'o." Finally the captain, finding that I was not to be choked off, took his long glass and came up himself. He could not see it either, with or without his glass.

After watching nearly an hour, he finally caught sight of the land with his glass, and headed the ship for it. A few hours later all hands could see it. I felt very proud to think that I could see farther with the naked eye than the captain could with his glass. We ran in, and, shipping more hands, soon left for another cruise.

We sailed away again for a month or two without finding anything larger than a sunfish and a few flying fish, which came on board and took passage with us. They made a very good fry, quite as good as trout.

We were nearing the Cape of Good Hope. We sighted the cape, where we saw some cattle grazing on shore, but we did not land. Not long after we put in at an island by the name of Trustinucuna. There was but one family on this island, old Governor Glass, who was monarch of all he surveyed. His subjects were mostly penguins and worgins. The latter are the male birds, if birds they can be called. They have feathers on their bodies, but nude wings, and cannot rise from land or water. They use their wings when they are in the water. They are amphibious and live on fish. We remained there about three hours, and then sailed away for Madagascar We had been living for several months on salt meats. The captain thought it time to freshen up a little. Too much salt meat, without vegetables or fresh meat, brings on the scurvy, a disease which softens the flesh and covers the limbs with boils, with considerable swelling. We ran into Dillago Bay, where we found other whaling ships. We found plenty of fresh meat. We could buy a whole ox, weighing eight or nine hundred pounds, for a common coffee mug of powder. The cattle are like our Texas cattle, except that they have a large hump on their foreshoulders, quite as large as that on the camel. Another animal, about the size of a three-months old calf, has its habitat there, seemingly half goat and half calf; the meat being much better than either mutton or veal. I have often wondered why some enterprising Yankee has not ere this shipped a few of those animals to this country. They would undoubtedly soon become acclimated and thrive well here. Then we could have veal at all times of the year. There was at that time, which was over forty years ago, plenty of turpin there, which, by the way, makes a superior soup. They are excellent to take to sea, as they will live in the ship's hole three or four months without food or water, and appear none the leaner for their long fast. We wanted water. To get it we would raft a lot of casks together, and tow them into the mouth of the river. We would then knock out the bungs and let them fill. While at this work I learned to swim, by holding to a cask and floating down stream with the current, at the same time kicking out with my feet. It afterwards proved very fortunate for me that I did take that occasion to learn to swim.

We got milk from the natives, which was served to us in an eggshell, or rather half of a shell, which made quite a respectable bowl, and would hold quite two quarts. It was the eggshell of a very large bird which has long been extinct.

The forest trees were quite tall and covered with vines which hung from the branches, many reaching the ground. The trees propagate this wise: they bear a spindle about as large and somewhat resembling the carbons which are used in arc lighting. At the proper season these spindles, which grow out from the limbs, fall to the ground endways and are driven two or three inches into the soft earth. There they take root and grow into trees.

Numerous species of the cactus were to be found on that island, some being ten or twelve feet high. They did not appear to have much trunk, but were nearly all leaves. Those near the bottom were six to eight feet long, about ten inches wide, and quite thin on the edge, which was rimmed with long thorns. The middle of the leaves would average about four inches in thickness.

The ruler of the island at that period was called Prince Willy; and it was a singular custom, that before a man became a prince there, he must have one eye taken out. This prince had had one of his " extracted." He looked as if he had been in a Texas fight with his one eye, his sinister-looking long goatee and hair pretty well on end. He looked quite the man, too, for a savage ruler. The natives were arrant thieves and adepts at their profession. They had a particular fancy for old hoop iron. We learned after we left that a blacksmith had a few months before escaped from a whaling ship, and to please the natives he made spearheads or points from hoop iron. When ships came into the harbor the natives would take the blacksmith into the forest and hide him until the vessels had left. They were afraid he would leave the island, and they wanted him for their own use. One of our men caught a native with a lot of hoop iron under his wrap, which he took away from him and gave the fellow a slap on the head with his hand. The thief yelled so one could hear him a mile off. A dozen natives were on deck at the time, and all set up a great howling. In less than a minute there were twenty or more canoes putting off from the shore, filled with natives with plenty of spears in their hands. As they pushed alongside the first to show above the ship's rail was that bushy-headed, one-eyed Prince, and close behind were his many followers. They swarmed around the captain on the quarter-deck, all wanting to talk at once. Such a medley I never heard before or since. They made the captain somewhat nervous. He could not make them understand, and they did not appear to want to understand. They wanted to fight right there and then apparently, but the captain had no intention of gratifying their wishes.

He signalled to other ships, for their captains to come on board, which they did, with the result that there was a deal of loud talk which no one understood. One had to guess what the other one said.

At one time I thought the captains would command all hands to take to the water and try to reach shore or find the bottom of the bay as a means of safety ; and yet to jump overboard would be like jumping out of the frying pan into the fire. If the sharks did not get us, the natives would soon run us down with their canoes.

I concluded to remain on deck, and if worse came to worst I could take to the rigging and skip aloft, for I knew they could not get up very fast over the ratlines. The affair was finally settled without any blood being spilt on either side; but the captain had a few plugs of tobacco less than before the trouble began. The natives are very fond of tobacco. On some of the islands one might buy a woman or a man for a plug of tobacco.

After the trouble was all over, Prince Willy left the vessel with his escort, and the decks were soon cleared of the vermin. We never, after that, allowed many on board at one time, by that means avoiding further trouble.

We shipped two men here, who had run away from vessels that had been before us. I shall have more to say of them. One was James Bertine of New York, a very tall, slim fellow, whose sobriquet was Long Jim The other's name I have forgotten. He was made third mate; we will call him Jack.

After lying in port for about a month, and having taken on board a good supply of meat both dressed and alive, and about one hundred turpin, we hoisted anchor and sailed out to sea again to have another hunt for whales. We had not been out many weeks before we found a right whale. The captain, taking three boats, went after him. The captain got fast to the fellow, and for some reason which I could never find out, he bent on what whalemen call a drag,—a piece of two-inch plank about twelve inches square, with a plug run through the centre, to which a line is attached. This line was bent to the one attached to the whale, and the balance of the line in the boat was held to, and the part that was overboard was cut on the gunwale of the boat. Strange to say, the captain pulled after the whale again, which, being frightened, went twice as fast as the boat, or as he did before he was struck. The captain pulled away until the fish was out of sight, then came on board, and I suppose entered on the log, "Chased a whale this day, could not catch him ; going two-forty and no bets."

That fish was the largest I had ever seen. Right whales feed on what is called brit, which is quite as fine as corn meal and of a reddish color ; in fact, the water looks quite red with it, and is apparently alive. A whale's lips are some three feet wide and from six to eight feet long. The bone which is in each side of the mouth under their lips, consists of slabs of bone, set pretty near together, with the edge having the hair on the inside. The tongue is very large, and fills the whole of the lower part of the mouth. It resembles a well-filled feather tick. The whale when feeding swims rapidly through the water, throwing his lips wide open, and the bone which is inside expands at the same time, which permits the water to flow into the mouth, and in closing their lips, the tongue, being very flexible, assists to force the water out through the hair which is attached to the inner edges of the two tiers of bones, act as a strainer. As the water is forced out, the whale swallows what he has caught, which is seldom too large to go down, since there is not usually anything found for whale food on what is called "right whale ground" that is of any considerable size.

The humpback whales gather their food in the same way, but the bone in their mouths is not much over two feet in length, and they feed on small fish about the size of herring. Frequently humpback whales when feeding go through the water with their noses sticking a few feet above it, scooping in large numbers of fish, with a windrow of fish rolling out of the water ahead, trying to get out of the way.

The throat or pharynx of the right and humpback whales is small, being not over four inches in diameter. It is doubtful if it was this species that swallowed Jonah. The sperm whale has a much larger throat. It feeds on squid, which is similar to the squid found around nearly all shores, but immensely larger. Before the whale has been through them and dismembered them, they will cover quite an acre of space on the water.

The sperm whale has quite a square head, the lower part of which is very much smaller than the upper. The lower jawbone, when stripped of flesh, looks much like a farmer's harrow with a long shaft running out at the point where the two arms meet. This shaft in a large whale is some six feet in length and twelve inches thick at the fork, tapering down to five or six at the other end. The upper surface of this long shaft is flat, while the under portion is rounded. Teeth that are from one and one half to two and three inches thick, and from six to ten inches long, are set about three inches apart on the flat side, that is, the upper side of the lower jaw. This arm of the lower jaw shuts into a groove in the under side of the head. In the groove are sockets into which the teeth fit. There are no teeth on the upper jaw, only these sockets; therefore it can readily be seen that they cannot chew their food. When feeding the lower jaw hangs down a little, and as they swim rapidly through the squid they cut them into many pieces; then they scoop in the mutilated fish and swallow them. Sometimes they leave pieces many feet long. I think a sperm whale could easily swallow a man.

We found no more whales although we spent many months searching for them in vain. We finally ran the bark into a group of islands called Rosemary Islands. We found plenty of humpback whales there. This species of whale is found in breeding time near shore where the water is shallow. They are more easily taken when they have young with them, as the female will not leave her little ones that cannot swim as fast as she can. The boats frequently fasten to a calf, and they are sure to get the mother whale, for she will never forsake her baby.

I have been in a boat that was carried several rods on a whale's fin, the whale thinking the boat was her calf. They often carry their young on their fins when hard pushed by a boat. The cow will seldom strike a boat when her calf is around, no doubt taking the boat for her calf. The bulls are vicious. I have travelled faster in a boat fastened to a whale when attacked than on steam cars, and I have travelled over a mile a minute on the cars. Many times have I heard humpback whales when under water make a whining sound similar to that which a lot of bees make when disturbed, a sound which can be heard a mile away.

The bull whales are frequently seen flapping their fins up and down. It is very dangerous to approach them when they are at that sport. Their fins are from ten to twelve feet long. Those of the other species are not more than four to six feet long. The humpback whale cutting through the water with those long fins and broad, heavy tail would make short work of a boat that got too near.

I have fastened to them when they were "finning," as it is called, and it was difficult to tell at times which was in the boat, the crew or the whale, or both. A broad fin would sweep over the entire length of the boat, feeling for something to strike, then disappear with a plunge into the seething waters, and up would come a head quite as large as a load of hay, behind which was an immense body. We would then put our hands against the mass, and others, with the boat hook, would push the boat from the creature, as one would from a ledge of rocks.

The humpback whale is the most dangerous creature to handle that can be found in the water or on land. We seldom go out of a scrape with one without several holes being stove in our boats. The whales taken at these islands sank after they were killed. We anchored them in about twenty fathoms. After they had lain at the bottom three days they would float. We would then tow them to the ship and cut them up.

The abdomen of the humpback whale is corrugated, and looks like the lid of a roll-top desk. The skin between these wrinkles is very elastic, quite as much so as rubber. If we happened to lose a whale, and not find it for a week or so, it would, by that time, be what the whalemen call "blasted,"—swollen to twice its natural size, perhaps even three times, and would look a little distance off like a very large vessel on her beam ends. When in that condition they are filled with a foul gas which can be scented ten miles to the leeward.

The Rosemary Islands are not very fertile. Many are merely sand banks thinly scattered with a sage brush, while others are a mass of ledge with sharp points. We found but one island in the group that had water or wood upon it. We saw few natives, eight or ten perhaps, and they were perfectly nude, and were as near the brute as could be. The only weapons they carried were bones from a bird's wing stuck through a hole in the end of their nose. That they used to kill turtles, in this way: They have a dry log which is about ten feet long and eight inches thick which they straddle in the water. Paddling with their hands and kicking with their feet, they get through the water quite rapidly, and when they espy a turtle sleeping on the surface, they approach noiselessly and catch it by one of the flippers, and turn him over on to his back. They then draw the peg out of their nose, and run it through the turtle's eyes. This soon kills the turtle, when they tow it ashore, and have a royal feast.

Turtle, fish, and birds are all they have to live upon when there is no whaling going on in the bays. When ships are taking whales, the carcasses, having been stripped of the blubber, frequently float ashore, and the natives strip the flesh from the bones for food. They paddle off to vessels when the whalemen are "cutting in" a whale and eat the scraps the sailors throw over to them.

We were "cutting in" a cow whale one day, and the man who was using the spade cut into the udder, and the milk began to flow at once. Being curious to know how whale's milk tasted, I took a dipper and jumped on to the staging and from there on to the whale and caught some of the milk. I then returned to the deck and took a sup of the milk, but it was too salt to taste. In dipping I unfortunately took in about as much salt water as milk, but I had tasted whale's milk, which I think no other person ever did. Although I could not tell how it tasted, it was quite as white as cow's milk. At another time, when we were "cutting in" on another large whale, the captain thought he would give us a fresh mess of whale steak; accordingly he had a large piece of lean meat cut off and hoisted on board. The cook was soon set to frying whale steak. He cooked up quite a lot of it. At dinner-time we found a well-filled kid sent down to us of fried whale. Each man took a slice and began trying to eat it. Each ate a little, and a little was quite as much as any of us wished for. The grain was as large as a man's finger, and as tough as an alligator's hide. We partook so very sparingly of our fresh meat that when the kid was returned to the cook, he thought there was more left than was first served. As in the feast of the multitude, there were left seven basketsful and much fish.

The cook seldom threw anything overboard except the water bucket, which he would throw on certain occasions. So he took the fine lot of meat or fish, call it what you may, and worked it over into a whale lobscouse. We supposed the cook would take the kid and throw the lot overboard, but we found at supper-time that he had not done so. The same old cat we rejected at noon was passed down to us steaming hot. The creature had been trimmed up a little, but the first mouthful revealed his presence. However, out of consideration for the cook, who had spent quite all of the afternoon wrestling with the problem of making the creature eatable, and who had used three or four pounds of hard bread therefor, we masticated a little of it ; more for the bread that was in it, than for anything else. What was left went over- board that night while the cook was tucked snug away in his blankets. The captain never afterwards tried to palm off whale steak on us for veal cutlets. Experience enabled me to say that I had eaten whale and drank whale's milk ; but as the student said of stewed crow peppered with Scotch snuff, I might say of the whale steak, " Whale meat is good meat, but I don't hanker after it."

The season for whales at that place was over. We had been there about three months. All hands were badly off with scurvy, having so long had salt beef for dinner, lobscouse for supper, and, for a change, lob- scouse for breakfast. On Sunday we would get a slice of plum duff, with about one plum to a man. It was then I recalled the plums heaped before me at my uncle's in Boston. However, I choked down my emotion with a chunk of salt beef that might have been around the world three or four times for aught I know, and waited until all the other sailors had had their hack at the duff, when, if any was left, came my chance. I was the " titman " on board, and, according to nautical etiquette, was the last to get served at the mess kid. As a general rule sailors live pretty well on whaleships ; but sometimes, when a ship has been out two or three years, her meats and breadstuffs get rather stale, so much so, that often the cook would find fully half the meat and bread served for the meal, left in the kid. A good cook is never at a loss to know what to do in such cases ; he knows all the mysteries of lobscouse, and it is doubtful if a chemist could analyze it to tell what its components are. All that is left over in all the kids, both fore and aft, goes into the pot together, good, bad, and indifferent, to complete the compound. To season this the cook puts in a couple of spoonfuls of "slush" with half a pint of molasses; then the mess is boiled, poured into the kid, and served to the crew for their inspection and consumption. Sometimes the sailors make for a change what is called, among high-toned jack-tars, "dundifunk." This is made of powdered hard bread, slush and molasses, then baked until brown on the top. They do not have it often, since it is considered a rare and delicate dish.

The Sunday before we left the islands all went on shore in company with the crew of another vessel that happened there. A man in the other vessel's crew had a fife which he took along with him, so we all had a march on shore, headed by the fifer. The captain wanted to give us a run on land, since it was a help to those who had the scurvy, and we had it badly. I wish to call attention to the man who played the fife, since I saw him again in a distant part of the world, and in a more lucrative business than whaling.

Our ramble on the shore over, we went on board and were soon under way and running for Geograph Bay, Australia, where we arrived without mishap. I was down with the scurvy. We were sent on shore, where with an old sail we rigged up a tent. We did not require much shelter, for the weather was warm and dry. We were fed on potatoes, milk, and beef, and were soon perfectly well.

I was glad to find many white people at that place. They were not only white, but spoke English. I had made up my mind to leave the vessel as soon as we came to a country where white people lived, and I concluded this was the place. I managed to board the ship two or three times a week under the pretence of getting something, and then when going ashore again would have on more than one suit of clothes, and sometimes carried a bundle. In that way I soon got everything I cared for ashore, since my outfit was not very large. I had used up all of my outfit with which I started from home, and was considerably in debt to the "slop chest," which is a sort of a country store on board the ship, and out of which the captain peddles goods to the sailors at whatever terms may suit himself. After finding my credit good at the store, I ran up quite a little bill. I owed at home between thirty and forty dollars, which was waiting to be paid out of the three or four hundred dollars that I was to get at the end of the voyage. I knew with what I was owing the captain and what I owed the store in Boston, with the voyage only half through, that if I stayed the entire voyage and filled the vessel with oil, I would not have, after my bills were paid, enough money to pay for a plate of Boston's baked beans. So I decided to leave the ship, with all its joys and sorrows behind. No fault was to be found with the vessel, its officers or crew, for I was treated well by all on board and liked the sea, but I did not hanker after whales which had no money in them for me.

We were camped near the beach. There was a lagoon running back from the beach about a half-mile wide. Beyond that was a small hamlet, with a little hotel and a few log-cabins. The principal store was on the beach near where we landed. We used to wade the lagoon when we wanted to go over to the hotel. In some places the lagoon was quite three feet deep.

The time had come at last for me to shoulder my kit and break camp. The vessel was about ready to go to sea. I slung all my worldly effects over my shoulder and in the night stole across the dark waters which lay between me and liberty. I passed through the little town and close to the hotel where the captain was sleeping, and sleeping soundly I hoped. I went through the town without waking even a dog, and plunged into the forest not far away. It was dark, but I liked that; no one could pursue me. I kept on for about a mile, when I came to an old log which was a pretty large one; one end was about two feet above the ground; I piled some brush against one side, and hid myself under it after the fashion of a bird that puts its head under a leaf and thinks itself out of sight.

I did not know whether there were any wild animals about or not, or whether there were any in the country; neither did I care much just then. I was under the log, and out of harm's way for the present. I did not make a fire, having no desire to attract attention, and being yet within the lines of the enemy. Finally I fell asleep, and slept well, considering the accommodations at my new hotel, for it was not quite so elaborate as was my room in Lowell, but luxuries were readily dispensed with.

I was not troubled by the bills I owed the ship, as after leaving Lowell, having got bravely over that compunction. On finding the coast clear and no signs of immediate attack, I was quite contented with the situation. Before retiring I partook of a slight repast, which consisted of a small piece of ship biscuit and a little molasses. When finally leaving the ship I took a bottle half full of molasses and six cakes of hard bread.

CHAPTER III.

FIRST DAY IN THE BUSH — ADVANCES TOWARDS THE SETTLE-
MENT — LEARNS BRICKMAKING AT THE COLONY — A JOUR-
NEY INLAND — KANGAROO HUNTING — BECOMES A CAR-
PENTER — STUDYING THE HABITS OF THE NATIVES — A
MILLERITE EVENT WHICH CAUSES THE LOSS OF A SHIP —
STARTS IN BUSINESS — POOR RESULTS AND BAD DEBTS —
BECOMES A LUMBERMAN — PERFORMS A SURGICAL OPER-
ATION — HOMESICKNESS — LITTLE MONEY FOR FIVE
YEARS' WORK — RESOLVES TO EMBARK — CHARACTER-
ISTICS AND ANECDOTES OF THE AUSTRALIAN NATIVES.

My first morning in the bush was spent in laying plans
for the future. My first duty was, like a good general,
to examine my supply of provisions, which were so
limited that all hands were put on short allowance at
once. I knew that I could not stand much of a siege.
My next work was to strengthen my position a little,
which was done by piling up more brush around the log.
I did not know whether my habitation there would be
temporary or of long duration, so prepared for the
worst.

Having plenty of tobacco, I did not wish to put myself
on allowance, for it had become a great solace to me.
When we left home, we all took along ten to twenty
pounds each ; not only for our own use, but to trade with
the natives at the different islands we might stop at. I
took ten pounds. At that time I had never used tobacco, but wanted to trade with those who did use it. I
was at the wheel one day when the captain came up from
the cabin with a box of broken cigars. He asked me if
I wanted them, holding them out to me. He told me

that he did not care for them, as they were so broken up. Taking them forward, I soon began to try their flavor, and it did not take me many days to use up every stump ; and since I had got a taste, and the captain had no more boxes of broken cigars to give away, I took at once to my stock in trade. That was quite fifty years ago, and I have never neglected the weed since, when it was to be obtained, although having sometimes been on rather short allowance.

I found plenty of time between meals to meditate and smoke. I began to think that if a dish of that mysterious compound which we used to see so often on board ship was placed before me, that it would neither be regretted nor neglected. Finding, however, that dwelling on the past would not help the future nor the present, I partook of a humble supper and retired to my couch under the log, cast aside all thought of what the morrow might reveal and went to sleep, feeling safe for that night if for no longer. Before morning I found that there were other dangers to guard against besides the captain and sheriff,— the danger of losing one's food. I was awakened in the middle of the night by a singular noise near me, but just outside my brush shelter. I laid perfectly quiet and waited to see what the creature would do, intending to let it be the first to make an attack, if there was to be a fight. I soon found that the animal, whatever it might be, appeared to be hunting for my hard bread ; he had managed to get his nose pretty near my bag, in which was kept all my worldly effects as well as my daily supply of food. I concluded by the noise that the animal was not a very large one, whatever it might be, but its nose was painfully near my rations, so believed it time to call a halt. Accordingly I gave the brush a kick, and with one bound it was a rod away, and with one or two more of such leaps, out of hearing.

This disturber was a little animal about the size of a rabbit that jumps like the kangaroo; which appears to be the way most of the animals get over the ground in that country. This animal is called the walaby by the natives; and they jump like grasshoppers, with their hind legs and tail. When feeding they use their fore legs, which are short.

Having had no water since leaving the beach, I was very thirsty in the morning. At the beach I had become acquainted with two men: one was a sailor, an American, who had run away from some ship; the other man was an Englishman and a hanger-on around the hotel. The Englishman we will call Sam; and the Yankee, Spaulding, which was his right name, and if he is alive now and should read this book, he will remember the incident. I thought that Sam was trustworthy, and would keep silent about me, therefore after dark one night I left my hiding place and made my way to the door of Sam's cabin. He seemed to be much pleased to see me, and gave me a good supper of fresh beef stew, and urged me to remain over night with him, saying that I could get away in the morning before any one was up. I hesitated at first, but at his earnest request I remained with him. In the morning I was up at daylight. I thought of my experience in Lowell, and had no intention of being caught napping. Sam made me promise to spend the next night with him. I returned to my fort before the garrison was up, and managed to get through the day without having a surprise. After dark I went to my friend's again; he was ready to receive me, but he had no steaming supper waiting for me as I expected. He said, however, that he would soon have supper, but was out of bread, and if I would lend him my hat he would run over to the hotel and get a loaf. I did so and he started off. I soon began to mistrust my new friend, and so followed after him and kept him in sight. He entered the hotel, while I stopped some four or five rods from the hotel and awaited developments. I had not long to wait, for in a very few minutes out came Sam and another man in his shirt sleeves. This man had on a white shirt, which neither Sam nor Spaulding wore. When they had got about twenty feet from the door I thought it time to challenge, so sang out to know who the man was with him. Sam appeared to be surprised to find me so near him, since he thought I was in the cabin awaiting his return; but he soon answered that it was Spaulding. I replied that Spaulding did not wear a white shirt. "Yes," said he, "Spaulding has changed his shirt to-day." "Now," said I, "let him speak, and if it is Spaulding I shall know his voice." So he told his companion to speak, but he did not seem to care to. I was well satisfied at the first sight of the white shirt that the man was Capt. Coffin, but at the same time I wanted to be doubly sure. Finally the captain, as he proved to be, gave a sort of a grunt. I sang out, "That is old Coffin," and started away for the bush on the run. The captain continued calling after me, and I continued running. Sam called until his friendly calls were soon lost in the distance that I had quickly made between us. I pushed on for about a mile, and then halted. I knew from the nature of the forest that there would be no further pursuit that night. I could not find my log-cabin, it was too dark; so I built a little fire and laid myself down to sleep, and managed to get a few short naps, but I kept one eye open, having no idea of being caught by the captain. I was fast learning the ways of my friends. I was up at daylight and went at once on a still hunt for my log, which I soon found and took possession of again, none the worse for my adventure. Towards ten o'clock as I lay snugly tucked away under my log, pondering over my narrow escape and wondering what next would happen to me, I presently heard steps approaching. I crawled partly out and was soon in a position to beat a hasty retreat if need be. The person causing me so much uneasiness came and stood before me with nothing to cover his person but a roll of twine, about the size of my arm, wound around his waist. He was one of the natives, and the twine was made of opossum fur. I waited in silence for him to introduce himself. Finally, after gazing at me a few moments, he made a half-scowl and half-grin and started on his way, and, as I believed, rejoicing to think of the reward he would get for his discovery from the captain. But I was not to be outgeneralled by a nude savage! He had hardly disappeared from sight before I had my grip on my shoulder and was off on my way to pastures new and fresh. I pushed on into the forest a mile farther, and pitched my tent this time under a tree, where there was nothing to obstruct my view, as I now had a desire to see before being seen if it was possible, that I might have time for flight. I occupied this camp about a week. Occasionally I ventured out past the little village to a brook after water, and sometimes passed through a field of potatoes, where I would fill my pockets, and when I got back to camp would have a treat on potatoes and molasses. I was without a hat, since I did not wait for Sam to return mine.

I had thread and needles in my outfit and a pair of old pants. Believing I could get along better without pants than without a hat, I cut up the pants and made a skull cap. It had no visor to it, and was rather a poor substitute for a cap. I looked quite as comical in it as I did with the beaver which I wore when I left Canada. But I was never very proud, and I cared little for the fashions of the country, knowing that if I got entirely out of pants I should then be in the very height of the fashion, since I had seen, a few days since, one of their latest fashion plates.

Becoming restless, I thought I would go over to the beach and see if the vessel had sailed. I had begun to get tired of the monotony of my life, and longed for a change. I put on what clothing I could wear, lest I should not find my bundle on my return, hid my sack, and at night crossed over the bayou to the beach. Hiding near my old camp, I waited for daylight. As soon as light dawned, I was out making observations over the water, and there the old vessel lay quietly at anchor. My courage did not fail me. I hid in the bushes where I could see who came ashore. It was not long before I saw a boat push off, which was soon on the beach. The officer in the boat was the third mate, Jack, whom we shipped in Madagascar. In him I always had a friend. I met him at the store, and he told me that the captain was at the hotel and would be there all day, and I was safe at the store part of the day, if not throughout the day. At about ten o'clock the Englishman came over, but before I saw him he had drank heavily. I told the mate how he had taken my hat, and how he had tried to sell me to the captain. The Englishman had a very nice hat on, so the mate exchanged with him and gave him my patent cap for his hat. The mate told me that the bark would not sail for another week, and if I wanted to get clear I had better go up to the Lashanault, a little town about thirty miles up the coast, and I concluded to take his advice. He bought a pound of biscuit at the store, which he gave to me to eat on my journey. It was too late then to start, since I wanted to make the trip in one day, so I concluded to camp a little way up the beach until morning. Before leaving the mate, he told me that the native who saw me at my first hiding place came straight to the hotel and told the captain where he could find me. On learning that, the captain hunted up the sheriff and the three started out after me. The native was not long in guiding them to the old log I had so hastily and recently left. The sheriff looked under the log, and told the captain that the nest was there, but the bird had flown. The captain had a self-acting revolver. The sheriff had never seen one. He was looking at it, and as he held it in both hands and pulled the trigger to see how the thing worked, he found out to his sorrow. It acted, and his thumb went off at the same time.

I saw the sheriff some three months later; he showed me his hand, and said that was all he got for trying to catch me. I told him it ought to have blown his head off for chasing a poor sailor. I learned, later on, that the Englishman had reported me to the captain after my first night with him. The captain offered him fifteen dollars if he would help him catch me, but he found that chaff was no good around his trap.

The next morning I started bright and early for Lashanault, a walk of thirty miles over a hot and sandy beach and without water. The ocean lay on one side of my route, and a wild, dark forest on the other. I left my bag with its contents behind, since I dared not go after it, knowing that danger lurked in every bush, and not wanting to take any risk. I pushed on with the rising of the sun, and had not gone over a mile when I came to a river some two hundred yards wide and quite deep and rapid. Thinking I might ford it, I pulled off my shoes and pants and started in, but found it too deep to go straight across and too rapid to think of swimming against the current, so I retreated. Upon further investigation I found that, where the river emptied into the bay, the water appeared to be quite shallow. I started in again and took a long half-moon circle and found the water some three feet deep, but I made the landing on the other side successfully. Soon dressed, again I went on my way, rejoicing to know that there was at least one barrier between me and pursuit. I pushed on about two miles farther, when another river lay before me. This river I found quite deep, but I thought I could get over in the same manner as the other; so I doffed my shoes and pants and plunged in and started on a long circuit. I had got about fifty yards from shore, when, to my dismay, I found myself slowly but surely sinking. The sand beneath my feet appeared to be alive, and I realized in a moment that I was on a bar of quicksand, and to think was to act under those circumstances. I whirled around and drew my feet from the sand and made for the shore again, which I soon reached.

My courage was yet unabated. Going up the stream some two hundred yards, to where the current was not quite so rapid, I stripped off my shirt, bundled up my effects and held them in one hand at arm's length, and waded in until the water reached my waist, then struck out with both feet and one hand. The current, as I expected, carried me down the stream rapidly, but I kept my eyes on the opposite shore and pulled as for dear life. I dared not turn my eyes toward the ocean which I knew was very near; and I thought if there was danger of my taking a fast trip to sea, I did not wish to know it. I finally reached the bank on the opposite side of the river, and was soon ready for the tramp, which I resumed at once, feeling then for the first time since I had left the vessel that I was a free man, with the world before me.

I pushed on at a good pace with a fair wind behind, the open sea beside me, and a clear sky overhead. I soon found myself much in want of what I recently had too much of,— water. With the heat and the sea breeze I found myself almost choked; I did not find a drop of fresh water during the whole journey of thirty miles. I knew that when I started, hence my desire to keep on the move. I would take a bite of cracker and a smoke after, to allay my thirst. I always found a good smoke, when very thirsty, would moisten my mouth and very much relieve me.

About mid-day I saw something ahead that made me feel that the end of trouble was not yet, notwithstanding I had flattered myself that I had passed all danger. Three natives came out of the bush and walked down to the water's edge. But since there were but three, I thought I might have some show in a fight, if there was to be one. My first thought was that the captain, anticipating my intended journey, had sent an advance to act as body guard and escort while on the way back to headquarters. Again I thought of the tales I had heard of the cannibals who inhabit the islands in that part of the world. On getting up to them, they took a careful survey of me and then gave a grunt and muttered a few words in a language which was all like Dutch to me, but I pretended to understand them and pointed ahead and said, "Yes," "Warm day," "Good morning," and started on again. I soon looked back, however, not wishing them to steal a march on me, and finding they were going the other way, felt much relieved. Perhaps they thought me too lean to make them a suitable meal, and thus let me pass, while looking further for fatter game.

I kept on, with now and then a little rest. About four in the afternoon I came to a point or bluff which extended out some way into the ocean, with a low neck running toward the sandhills which were back of the beach at that place. I climbed over the neck, thinking to save a mile or two, for I was by that time pretty well

TREADING THE MIXTURE FOR BRICKMAKING IN AUSTRALIA.

tired out.　When I mounted to the top of the neck and looked over, my heart leaped to my mouth.　Spread out before me was a beautiful river, on whose banks, dotted here and there, were little cottages, while in the background could be seen the verdure of many a native plant and shrub.　There was one solitary hut not far ahead, toward which I bent my steps with some haste.

As I approached the shanty I saw a very pretty young woman standing at the open door.　I gazed with admiration, while she looked at me with disgust I suppose ; for I must admit I was rather a pitiable looking object, being completely worn out.　She opened her ruby lips and greeted me with, "Why, young man, you look as if you were completely worn out."　I answered her that I was, and that I was almost choked, as I had drank no water since the night before.　She soon supplied me, not only with water, but with a good hearty meal of sheep's head and pluck.　Not long after, her husband came in.　I learned that his name was Salter.　He was accompanied by another man, whose name was Penny, for whom Salter was employed in making brick.　I soon struck a bargain with Penny to help them make bricks.　Although I had never seen a brick made, I was willing to learn how.　The next morning we started for the brickyard, which was about two miles back from the coast, in the forest.　The yard consisted of nothing but a few boards put together on the ground like a mortar bed, into which a few wheelbarrow loads of clay were thrown, with a load or two of sand.　Then the process began with slashing and cutting at the pile with a long wooden sword. When pretty well hewn down, we would strip off shoes and stockings and wade in and tread and mix the clay and sand in that way until it was in condition to mould. I found it hard for my feet for the first two or three days, but did not complain.　Not only was I learning the trade,

but was getting my food, which was the main consideration with me just then.

I served about two weeks' apprenticeship at the clay
pile, keeping my eyes open during the time for something better than brickmaking. There were soldiers
stationed near by the place; and the lieutenant who was
in command of them seemed a very fine officer. I had
become somewhat acquainted with him, while passing
frequently near his quarters. Meeting me one day, he
inquired how I liked brickmaking. I replied that I did
not like the business. He then asked how I would like
to go out a few miles into the country with him to help
him get a few tons of hay. I told him I should like to
go, and that I was more used to that kind of work than
making bricks. He informed me what day he was going
to start, and said if I wanted to go to be ready. When
the appointed day came, he did not have to wait for me.
I notified Mr. Penny that I had found work that suited
me better, and left him without further notice.

There were four in our haying party. We travelled
about twenty miles, and were three weeks making about
one ton of hay. The blades of grass were few and far
between. My work was not very hard; for the lieutenant often took me and two natives, with a couple of
dogs, to go out after kangaroo, which were numerous,
and we used to keep the camp supplied with fresh meat.

The manner in which the white people catch the kangaroo is very interesting. They have large dogs, called
kangaroo dogs, trained expressly to hunt this animal. They
range in value from fifty to five hundred dollars. Two
dogs and one or two natives are taken along to hunt.
The kangaroo is generally found in herds of ten to
twenty, sometimes more; occasionally only two or three
are found together. Very much depends upon the
season of the year. When the game is sighted, the dogs

start out, and the kangaroo is away at the first jump of the dog.

A well-trained dog will soon run one down, kill it, and return to his master, who looks in the dog's mouth. If he has killed the kangaroo there will always be found some hair in the corners of his mouth. The master tells the dog to find him, and he starts off on a trot leading directly to the dead animal. The hunters take the natives along to pack and tow in the game, and to track it. When hunting kangaroo and they discover a trail, the natives track the animals much better than the dogs. The kangaroo dog goes by sight, and not by scent. It has been said that the Australian natives track by instinct, but such is not the case; for the one who made the discovery of myself under the old log could have tried his skill on a new trail, for I certainly did not try to cover up my tracks.

The kangaroo has a long claw, like a finger, only much longer, with a talon at the end; from the point of that talon to the heel of the male is nearly two feet. They stand on the lower parts of their legs, and their tail rests on the ground back of them some two feet, in such a way that it acts as a spring. When they run, they give a spring with their hind legs and a push with their tail at the same time. Every time they strike they leave a mark with that long claw. The tail is not used after the first spring, but is elevated a little above the ground. The tail of a large male is about four feet long, and some four inches broad at the body, and tapers down to about one inch at the end. It is brought into use when the animal is feeding; he rests on his shanks and tail, and will reach forward as far as he can, then he puts down his two fore paws, which are quite short, and draws his tail up, keeping about eighteen inches of the end of it snug to the ground, while the other part is bent up in the form of a bow. Their weight is then on their tail and fore feet: they lift their hind feet together and swing them forward, placing them on the ground again. In this manner they make a different track from that made when jumping. As they drag the tail it bends the grass the way the animal is going, his fore feet also leave marks as well. When the native is in the neighborhood of the kangaroo feeding grounds, he scans the grounds closely, and when he sees the dry grass bent over he drops down on his hands and knees to examine the ground. He will soon tell which way the animal was travelling, and, if feeding, will find the marks made by his tail and fore feet. The native, keeping the tracks in view until he finally loses them, will very soon find the last track of the fore paws and tail; and on looking very closely, he observes the two marks made by the long claw or finger on each hind foot. He knows by this time how large the animal is by the marks left by the tail and fore paws, and he knows about how far the animal will jump, and also whether the animal was frightened or not. He soon gets his eye on the spot where the dry grass is bent down, with one or both of the toe scratches.

His knowledge of the tracks of the different animals is so excellent that when the track is found he will start off on a trot and keep that gait up until he starts the animal from his lair or his feeding ground. If large game happens to pass, while on the run, over several yards of ledge, they invariably leave some slight scratches, and then the native has the course, which is generally nearly a straight one. I became quite expert in the art of tracking the kangaroo before leaving the country.

There is many a sorry-looking dog after the chase is over. If the dog is green or not properly trained, he will attack at once after running the kangaroo to bay, thinking that he has the killing all his own way, but he soon finds out to his sorrow that he is not alone in the fight. The kangaroo strikes out with that long claw and strikes the dog in the head or neck, and sends him a rod or two through the air. After a kick or two, the plucky dog renews the attack, but somewhat on his guard, having learned cautiousness by experience. He then plays about the animal, worrying him until he gets him tired out, and then when a good chance offers catches the kangaroo by the neck, and after pulling him down it takes but a short time for the dog to despatch him.

Dogs sometimes have their heads and necks so terribly lacerated that they have to be doctored many weeks before they go out again on the chase. The kangaroo has been known to catch small dogs in their fore paws and carry them to a pool of water and hold them under the surface till they were drowned.

The white people never save the fore quarters ; the hind quarters, tail, and hide are all that are carried from the field. The hind quarters make good steak or meat to stew, but is rather dry, having no fat. The tail makes excellent soup, much better to my taste than ox tail or turtle. All the fat on the animal is in the tail. The fore quarters are little else than bones and claws. I used to think that if some enterprising Yankee was there, he might start an industry and make a fortune gathering up the kangaroo fore quarters and canning them for the sailors. They would keep in any climate, and would come handy for the cook failing to find odds and ends enough for the scouse, pot; the preparation might season if it did not fatten.

After three weeks of haying and hunting, we returned to town. Lieut. Northy paid me with two sovereigns, the first money I had seen since leaving Boston. It soon burned a hole through my pocket, but I was looking about for employment before the bottom of my pocket dropped out. I soon found a carpenter named Leighton, who some three years before came from London, England. He had a large shop, covered with what is called paper bark, light colored and about one inch thick. The bark can be split to the thickness of letter paper. It is taken from trees in strips about three feet wide and from eight to ten feet long, then split to the desired thickness and sewed to frames. The natives use it to make huts very much like an American Indian wigwam. When the natives move, the females pack the bark on their backs.

To my surprise, I found my old shipmate Long Jim here, and learned, through him, that two or three sailors besides myself had run away from the ship at Geograph Bay. He was at work for Mr. Leighton, and through him I obtained work at the same place, with the promise of two sovereigns a month and board. I thought it would suit me better to be a carpenter than a brickmaker or to follow farming.

The wood commonly used there was mahogany. It resembled the Honduras very much in color, and some of it was quite soft. It sank quite readily in water. There were many other kinds of trees in that part of the country, but mahogany was the most common. Houses, fences, and boats were built of it. I helped build a bridge with it, also a brig of two hundred and fifty tons burden.

Mr. Leighton had worked on the king's palace in England when King George was alive. He said when the king came, all dropped to their knees until the king had passed. I told him no Yankee would do that. He replied that it was done out of respect to their sovereign. He brought from England a chest of tools that cost him $2,500. Then all woodwork was done by hand, and he had a tool for everything used in woodworking.

He had some fifteen men at work when he employed me, and in less than one year all left him but myself. He got to drinking very hard, and neglected his business, soon going from bad to worse. I remained with him for nearly three years. We used to do about enough to pay for our food and to furnish him with beer.

One day a vessel from England came into the harbor with emigrants. Among them was a young Italian woman whose father was the modeller in marble of the big elephant which was shot in London a few years previous to her emigration. Mr. Leighton married her in about three weeks after she landed. That stopped his drinking for a short time, but after a little he began drinking again worse than ever. I frequently led him home and put him to bed, for his wife could do nothing with him

During this period I had plenty of time to study the natives, the habits, costumes, and peculiarities which belonged to that people exclusively.

In 1843, when the great comet of that year became visible, it was seen in Australia in all its beauty and grandeur, and viewed with wonder and astonishment by many, by others with fear and dread. Many knew or had read of Miller, the Adventist, and thought the world was coming to an end.

An American captain with his ship, which belonged in Fairhaven, arrived off the coast when the comet appeared in sight. He thought the world was about to collapse, and he pointed his ship for the Lashanault, our port, thinking, perhaps, that he could run faster than he could swim, with the result that some of the ship's ribs and truck are rotting to-day on the sandy shores of Australia.

In common with my old friend Mr. Penny of the brickyard and a Mr. Stafford, an American from Salem, Mass., and one or two others, I went off in the night in a long-boat to the ship. We saw that she was going ashore. The bay at that time was a mass of rolling billows, but there were stout hearts and strong limbs in the boat, and we made the ship and were pulled in over the stern. She was aground, and we could do nothing but send down a few spars. In the morning the wind abated a little. We got out her anchors and hove her into deep water again. In the afternoon the gale renewed its fury and drove her up high and dry. The captain thought it impossible to float her again, and after two or three weeks unloading, she was sold for two hundred pounds sterling. The captain sold the effects and started for home to wait a little longer before he started for that foreign shore so far away and yet so painfully near to him. The vessel was the " North America," of Fairhaven, Mass., and the men who bought her were two brothers, who, after a week's work, got her afloat off shore, where she lay for three weeks, apparently sound and perfectly tight. They were about ready to start with her to Freemantle, a port at Swan River. The day before they were to sail she began to leak so badly they could not keep her afloat, and finally they had to let her go on to the beach, where they broke her up.

Some of her ribs are yet bleaching on that sandy beach not far from the spot where a ship called the " Samuel Wright," from New Bedford, commanded by a Capt. Coffin, was cast away a few years previous to the wreck of the " North America."

One summer we found ourselves running very short of provisions. For three months we lived on sheep's head and pluck for meat, and rice for bread, and we were without tobacco. During that time I spent hours hunting over piles of shavings in the shop for old stumps and bits of tobacco. It was like hunting for diamonds, every one that was found was valued as one might a gem of the first water. At this time hearing that there was an American whaler lying at Geograph Bay, I started at once for the Bay, where I obtained a month or two's supply of tobacco and returned. At another time, when I was out of the weed, I persuaded a native to loiter around the house of the chief judge of the place, knowing the judge used tobacco. The natives have access to all parts of the settlers' dwellings. They seldom steal, nor do they smoke; but this old native was very friendly to me, and quite willing to filch tobacco for me. He seldom came out of the judge's parlors without half a plug of Yankee tobacco tucked under his skin cloak.

Finding that I was not getting rich very fast at Leighton's, while he was getting drunk nearly every day, I finally informed him that I could not remain longer with him, but was going down to Geograph Bay and see what I could find to do there. I had learned the trade so well that I thought myself capable of building a house, and make my own bricks also, if need be. Mr. Leighton objected to have me leave him, but I had determined to start in business for myself. Finding moral suasion unsuccessful, he concluded to let me go, and gave me quite a kit of tools, which I gratefully received and shipped for Geograph Bay. There I located at a farmhouse, hung out my sign, and was soon ready for any kind of a job. I soon got one, the first and the last in that locality. An Irishwoman came to me one morning and said that her little boy had died the day before, and she wanted a coffin made for the little fellow. I was ready to make it for her. She wanted to know the cost, and I informed her that I could make it for her for about ten shillings.

"Oh!" said she, "that is too much; I cannot afford to pay that."

I did not wish to drive away my first customer, as it might injure my business, so told her, as she was poor, I would get her up something for eight shillings.

"Why," said she, "I cannot pay even that much." I thought she was trying to drive a close bargain. "Well," said she, "I will give you two pounds of butter, since I have not got any money at all, at all."

I thought the matter over, wondering what I could do with two pounds of butter. Finally, I concluded to take the butter, as Geograph Bay was often visited by the whalers, and I thought I might trade it for tobacco or something that would sell for cash, so accepted the woman's offer for the coffin, but told her she must not tell what she gave me for the job. She promised, and was very profuse with her thanks. I made the box and delivered it to her. She said that in a few days she would pay me. The net result of that job was one pair of shoe soles faithfully worn out running for that butter, which never materialized. My business venture did not meet with success, for I found there was neither money nor butter in that locality for me.

I left the place and began work on a farm, and helped the owner to cut some ten acres of wheat. While helping the farmer an American whaler came into port, and a boat came ashore with the colored steward. He came to the farm and said the ship was to start for home in about three months. I gave him a letter, and a portrait of myself that I had paid a friend to paint for me, by making a box to keep his brushes and paints in. The letter and picture were all the tidings my friends received of me during the seven years of my absence.

After the harvest I gave my tools away and started for Swan River, arriving there in due time. I put up at a hotel for a few days, and did little jobs around for my board. After a while I met a man whose business was to saw lumber by hand. He wanted me to dig pits for him.

A pit is dug in the ground about five feet deep, about twenty feet long, and five wide. Skids are laid across the pit so the logs when rolled upon them will be about six feet above the bottom of the pit. When the log is in position, one man stands in the bottom of the pit while the other stands on the log; then they proceed to saw and make the log into boards. After working two weeks at pit digging, the man who engaged me went to a place called Murray River to saw timber for a brig which he was to build. He and a partner did business under the name of Morris & Wested; they took a number of men, and I went with them. We all camped in the woods, and a cook was needed, so they put me to cooking. They taught me to make what they called dampers, that being what they call their bread. They first make a hot fire; a good bed of ashes and coals obtained, they put the dough into the hot ashes and cover it up. It will bake or roast in this manner, and comes out in fine condition, and is very palatable.

Bread baked in that way is much better than in an oven, and far sweeter. The ashes brush off and leave the bread white and perfectly clean. The flavor is retained by the ashes, and the bread is better.

My adventures were various during the eleven months of my stay in that place. A young man about my age tended a sort of country store that Mr. Morris kept at Freemantle. I call him Mr. S. He will figure prominently later in my adventures and in other parts of the world. His father was a wealthy merchant and a member of the London Stock Exchange. Something like myself, he wanted to see the world, so his father gave him £1,000 a year for spending money, and sent him to Swan River. He used to spend his allowance in three or four months, having what he thought was a " good time." He was not one who would sit down and suck his thumbs after his money was gone and wait for another remittance, but would pitch in and do anything to bring him an honest loaf of bread.

When I first knew him he was tending Mr. Morris's store. I was wanted in the woods to dig pits, and, since business was not very brisk at the store, Mr. S. came to Murray River and took my position as cook for the camp.

He held that lofty position for the eleven months I was there, and how much longer, after I left, I never knew.

A gentleman lived not far from the banks of the river whose name was Peel. His brother was Prime Minister of England. He owned a large tract of land in that locality, and it was said that he bought it of the English government for sixpence an acre.

I was told by a friend, a few years later, that he gave it back to the government, as he could not pay for it. The land was poor and sandy, but well timbered with mahogany and other timber common to the country.

Mr. Peel gave Mr. Morris permission to cut all the timber he wanted from his land. We had to scour the forest for what natural crooks, bends, and knees we wanted, which consisted of one or two thousand acres. That place is now called Peel.

There were but three buildings at Murray River at that time, and they were mere log-cabins. Up the river about ten miles was a small hamlet called Penjarah. I soon learned to saw boards and planks, so I was kept at that, and others dug the pits. I cut one tree called by the settlers *tuit*, a very hard and close-grained wood, and very hard to split. This tree was twenty inches at the ground, and from it were taken two sticks four by eight and eighty feet long, without a waney edge on either one. How much longer the tree was I do not know, as I did not measure it. This statement gives some idea of the height of small trees in that country. The color of the bark on this species is something like that on our horse-chestnuts and about as thick. The wood is of a light color; it is impossible to split it, and it looks like the lignum-vitæ. My mate and myself sawed two stringers for the brig out of that four by eight stick, which were eighty feet long, and without a blemish the entire length. Those two stringers and her spars were the only two kinds of timber in the entire vessel differing from mahogany, which composed the balance of the ship. Mahogany was shipped by them to England for ship's planking, it being commonly said that the worms would not work in it.

I was in the habit of going to Swan River, forty miles above, about every two months after sheep that Mr. Morris would have driven to that place, and from there to the river below, on which to feed his men. On the road out I frequently met my friend S. going to town to spend a few days.

When I had a little change in my pocket, knowing that he had none since Morris paid about all his debts with promises, I would say, " S., have you any money ? "

" No," he would invariably answer, "not a red."

" Here is half a crown, it will pay for your dinner."

He would then push on to town, having the satisfaction of knowing that he was not " broke." I always felt quite independent when I could feel a coin in my pocket, let it be ever so small, and I thought that was the way S. would feel on arriving in town.

I may mention a little incident that happened one day when I was at Freemantle after sheep, to show how easily a young fellow can get into trouble where there are meddlesome people around who do not stop to investigate, but who jump at swift conclusions. If people would only investigate a little, they would save themselves a great amount of misery and trouble.

A little mistake of a lady nearly caused me to lose my situation. On my arrival in town I was sometimes obliged to wait two or three days for the sheep to arrive from over "the hills." The general store of the place was in a double house, one part being used as a store, and the other as a tenement, and its occupant was a meddlesome lady. The store was closed since its clerk had been promoted to cook, and the key was left at the next door. While waiting for the sheep I was permitted to occupy the store until the drove arrived.

Near the store lived a woman whose husband was at work on the vessel which we were building. She was considered of rather doubtful character, as gossip went. On one trip her husband was coming in with the sheep from the hills, and was expected to help me drive them down to Murray River. I had to wait two or three days for him, but found enough in the store to cook, excepting meat. To supply this need I went to the butcher's and bought a leg of mutton, and salted it well, as I supposed, from a barrel of salt found in the store, then carried it to the next door to let the lady bake it for me. Soon after my roast was under way, the other lady came in and said that since her husband was going down with me, we would need something to eat on the road, and if I would give her a bowl of flour, she would bake a few biscuits for us. I was very glad to do so, thinking that what meat I did not eat while waiting, with the biscuits, would last us during our trip down to the river. The next-door neighbor saw her come with an empty bowl, and go away with it full. I went for my mutton, which was nicely baked. She said nothing to me about the flour. I got my biscuits and sat down to my repast. From a slice of the rich brown roast I took a good mouthful, but it came out quicker than it went in.   I found, upon investigation, that I had salted the mutton with saltpetre instead of salt.   Mr. Wested came in during the day, and I gave the roast to him, which he devoured with apparent relish. My friend did not go down with me as was expected, nor did the roast, but I was supplied with bread.

The distance from Freemantle to Murray River is forty miles, very dry and sandy, with but one place where water could be had, and that scarcely large enough to satisfy a dog's thirst.

A large number of native dogs prowl around those wild deserts. They are as ravenous as wolves, and a few of them will soon destroy a large flock of sheep by sucking their blood.   I started out at sunrise with twenty sheep ahead of me, and pushed on rapidly, knowing that if night overtook me I would not have many sheep to drive in the morning.   I came to the little water hole about mid-day.   It was very dry and hot.   I drove my flock up to the hole, which was about large enough for one sheep to get his nose into.   They would look at the hole, and then jumped over it, one after another, until they had all passed over.   I found it was no use tying to get them to drink, for I was losing valuable time ; and every one who knows anything about sheep knows they are something as a woman is said to be, for when she says she *won't*, she *won't*, and it is no use to coax her.

By keeping them on the move I finally arrived at the camp just as the sun was setting, for which I felt grateful, as a little previous to this a man was attacked by dogs in the night.   He had to climb a black boy stump, and sit and see his flock killed to the last sheep without being able to prevent it, being only too glad to think himself out of their reach, although his perch was not a very comfortable one.

A few days later Mr. Morris came down, and he was

not long in finding me. He wanted to know why I gave that woman the flour. I told him, and he was satisfied; but the next-door neighbor would not be convinced.

The carpenter who was building the vessel upon which we were working had run away from a British man-of-war, on which he was carpenter. Previous to beginning the vessel he had agreed to build a bridge for a Mr. Moore across a river some twenty miles above Perth, the capital of Western Australia, and eleven miles above the seaport of Freemantle. When the carpenter contracted to build this vessel he left the bridge unfinished, but his peculiar way of doing business was not satisfactory, and he was obliged to return and fulfil his contract. He was a man with many peculiarities, and one of the peculiar features about his personal appearance was a large wart in the corner of his left eye. It was as large as a marble, and he frequently complained about its preventing him from seeing clearly. I asked him why he did not have it removed.

He replied that the doctors on board the man-of-war said, if it was cut out, he would bleed to death; and since he was not ready to die, he let it remain, although it troubled him greatly.

I offered to remove it, and guaranteed that the operation would not hurt nor kill.

He said that if I would do so, he would give me two sovereigns, to which I agreed.

One Sunday morning I informed him I was ready to perform the operation. The men not being at work, they gathered around to see the operation performed.

I wanted some fun with the fellow, and gave the boys a hint. One man wanted to know if it would not be well to strap him to the table, while another thought they could hold him.

I told them it would not be necessary, but they might

lock the door and guard the windows and also the chimney, if they thought there would be any danger. I asked the victim if he would let them hold him. He answered, "No," saying further, that if the operation was going to kill him, he wanted one last chance to kick before his life was snuffed out.

I reminded him that I had agreed not to hurt him, and that I would not do so.

I had at home practised on my own warts. I thought a successful operation of this magnitude in the colonies might establish my reputation, and my fortune would be certain. I could make brick, build houses and ships, but there was no money in any of those trades for me. This operation, however, bid fair to yield me more money than I had seen for years. I called for a pair of scissors and a silk thread. The contractor, seated before me, began to look pale, and, as he used a deal of tobacoo, I told him a good smoke would quiet his nerves.

He consented, and the way he blew out the smoke one might think it was to be his last indulgence. Finally, laying aside his pipe, he announced that he was ready.

I simply tied the thread around the wart, drew the ends tight and cut them off, leaving half an inch hanging down on his cheek, and told him that he would have to wait a few hours before the operation would be complete. The wart soon began to turn black and in three hours it was jet black.

My patient began to be uneasy for fear his head might turn black and drop off. He hastened to a little glass that hung against the wall and began to pick at the ends of the thread that hung down, and the wart dropped into his hand. He came to me at once with joy in his eye, and upon examination there was scarcely a mark where the wart had been. I told him that he would have no further trouble with it.

He was very profuse with his thanks, and promised to pay me soon, saying that he was rather short just then.

His stock of promises held out well; and when he found how easy he had been rid of his pet wart, he thought he might pay for the operation in the same easy way, which he did.

Finally, his stock of promises gave out and left nothing to pin my hopes on, and to my disgust they also gave out. Thus my hope of establishing a new profession began in smoke and ended in misty promises. He might, I thought, have written to the queen what a wonderful operation had been performed by a young American who was travelling through her Majesty's domain in the southern hemisphere for health and pleasure, and who had by chance stopped at that town and volunteered without charge to relieve one of her loyal subjects of a troublesome and extraneous growth, and had performed an operation that the skilled surgeons on her Majesty's ships dared not attempt. I thought possibly that after reading such a token of regard for me from one of her subjects, if she did not send me a pension for life, she might at least transport me from that place, since I could see no future operations whereby I could realize sufficient cash to take me out of the country. Such a letter might give me some little notoriety, especially in that country where so many wealthy men had preceded me, not only for their own health, but for the good of their mother country. Anything would be accepted with thanks at that time; but alas! the patient forgot that he ever had a wart.

We had the vessel ready to plank, when the carpenter received a letter to come up at once and finish the bridge. He was threatened with suit at once if he did not come and fulfil his contract. To leave then would place Mr. Morris in a tight place, but there was no other way.

The two owners, the carpenters, and two other men went to finish the bridge, a task which would take them about four weeks. They had been gone only about a week, when one evening I overheard the men who were left behind, some eight or ten, plotting to finish the vessel themselves. They had received no money for their work, since money was one of the exceptions at that place, and they could claim the whole contract money for what they had done. I knew poor old Morris had everything at stake in the vessel; and he having always treated me well, although unable to pay me money, I could not consent to see him wronged.

The next morning I took a lunch and started for Mr. Moore's, nearly seventy miles away. After two days of forced travelling I reached my employers and laid before them what was going on at the vessel.

Mr. Wested went down at once and put an end to their plotting. I then remained and helped finish the bridge. It was at this time that I first began to feel homesick; the nature of the work was the direct cause of my homesickness. We had to put together two piles with a cap secured to the top, then with a flat boat, with a derrick in the centre, get the "bents" into the right position. With a wooden monkey—a log of wood about twelve inches through and three feet long, with a rope tied to one end, and driven through a block at the top of the derrick — we did our pile driving. We would hoist the monkey by the rope, then let it drop: if it hit the mark, the pile went down a little; and if it did not hit, why the monkey went farther down than the pile did.

After a week of hitting and missing, we got four bents driven into the mud so that they would stand without a a rope to hold them up, which was a very poor result for our labor. Pulling that monkey up was what made me homesick, since it reminded me of Boston, where I

first saw pile driving.   So forcibly was I reminded
of home by that experience that I could not keep *home*
out of mind day or night thereafter.

We got the bridge finished without serious mishap,
though we thought one night we were attacked by
savages.   We slept in one field bed; that is, we slept
on the ground, in an old deserted cabin with many big
cracks open, and no door to close, and with only a few
logs overhead.   In the middle of the night, when all
were soundly sleeping, we were rudely awakened by a
monster of some sort falling on us.   There appeared to
be arms or claws scooping us all in, and each thought
he was the particular victim.   On our feet, we saw the
object that had aroused us from slumber dart away.   It
was the Australian iguana, a creature much like a lizard.
It has a body about twenty inches long and a tail about
three feet long ; the body of a full-grown one measuring
about five inches across the back, and the legs are about
twelve inches long.   They are very strong, and that one
particularly was very lively, at least while struggling
about among our blankets.   The natives spear them and
use them for food.

After getting the bridge so that a man could pass over it
in safety, we returned to Murray River, but I did not get
over my homesickness and longing to leave the country.
I found plenty of work but no money, although I got
along pretty well without the latter.   Provisions were
cheap and plenty, such as they were, and good enough,
although of the simplest kind, but I was anxious to get
where I could handle a little money.

Our blacksmith leaving about this time, I told the boss
that I could do the work, so he set me to making bolts.
I served a brief apprenticeship, with credit to myself and
possibly honor to the trade.   That trade, however, like
all the many trades which I had mastered, had no money

in it. All the money I had received since I had left home was about twenty dollars during about five years of work.

Still I thought, if I learned all the trades, I might yet see the day and place where I could earn a few dollars by my knowledge of so many trades. In addition to the four sovereigns received, I had also a promise of two pounds of butter.

About this time a vessel called the " Falco," of Lynn, Mass., Capt. Mosely, came into Swan River. She was on a trading voyage around the world, and was loaded with all the Yankee notions, from a clock to a canoe. On board was a man named Williams, who appeared to be the supercargo. He was also an American consul, going somewhere to represent Uncle Sam, I never learned just where, and I don't think he knew himself; he intended probably to locate where he found the most money, since he concluded not to stop long at Swan River. I thought, as he was an American consul, he would be obliged to look after the interests of Americans in foreign countries, especially those who were cast away on a foreign shore; and wasn't I a cast-away sailor and an American? To be sure, I was cast away in the " North America " at the Lashanault. Armed with these facts, I hurried to town and to the hotel where the consul was staying. Being ushered into his presence, I found him in all his regalia, even to the cocked hat. I stated my case, and he appeared to appreciate my remarks, and said he only felt too happy to be able to extend a helping hand to a poor fellow-countryman, and I considered it a godsend that his arrival was so opportune. It was understood that I should depart with him.

Before entering upon a new chapter of my adventures, and ere I leave this land of milk and honey, I would devote a few descriptive words to the natives and to their customs and habits.

The natives of Australia resemble Kaffirs of the Cape of Good Hope and the natives of India more than any other peoples I have seen. About medium height, they are well proportioned and have invariably double teeth all around on both jaws, in which they appeared to be especially favored, since they have to eat very tough, half-cooked, and sometimes raw food. They wear little or nothing in the warm weather; but in winter, which is the rainy season, both male and female, when it is chilly, wear what is called a *booker*. The booker is a kangaroo-skin, with two corners tied together, drawn over the head. This falls over the shoulders and down about to the knees.

When it is very chilly they take what they call *mongit*, which is much like a knot; they then build a fire with a lot of these knots. They place these knots in the form of a star with many points, and light the fire in the centre. The knots burn very slowly and last for many hours. The natives will start one of these fires before going on a journey; then when ready to start they take one of the brands, which has had time to become thoroughly lighted, by the outer end, which is scarcely warm, and hold it with both hands under their skin robes and in front of them; the heat from the brand keeps them warm. These brands will last hours before they are consumed.

If the natives are on a very long journey and the brand should burn out before they get to its end, if they have further need of it, they stop where they can get two dry sticks, usually preferring the spindle that grows at the top of the black boy. It is about the size of a man's thumb, and has a dry pith in the centre. They take two pieces of this, making a notch in one and a point on the other, then put the pointed end into the notch, using a flint knife with which to do their whittling. One is placed on the ground, the other upright. They grasp the upright stick, a foot perhaps in length, with both hands, and rub back and forth, their hands naturally working downward. When near the bottom they let go and grasp the top again, and so quickly the stick does not have time to fall. In this way a dust is produced at the bottom, and fire immediately follows. It takes about a minute to start a fire, and then their knot is soon aglow again.

The weapons used by the Australians in war or in the chase are the glass knife or flint, the stone hatchet, the spear, the shield, and that wonderful weapon the boomerang.

The knife is composed of a stick about ten inches long and an inch thick, with a bit of glass or flint stuck into one side near the end, which is held on with black boy gum. The stone hatchet has a handle similar to the knife, with a piece of flint stone about two inches wide and one and a half long, shaped like a flint and stuck to the handle with gum like the knife. The other end of the hatchet handle is pointed. The spear is made of wattle, a little sapling common to the country. The early settlers built their houses of it, by winding strips of wattle between posts and then plastering them with mud, which was called wattling and daubing. The natives cut the wattles with their hatchets, and then cut them into lengths of about six feet and scrape off the bark. Then they sit down, and throwing their left foot high upon their right thigh, with the bottom of the foot turned up, place the but-end of the stick on the ball of the heel, with the other end extending out before them, and scrape the spear down to a point. They always draw the knife toward them, using their heel as a bench for all work where a rest or support is required. The spear, when pointed, is reversed and placed between the toes of the right foot; they then dig a small hole in the small

AUSTRALIAN CHIEF IN THE ATTITUDE TAKEN WHEN THROWING THE SPEAR.

end of the spear. If it is to be a battle spear, they attach glass or flint near the point with gum. This makes it a formidable weapon. The shield is a flat piece of wood about two feet long and four in width, three eighths of an inch thick in the middle, with thin edges, and it also tapers toward the ends, where it is about one half an inch thick. On one end is a knob about the size of a walnut, and on the other a little peg. When they throw the spear from the shield, they slip the small end of the spear on to the peg, then grasp the knob end between the fore and middle fingers of the right hand, holding the spear between the thumb and forefinger. They advance their left foot and turn their left side to whatever they wish to spear, raise the left arm bent inward a little above the shoulder. The right arm is extended at length, while the spear rests on the left near the elbow. When they throw, they sweep the right hand nearly over the head, releasing the spear from between the thumb and forefinger. The spear will rise and keep a level until the peg is thrown out of the little hole, when it speeds on its mission of death, which is certain at a distance of two hundred and fifty feet and sometimes much farther. One can readily see what an impetus is derived from leverage and so much strength of arm and body, for they turn their body partly round as they raise their arm, so that when the spear leaves their hand they face the enemy or game. For small game they throw with the hand only.

The boomerang they make of the limbs of trees, reducing them in size. The natives find a limb that is bent into an elbow, and cut off the ends, leaving about six inches each way from the elbow. Then it is scraped down to about three eighths of an inch, the ends tapered slightly and the edges quite thin. In shaping it they make one side concave and the other convex. They throw it with great force, so that it will wind itself high

NATIVE OF AUSTRALIA CLIMBING UP A TREE BY THE BARK.

up into the air and keep spinning around until it strikes the ground quite near the man who throws it. I have seen them thrown around a tree before they returned to the ground again. The natives will throw them to the ground, and the weapon will rise like a bird and sail away; and they can throw them quite straight, if they desire to do so.

The boomerang has been called a wonderful and mysterious weapon, but there is nothing wonderful or mysterious about it. A child of five years could make one of a piece of pasteboard in a few minutes that would perform all the tricks the Australian boomerangs will, but without the latter's force.

The natives climb trees after small game very readily. No matter how large, how tall, or how straight the tree, they will go to its top in a very short time. With their stone hatchet they bruise the bark and make notches as high as they can reach. Then they stick the pointed end of the hammer handle into the upper notch and their great toe into the lower, and, with the fingers of the left hand in another notch, pull themselves up so that they can reach still another with the big toe of their other foot. They hold on with their left hand while they make more notches with their right. In this manner they will walk up the bark of a tree a hundred feet, if need be, to get the game, which is oftentimes well out on a limb and perhaps in a hole. If the latter is the case, when they reach the limb they will manage to crawl out upon it until they get to the hole, then cut the game out with their stone hatchet, kill it, and throw it down, then retrace their steps. They seldom or never fall.

The young natives get together and, with reeds for spears, have sham battles. In this manner they not only learn to throw the spear, but to dodge it, which they do very cleverly. The little ones will play with the boomerang, so that when grown up they have become experts in all their modes of warfare and hunting.

Seeing two natives once quarrelling, and always being interested in anything which showed their peculiarities, I was curious to know how they would settle their troubles. I watched to see the result. They stood about twenty feet apart with their spears shipped on their shields, and arms thrown back, watching a chance to throw, at the same time going around in a circle, and keeping up a terrible wrangle in their own language. After ten minutes of this performance, one of them darted his spear at the other's legs; he dodged the shaft and caught it before it got past, and broke it across his knee. It is quite common for them to carry two or three spears when they are travelling about. The one who threw the spear had another in position, and was on guard before the other had time to recover after breaking the spear. Finally, after much parading and scolding, they appeared to make a truce, and one approached the other until within six feet, then threw his spear so that it just touched the other's leg without piercing the skin. They did this because I was looking on, and they may have put off the settlement of their trouble for that reason.

Sometimes a number of the natives will go out and capture a number of kangaroo, which will last them for some days. When they find a herd of kangaroo feeding, they set the dry grass on fire in a circle around them, leaving an opening through which the animals must pass or perish. Then they station themselves on each side of the gap, and spear the game as it passes out. They seldom miss their mark, no matter how fast the game may be running. I paced the leap of what is called the flying doe; it was on a slight incline, and measured a little less than thirty feet. It takes an unusually good dog to catch one.

When the natives kill small game, they build a fire, roast the animal, and eat it on the spot. When they have an abundance, they will eat enough at one sitting to last them a week. I have known them to eat so much that they could not walk until some of their companions took them and rolled them on the ground and limbered them up a little.

I cannot recall the manner in which they eat without disgust; and yet, to give a correct idea of how low mankind can descend, I must state the facts as they are, and put aside all my own thought. They kill the game, then build a fire, and the animal, if a small one, like the rabbit, is thrown on to the coals. After it has roasted awhile they will remove it, pull off a leg, and throw the larger part upon the coals again. They give the leg a snap with their fingers to knock off the ashes, then it is devoured. By that time another leg is ready to be served by the same means, and so on until the creature is all devoured. It has been said that all savage races begin to eat, like animals, on the entrails first; such is not always the case, as I have seen them eat as often one way as the other. There is a large variety of small animals and reptiles, such as frogs, snakes, grubs, snails, and many others, that they use as food.

There is a very delicate little creature, a treat indeed for the whites as well, when they can get them, which is called *gonack*. It is a perfect little lobster, about four inches long, with a big claw which is much larger than the body. The natives dig them out of the mud in swampy places. There is also what the natives call *mungite*, the whites call it honeysuckle; it grows on a tree called the she-oak, which is used quite commonly for firewood. The mungite is, so to speak, the fruit and blossom. They are about the size of an ear of corn, with a yellow blossom putting out all over it, and appear something like a round brush at some seasons of the year. These blossoms are filled with honey. The natives pluck them and suck the honey. Every year they dry up and fall off, and soon become hard. They are then used by the natives to make fires, and also as fagots to keep them warm when on their travels, as previously stated.

The natives have a method of talking long distances. They will talk so as to be understood as far as the voice can be heard. If they wish to say " you go," — which in their language is, "*yo ne watoo*," — they will halloo the "*yo*" and keep up that sound for half a minute, then the sound "*ne*" the same length of time, and then the "*wa*" pronounced very broad, and at the end comes the rest of the word, "*too*." They bring the last part of the sound out with a deep guttural sound. This manner of talking at a long distance is so well understood that they know the meaning of every sound, no matter how far away, if the least sound of the voice can be heard.

The natives work for the whites, bring wood and water, and take whatever the whites may give them for food. Sometimes it is flour, to mix and bake in ashes. They mix this flour on a piece of bark. Sitting down with the bark between their legs, they fill the mouth with water and let it run on to the flour while they mix it with both hands.

They are seldom sick, and it is a rare case if one of them dies of anything other than old age. To bury their dead they dig a hole some three feet deep, and then put the corpse in the hole in a sitting position, cover it up, and build a fire on the grave. They cut notches in the trees around the grave, and by the notches every native can tell who lies there. If it be a man of note among them, he will have marks or ridges across the abdomen. All important natives have these marks, which are made by cutting the skin with glass or some poisonous article, which, after healing, leaves a scar which rises up from a quarter to half an inch. These scars extend from side to side. When one of these favored ones performs anything out of common, he adds a scar as a token of honor. I have seen some of them where the scars covered the width of ten inches and were close together, something like the humpback whale, except that on a whale they run lengthways, while on the natives they run across. The marks at the grave denote the rank or title.

The men do not mourn for the dead, but the women do. They sit down and keep up a half-whine and half-cry, at the same time they scratch their faces with their nails. They will continue this way for hours, until their cheeks are terribly cut and covered by blood.

What their religion was before the whites came I cannot say; but at this period they believed that a native, when he died, came up a white man, and would say that man was once his brother, but had gone away and came back a white man. The natives have been called the lowest in the human scale, but I do not deem them so.

They have been called cannibals, but facts do not lead me to believe it.

In the early colonial days the English crowded and imposed upon the natives as we have the Indians in this country, and of course they retaliated, which was natural and to be expected. But in cases of this kind " might makes right," so the aborigines were driven to the wall. These natives fought the English, who used muskets, with spears. The natives whipped the soldiers in a fair fight. It was at Penjarah, about ten miles inland on the Murray River. Soon after the soldiers received orders to turn out and shoot every male, no matter where found, and they obeyed orders. One old native was partly concealed in a bunch of bushes, and as the soldiers came up he stretched his head out and cried, " Me womanny! womanny!" but the soldiers knew by his head of hair of what sex he was, and soon spattered the bushes with his brains. The natives, after that, concluded to submit to the inevitable, and they now remain a downtrodden race.

No pen can describe the native costume nor do the subject justice. One article of dress beside the fur cloak, which is only worn in cool weather, is made of opossum fur twisted into a string many feet in length, that is wound around their loins until it makes a roll the size of a man's arm. This serves as a place to put their hatchet and knife and sometimes the legs of small game, if more than they can eat is killed while on the chase. They have another string made of the same material, but not so long, used in dressing the hair. The hair of the chief is quite long. They brush the hair up all around, and grasp it at the top of the head, and then wind this string around it as a woman will when she wants to do her hair in a coil. They will wind up about two inches and fasten the end, then insert different colored feathers all around where they wind it. They are then fully dressed. About once a week they remove the strings and take a bath. They use a clay, which when burnt is red. They mix it with opossum fat, and sometimes spend an hour in greasing themselves from the feet to the top of the head. Their hair will be so full of the fat that it will run down over their bodies. After rubbing the body with fat they wind the string around their bodies again ; their head is dressed as before described, and they are once more in full attire, ready for a dance or a reception. They quite often gather together for what they call a *carabbray*, which is similar to the powwow of our own Indian natives. They are singularly painted and in different colors.

They catch parrots alive by taking a bough thickly

foliaged, and watch the water holes where the birds go to drink. When a bird comes down to the water they squat, with the bush in front, and creep carefully along, hiding behind the bush, until they can reach the bird. Then, with a quick movement, they catch it before it is aware of its danger.

They seldom lay up anything for the morrow. They have no frugal traits. All they care for is sufficient for the present day. I have known the carcass of a whale to float ashore, which would attract the natives for many miles around; and they would camp near by and live on the flesh until the bones were stripped clean.

As regards the animals, fowls, etc., used by them as food, they have been described by others. All animals and birds and vegetation, and in fact about everything connected with the country, with but very few exceptions, differs enough from all other products in other countries to warrant the opinion that Australia was once a satellite to this earth, in common with the moon, and has come to us in a manner described elsewhere. I do not believe, however, that the present natives came with it. Undoubtedly, another people were the first inhabitants of the island, perhaps Chinese, who have long since left it for other lands, and the present natives came from the continent on flats, or logs, or, as called in South America, on catamarans.

Bald heads, white or gray heads, are unknown among the natives. They wear no covering on the head. The hair of the women hangs down in ringlets to their shoulders. Some of them would be quite pretty if they were clean and were dressed in European style; but in their native costume, garnished with plenty of mother earth and opossum fat, they are more objects of disgust than admiration.

The narrative of life in Western Australia would be

incomplete without mentioning a sad circumstance which happened a short time previous to my arrival in the country, which is not without interest, showing, as it does, how much like civilized people savages can be, and also that humanity is actuated by the same impulses, whether cultured or uncultured. A native chief abducted a beautiful young lady named Drummond from her father's home near Perth, the capital of Western Australia. When the abduction became known, the whites got quite a number of the settlers together and went in pursuit. They were prepared for a long chase. They got the trail and made a long tramp through a wild country, some parts of which were very much tangled with a wild vine called scrub, which is woven together so firmly that one can sometimes walk for half a mile on the top of the mass without seeing the ground in that distance. There were also open forests with luxuriant fields of grass, with trees thinly scattered around, such as form the sheep and cattle ranches in that country. They came in sight of the captors in their temporary camp, in one of those open places in the forest.

The captors had camped so that they could see the approach of any one who might be in pursuit, in time either to defend themselves or make their escape. The chief saw that he could not escape, since the girl would not run, and they could not carry her and get over the ground fast enough to escape capture.

When the whites, the girl's father being among them, got within three hundred yards, the natives halted and the chief at once shipped his spear to the shield and stepped back a few paces from the girl, placed himself in the proper attitude to throw the spear, and shouted to the guide, a native whom the rescuing party had taken along, that if they advanced one step nearer he would put his spear through the girl's body. At that the pursuers halted. The father could not see his child murdered before his eyes, and was obliged to allow the natives to run away. The party had nothing but old English flintlock muskets. They found it was useless to try to run them down, so returned to devise other methods. After many failures in trying to trap the natives, or secure the girl who was closely guarded among the deep forests and jungles, and after many months of fruitless search, a tree was discovered that had rudely outlined ships on the bark. No white man had been in that section of the country to make those marks, and they knew they were made by a white person, and who else could it have been but the white girl captive? On this supposition they formulated a plan which nearly proved successful for the girl's rescue. A reward was offered of one thousand pounds, quite a fortune in the colonies at that time. The authorities had a lot of cheap handkerchiefs made, with printed instructions on them directing the girl how to proceed and where to go in case she saw the handkerchiefs. These were given to the natives of different tribes. Natives call writing on paper, paper talk. They were frequently sent with letters to different parties by the settlers, and so knew that there was some talk on the paper; but they knew nothing of printed letters, therefore they suspected nothing wrong with the handkerchiefs. The girl was told to go to a certain place in the forest, and if she succeeded in getting there without being suspected by her captors, she was to make a smoke by building a fire. The whites placed themselves at different places of observation, where they could scan a large scope of the country, and waited and watched. Finally one day they were rewarded, for their long and patient watching, by seeing curling smoke rising slowly up among the trees. The volume of smoke increased in size until quite a cloud was floating over the forest, while below, no doubt, the maiden stood silent and alone, straining her eyes to their utmost to catch a glimpse of her rescuers. Presently moving objects appear on a hill beyond a valley. They draw nearer. She knows that it is her rescuers, that her signal has been seen. Home and dear ones rise before her eyes; she stretches her hands to grasp them, but alas! she seizes but a phantom in her despair. A quick, cat-like step from behind, and she turns to be clasped in the brawny arms of her captors. She was again borne away into the trackless forest by the savages who had missed her. They saw the smoke, and their experienced eyes told them it was a signal of some kind. They hurried to the spot, and when her would-be rescuers arrived all that remained to reward them for their long and vigilant watch was a few smouldering brands.

The party returned with the sad news to the broken-hearted parents of the unfortunate girl, who was believed to have spent her life with her captors, and may yet be alive at the present time. It was some sixty years ago, but she was then young, and the manner in which the natives live prolongs life. The last heard of the Drummond girl was that she had borne two children to her captor chief.

Good health is a native characteristic, for I never saw a native sick or ill otherwise than by accident. Some old fellows whom I met must have been one hundred and fifty years old, if we can compare our old people with theirs. Should you ask one of their old men how old he is, he will raise both hands and say, "*Tatlum*," and lower them, and he will continue to raise and lower his hands, and repeat this word for half a day if you will listen to him. They mean they have lived so many moons. Generally the virtue of tribes of natives—and I have seen a good many native tribes—is sterling in every respect, until the advance guard of civilization appears, when they soon learn all the vices that civilization carries.

By some it has been thought that the sun, being so powerful and hot, sets dry grass on fire, but this is not true. The natives make a fire whenever they have game to roast, and they do not care whether it spreads or not. They prefer that it would, because it drives the game out so it can be seen better ; especialy is this true of small game. It also compels the kangaroo to seek small patches that are not burnt over, where they will be sure to find them. These frequent fires have sometimes led to the idea of spontaneous combustion.

It has often been said that kangaroos burrow, but this is not true. Knowing their habits, I should as soon think of seeing sheep burrow as kangaroos. They may have gotten into that habit since I left the country.

CHAPTER IV.

SAILS IN THE SHIP "FALCO" — SUSPECTS THE SHIP BEING IN UNLAWFUL SERVICE — TAKES TO WHALING AGAIN — DESERTS ONE WHALER FOR ANOTHER — TICKET-OF-LEAVE MEN — SAILING UNDER HER MAJESTY'S FLAG — HELPING A PRISONER ESCAPE — TRIES WHALING AGAIN — ANECDOTES ABOUT THE FIJIANS — BATTLE BETWEEN THE NATIVES — THE BANYAN-TREE — AGAIN DESERTS SHIP AND TRAMPS ACROSS COUNTRY — THE DISCOVERY OF GOLD IN AUSTRALIA — SAILS FOR ENGLAND — DOUBLING CAPE HORN — ARRIVES IN LONDON — SIGHTS THEN TO BE SEEN — EMBARKS FOR NEW YORK.

At last the day arrived for the "Falco" to leave port, and for me to leave the country where I had spent so many days mingled with joys, regrets, and occasionally disgust. I bade my companions adieu. My dear friend S. wrung my hand with a "God speed you," and directed me where to find him if I should ever reach London.

I started for Freemantle, where I soon arrived and went aboard the "Falco." It was quite a contrast to see the American consul and the governor together. The consul wore his uniform complete, — cocked hat with tassels, and coat and pants trimmed with gold-lace, — while the governor wore the dress of fashion at that time, — a red shirt, with black patent leather belt around the waist, looking like a fireman when on parade.

Perhaps the consul wished to impress on the governor the greatness of the country to which he belonged. I felt proud to acknowledge him as a fellow-countryman; while looking at him seemed to elevate me to his lofty height: The governor smiled on us as we stepped into the boat, and the words "bye-bye, governor," forced themselves unbidden to my lips, while they faded away in the distance as the sailors pulled rapidly to the brig, which was to carry me I knew not where, nor did I care much so that I was again on the ocean, with the star-spangled banner waving over me. The vessel was soon under way and rapidly sailing out of the harbor. I gave one last look toward the fast-receding shore. My thoughts were mingled with pleasure and regrets, — with pleasure to know I was leaving the country, and regret to think what might be the fate of those left behind who might not be so fortunate in getting away. The country was not then what it is now. I do not know of a country where I would sooner spend my remaining days than in any part of Australia, where I have been, and I have lived in many places on the coast from New Castle to Freemantle. From the fading shore I turned my eyes seaward, and was soon lost in speculation as to the future.

I was not long at sea before renewing my acquaintance with my old and tried friends, lobscouse and hard-tack; and for meat I found the same old horse in the traces and doing good service, and likely to survive very many voyages.

We soon made another port. The "Falco" was on a trading voyage around the world, and, as a matter of business, called at small as at larger ports to dispose of her Yankee notions. This port, King George's Sound, is one of the prettiest little harbors in the world. The passage in is about one hundred yards wide, while inside one hundred line-of-battle ships could ride quietly at anchor, whatever the weather outside.

The town consisted of about ten huts, inhabited by a company of soldiers and a few natives. The supercargo did not sell much there, since the soldiers were supplied by the government. The natives were also well supplied with home products. An American whaler lay in the harbor when we arrived, the "Hope," commanded by Capt. Wilcox. I had learned soon after boarding the "Falco" that trading was not her only business. It was said by some of her crew that she had a number of big guns in her hold, as well as a few cases of muskets, pikes, etc. I noted a number of small boats stowed between decks; all of which made me think, perhaps I had jumped from the frying pan into the fire, which caused me to cast a wistful eye at the whaler. I managed to see Capt. Wilcox, and told him I would like to ship with him if he was going home soon. He said that after one more cruise of four months he would start for home, and he would ship me if I wanted to go.

I told the consul on board of the "Falco" that I had a chance to go home on the whaler.

"Well," said he, "go if you want to."

The mate came to me to persuade me to remain. He said I would do much better with them, and hinted a deal; but I would not be persuaded. I had seen enough to cause me to suspect the craft.

I went on board the whaler, and little anticipated under what circumstances I should meet the consul a year later.

On the whaler I found the same lay-out at the mess table, and very soon became acquainted with my new shipmates. We made the cruise of four months, but captured no whales. Then the captain run the ship into what is called the Great Australian Bite, and anchored near shore, where he intended to lay a few months and bag whales; that is to say, lay at anchor and send the boats on shore, land the men and have them climb to the elevated points and look out for whales. When they saw one they would give chase with the boats and capture him if they could, tow him to the ship and "cut him in." Both right and humpback whales go in near the shore at certain seasons of the year, but sperm whales seldom do.

I saw my show for getting home was deferred indefinitely. Perhaps I had better have stayed on the brig. In the course of a week or two we heard that there was an English brig anchored in a bay one hundred miles farther up the coast; she was a whaler from Hobartstown, Van Dieman's Land. To go to her by water was some hundred and fifty miles, but across country one hundred miles. I concluded to run away and strike across the country and reach that vessel if I could. I knew that it was quite an undertaking, since it was a wild and trackless country, and no water to be had the entire distance. Australia is a very dry country as a general rule, especially in the summer time. By getting to Hobartstown I believed it possible to have a better chance to ship direct home. As desperate as were the chances, I considered myself equal to the task.

One morning I filled my bag, which held about four pounds of beef and hard bread, and flattened it well so that I could carry it under my frock secured to a belt. The boat went ashore; and I, with a week's supply of hard-tack, went with it. It was customary to leave a man in the boat to keep her off a little from the rough shore, and to haul her quickly in when the whales are in sight. I readily undertook the task of watching the boat that morning. The crew soon clambered up over the rocks and out of my sight. In five minutes I was going the other way on the run. A quarter of a mile away the land began to rise, and continued to rise for another quarter of a mile, so that the top of the hill, was about five hundred feet above the boat. When I began the up grade, I looked back and could plainly see the crew on the lookout on a prominence half a mile away. A low shrubbery grew on the slope of the hill, which would partly conceal me when on my hands and knees. When there was danger of being seen, I went on all fours to the top. The sun was uncomfortable, but I made the trip in safety and passed out of sight of my late companions, over the brow of the hill. I travelled around the bay, which was quite large, and reached the place where I wished to enter the forest about sundown. I had travelled about twenty miles that day, and was five miles in a straight line from the place from which I started in the morning. I camped in the edge of the woods for the night, but made no fire. At daylight I lunched and shaped my course by the sun and struck a " bee line " for the bay, one hundred miles away. I pushed on at a good pace until towards sundown ; then cut a few boughs and built a fire, took a lunch, and a long smoke, finally retiring on a bed of leaves for the night. I rested quietly and awoke much refreshed at daylight. Pushing on again that day until about two in the afternoon, I came in sight of a considerable opening in the forest, where a fire had burnt over the ground, leaving many black stumps and partly burnt brush.

I thought I saw a number of natives with their spears shipped to their shields, deliberately waiting for me. Not knowing whether I was pursued or not, every little noise startled me, and an old stump or crooked limb would assume any shape that my imagination shaped for it, from nude savages to many species of animals. I fancied I saw everything amongst that burnt timber that I did not wish to meet.

The only weapon which I possessed was a sheath knife. I drew that and ran my thumb down the edge, and I found that it would do at close range, although the chances were against my getting near enough to use the knife before I had been hit with the spears. It would not do to tarry, so I started on, knife in hand, fully determined to sell my life dearly if danger overtook me. I found the nearer I approached, the less warlike things appeared. The hosts soon vanished, and nothing remained but black stumps and charred branches which had fallen from trees. My imagination had evolved creatures that did not exist. The supposed danger past, I pushed forward again, half wishing that there had been just one savage, to relieve me of the monotony of the journey.

I camped at sundown by the side of an old log. I thought it quite safe to camp without much shelter, since I was now too far from the anchorage to think of hiding. By this time I keenly felt the want of water, but I would not allow my mind to dwell upon the subject. I ate my lunch, and after taking my regular smoke retired to rest and dreamed of water afar off. Up betimes I was early on the march, believing that the day's tramp would end the journey, and I was not mistaken in my judgment.

About four in the afternoon I went over a little rolling hill which I began to descend gradually, and after going a half-mile I saw a beacon light ahead. It was the gleam of the ocean through the trees. Another half-mile brought me in full view of the bay I was searching for. A little farther on lay the vessel that I expected to find. A surveyor could not have drawn a line any straighter from shore to shore than I had taken during my journey; while to end the journey happily, I reached the beach just as the last man of a boat's crew stepped into the boat, and I stepped in also. They were going aboard after spending the day on land watching for whales.

I told them my story, and the first man I met when we got on board the ship was an old friend whom I knew at the Lashanault. He had got around to Hobartstown and had shipped as cook on the brig. I considered it a happy termination of my journey, and soon made myself at ease, although I found things somewhat different on this colonial ship. She carried plenty of soft white bread and fresh meat, and canned fruits and vegetables. The ship had been out only on a short trip, which made it unnecessary to carry salt meats except in limited quantity. The crew had taken no whales, but about a week after my advent one was sighted. The captain finding me a good hand at the oar, I was put into the mate's boat to pull the after or stroke oar, a position I preferred because it was the farthest from the whale when the man forward fastened to him. The whale almost invariably, when struck with the harpoon, will strike back with his fins or big fan-like tail. I found that this particular whale worked both ways. The mate, a native of New Zealand, was a good sailor and a good whaleman, but very excitable when on the chase. We started out three boats. The mate's boat got ahead of the others and we soon got fast. The whale managed to strike both ends of the boat at once, and knocked me out at the stern and the boat steerer at the forward end at one blow. The boat moved forward a little, and the mate in the stern grasped the man who was thrown out forward as he was floating past. I, being thrown out from the after end, went astern of the boat. The black mate, after hauling his man in, held to his whale. I was very soon left far behind. I looked to see how far away the land was. The nearest point was fully three miles ; but now the other boats hove in sight and one was soon alongside. I was pulled in. The whale ran toward the other boats, and as the mate was passing them he sang out a man was overboard, and pointed toward where I was. Had it not been for the other boats, I should have had a long swim to reach the land, or a short dive to get to the bottom. We towed the whale alongside and soon had it stripped, tried out, and stowed in the hold. After a week longer watching, seeing no more whales, we sailed for Hobartstown, where all hands were paid off.

I had six dollars to repay me for my ducking. Six dollars would go a long way at that place in those days. After a few days of sight-seeing, I wandered down to the wharf, and discovered in a little coasting craft my old friend Long Jim. He had arrived at that port some time previous, and had managed to get money enough to buy the little craft, of which he was not only owner, but captain and crew. He was engaged in bringing wood across the harbor. He offered me a berth on board with him, but I declined his kind offer, having loftier aspirations. I wanted to get into a large vessel that was soon going home, or headed in that direction at least. Kicking around a week, my money about all gone, and no ship likely to start soon for home, I sought something to do. There was little that I could do, since nearly all the work was done by ticket-of-leave men. Van Dieman's Land was a convict colony, and these ticket-of-leave men were such as had served for some time and through good behavior got out on a ticket. They could not leave the country, but could work where they chose and have what they earned for themselves. They reported at headquarters once in three months. They got about all the work ashore.

I hunted for a vessel that belonged to the port, thinking that I would ship for a short time, until I could get a voyage toward home. There were two vessels belonging to the government, — one a bark called the " Lady Franklin "; the other a brig called " Governor Phillips." They were for carrying prisoners from Hobartstown to the penal settlements along the coast, where they were put at government work. There the convicts do all of the government work on shore. Being told these vessels frequently needed hands, I went on board of the " Governor Phillips," and applied for a chance to go before the mast. The captain looked me over a little, and said he thought I would do, and shipped me at once at two pounds a month. Things were in pretty good shape in that vessel, with plenty of everything the market afforded. The wages were small, but they were sure. The British government was paymaster.

When a ship came in with convicts from England, we would take the prisoners on board of the brig, some fifty or more, and carry them to some penal station along the coast. Sometimes we would have a load of young women. When we had men, we always had a dozen soldiers to guard them ; but the women, well, the sailors could take care of them.

A few months before I joined the brig the prisoners captured her. Every day they allowed about ten of the prisoners on deck out of the lock-up between decks. They remained on deck about an hour, and then were sent below, and others came up, and so on until all had been aired. One day ten of the most desperate fellows managed to get on deck together. Guards sometimes get careless, and this particular guard was careless. They sprang upon them and wrenched their muskets from them. Before the soldiers knew what was being done, they found themselves disarmed. The prisoners then made the relief, which was below, hand their muskets up. But while this was going on the officers of the vessel, taking in the situation, saw an opportunity to secure two guns with which they covered two men. In the excitement the soldiers secured more guns, and the prisoners were soon in the prison again.

Things were so pleasant on the brig that I forgot about home. We had an American colored cook, whose wife lived in town. As we were out and in every two or three days, the cook would go on shore as soon as the brig hauled up to the wharf. The steward found the cook was stealing the ship's stores and taking them to his wife, which he reported to the captain, and he was discharged; and that fact made a difference to me, for being the youngest one on board, I was installed as cook. I found my work quite easy, and I had all night in. When there were soldiers on board, it made extra work to do, and rather more cooking for the male prisoners.

The soldiers would often get up a little extra mess, for which they would pay me extra, and frequently in grog when they had no cash. I did not use liquor, but knew where to turn it into cash with a good profit. When the prisoners were on deck for an airing, they would come to the galley, and it was surprising how soon those fellows would discover that I had a little something on tap. I exchanged my whiskey for spot cash, at one shilling a glass. In this way I made considerable money.

When the vessel was in port I was sometimes alone on her for several hours at a time. One day I saw a young man on the dock. He beckoned to me to come ashore, which I did. He came to me and wanted to know if I was not an American. Telling him I was, he said, pointing to an American whaler that had been in port some three weeks, that he was an American also, and wanted to sail in that vessel. The crew, he said, had agreed to stow him away, and he wanted to go on board that night, for in the morning a guard was to be placed on board to remain until she sailed and was well down the harbor. This guard was to prevent prisoners from leaving the country. He said he could not go on any of the boats belonging to the whaler, because the harbor police overhauled all boats except the government boats. He wanted me to take him in one of the government boats that night. I asked him why he was afraid of being seen.

Then he said he was a prisoner, and out on a ticket of leave; that he was on a ship where the crew mutinied. The rest of the crew got seven years, but he being an American, the queen sent him out during her pleasure. Her pleasure might last his lifetime, for aught he knew.

I sympathized with the fellow, as he appeared to be honest, and told him if he would come to the wharf precisely at eight o'clock, and say nothing while in the boat, I would be there. I expected to be alone till nine o'clock.

I had a boat ready to slip over the ship's side at the first glimpse of the fellow. I saw him and reached the dock just as he arrived. He stepped into the boat without a word, and I sculled for the whaleship, which we reached in safety, and the fellow clambered over the ship's side out of sight. I have no doubt but he got away. On my return to the ship I saw two police boats not far off, but they did not hail me. Getting that fellow off made me feel homesick, and I determined the next American ship that came into that port that was homeward bound would take me in her.

About that time a man who was a shipowner began to build a large ship. The keel, stern, and stern posts were in position, — a fact which is mentioned because that ship when finished had something to do with my getting home.

I was contented on the brig as long as my business was brisk, and that was when we had male prisoners. When we had female prisoners, work was dull and monotonous and made me quite homesick. One day a Yankee whaler dropped anchor near where we lay. I was not long in getting on board, since I had plenty of leisure when in port.

I found her to be the bark "Kingston," Fairhaven, Capt. Ellis, master; first mate, Mr. Barker; and second,

Mr. Pearce.   I was pleased with the appearance of things the little time that I was on board.   She was to lay in port about three weeks, and then was to make one cruise of four months, then steering for home.   I thought that would suit me.   I frequently saw both men and officers on shore, and finally I met the captain and made a bargain with him.

He wanted a carpenter; and on the strength of what I had learned at shipbuilding on Murray River, I told him I could suit him.   I thought I had only to ask for my discharge from the brig to get it at once, as we had to ship a new crew about every trip on account of the sailors leaving, while I had stuck to the ship through thick and thin.   So one day before the whaler was to sail I asked my captain if he would give me my discharge.

" Why do you want to leave me ? " said he.

I told him I wanted to go home, and that the whale-ship was going home, and was to sail in about a week. He said, if I would go one trip more, which would only take about four days, I could have my discharge.

That was satisfactory, so I returned to my pots and kettles, singing my well-worn song : —

> Will I ever get home, far over the sea, —
> Will I ever get home to the land of the free,
> To the home of my childhood, the land of my birth,
> To the spot which to me is the best upon earth?
> I have been the world o'er, and trades have learned many,
> But, alas ! in this country they're not worth a penny.
> I'll forsake these wild shores, and cross the blue sea,
> I'll steer my course homeward and happy will be,
> And live among friends, the friends I once knew,
> Then I'll forget my experience eating lobscouse stew !

We returned in due time, and I cleared everything up in the galley, gave the pots an extra shine, and then went aft.   The captain was in the cabin, and the mate aloft doing some work; the other hands, as usual, had left for other pastures, fresh and green. I told the captain that I wanted my discharge; he looked up with a glitter in his eyes and asked me what I wanted my discharge for. I then repeated what I told him before, that I wanted to go on the whaleship.

"You go forward at once!" said he.

"But, Captain," said I, "you know you promised me my discharge on our return, and I must have it."

"Well," said he, "I would much rather you would stay; but if you are determined to go, I shall have to give you your discharge."

He then called the mate down and told him to write out my discharge, which he did. I went on shore at once and to the harbor master's office to get my pay.

Several months later I met this captain again, when he showed what regard he had for me.

I went at once on board my new ship, which was soon under way sailing out of the harbor. I took, as I supposed, one last look at Tasmania's Head, and we passed out to sea.

Tasmania's Head is a large cliff of rocks, which was long ago broken from the mainland, leaving a passage between the Head and the mainland of about one hundred yards, and so situated that the channel cannot be seen until you get near it. Tasmania was the name of the Dutch captain who first sighted the island, and that point of rock being a prominent point at the mouth of the harbor, he planted his flag on it, believing it to be the mainland. Later on Van Dieman came along, and exploring around the mouth of the harbor found that bluff to be only an island, so he planted his flag on the mainland and called it Van Dieman's Land.

On the "Kingston" I found we had a good ship, good officers, and a good crew, all jolly good fellows well met.

We cruised about on sperm whale grounds, seeing plenty of whales, and caught one by running him down in a fair race. I did not go in the boats much, since I was the ship's carpenter, and was kept busy repairing stoven boats. The boat steerers would manage to miss the whale about every time they got up to it. They would throw the harpoon either over or under him, but the whale seldom missed his mark. Once I repaired one boat three times before breakfast. Everything was fitted at the home port, and I had only to remove the broken parts and put in the new. The captain seldom went in the boats, but one day we saw whales, and he thought he would try his luck. He chose a crew from the company. I was to pull the stroke oar, which I preferred, although experience taught me there was little choice as to safety, for some whales attack both ends of the boat. We started after the whale, but before we got near enough to fasten, the leviathan saw us and swam at a little faster gait. We pulled a little faster too, but the whale managed to keep ahead about so far. If we gained a little, the object of our pursuit would make a spurt and double the distance between us. The captain got tired of that and said, " Now, boys, let us run the fellow down, or perish in the attempt."

We braced ouselves for the chase with all the strength we could muster. The captain gave the word, and every man bent his blade like a rainbow. We soon began to gain, and we kept a steady gain until we shot alongside, and the boat steerer soon had two harpoons into him clear to the hilt. The captain soon killed him, and we had him alongside the vessel.

Here may be stated how a whale dies, and some other things not generally known. Many believe that when a whale spouts or blows, that they spout water. Such is not the case. It is their breath, the same as our breath is seen as a stream of mist on a cold day. The air is colder than the water, hence the fog or steam that we see when a whale blows. Sometimes they blow before they get their spout holes quite above the water, and at such times they blow up a little water. During a very warm, still day you may see them raise their heads out of the water and hear a loud puff like drawing a sponge from a cannon, but there may be no sign of mist whatever. After a whale has been lanced and some vital spot has been struck by the point of the lance, the whale will throw up large quantities of blood when he spouts. Many times I have been completely drenched with it. About half an hour before a whale dies, he goes into what is called his "flurry": he will begin to go round in a circle, taking in half a mile; he will thrash, kick, and roll, leaving a boiling, foaming wake behind. The boats must then keep at a distance, or they would soon be knocked into splinters. As the whale becomes weaker it goes slower, and when the breath leaves the body invariably their eyes are toward the sun, possibly because the sun is the brightest object to be seen, and they keep their eyes on it until the last breath is drawn.

In the head of the sperm whale is what is called the case and junk. The case is a large bag filled with oil called spermaceti. The walls of this bag are composed of a soft spongy blubber; the junk is some five or six feet thick. Sometimes I have run my arm into this blubber up to the shoulder, and in withdrawing it would bring out a pint of oil. In saving this rich oil, we cut off the whale's head, and, with large hooks, blocks, and falls, hoist it to the level of the deck, then with a long-handled spade we cut a hole through the flesh to the case, then hoist it with a bucket and a rope run through a block attached to the yard leading to the deck, and tended by a man. A pole is thrust into the bottom of the bucket and pushed down into the hole which leads to the case, and the man at the end of the rope pulls the bucket out full of oil, which is emptied into a hogshead. This is continued until all the pure oil is out. A long-handled spade is now run in and cut around awhile, and the bucket is used again and again, until all worth saving is obtained. The soft blubber which is cut with the spade is also squeezed with the hands until the oil is all out of it. This spermaceti will, before being scalded, cool like lard, but will not become quite so firm.

The season was over on this ground, and only one whale had been caught. Going home was out of question as yet. The captain had been to the Fiji Islands the year before, and found sperm whales were plenty around the islands, and had captured one which gave a hundred barrels of oil. He thought he must try another season there. We accordingly ran for the islands, where we soon arrived and anchored at a place called Ovalau. I was then in a different country, and they were a far different people than those I left at Swan River.

Though these people and their island are quite fully understood, yet some account of them by one who lived among them fifty years ago may still be of interest at the present day.

At that time but few missionaries had been stationed there, yet there were but very few cases of cannibalism to be heard of. There were a few cases in the isolated parts. Two authenticated cases I heard of.

The captain said when he was there the year before, he was one day invited to dine with one of the chiefs, and when they had all sat down to the spread on the ground, they had roast pork, yam, and fruits in variety. There was one particular dish that the captain did not like the appearance of. He finally asked the chief what it was. He replied that it was *buccolo*. The captain then

NATIVE HIGH CHIEF OF THE FIJI ISLANDS.

inquired what *buccolo* was. The chief gave him to understand that it was human flesh, and urged the captain to partake, but he declined with thanks.

On another occasion the crew were on shore one Sunday and there were many natives, both male and female, scattered around among them. Presently a native, with a wig on his head, and with what is called a pineapple club in his hand, walked up behind a woman and drove the point into the woman's skull. She fell dead, and the fellow took her on his shoulder and carried her off. The other natives said, " *Turonger eat*," which meant chief eat. These were the only cases that ever came to my knowledge while among them during five months.

They have a bark which is very much like our wicopy bark. They strip it off the trees, lay it on a smooth log, and then pound it with a wooden mallet. In this manner they expand it to a great width. The process is similar to gold beating. A strip of two inches wide will be hammered out to two feet wide, and quite as thin as muslin. This fabric they call *tapper*. They put the edges of a number of strips together, and by that means make quite a respectable carpet. In making very large articles of it, they make it much thicker than for a headdress or a wrap for body covering. They print some of it in this way: They have the half of a log that would be twenty inches in diameter with the bark scraped off clean ; then they take little reeds about the size of a lead pencil and split them and wrap them over the log in different ways and secure them. In this manner they form the designs by cutting pieces and bending them in different ways. They make a dye by some process and spread it over their type ; then spread the cloth to be printed over the top. They then run a wooden roller over the cloth once or twice, and the work is completed.

Every tribe has its chief and its captains, who have

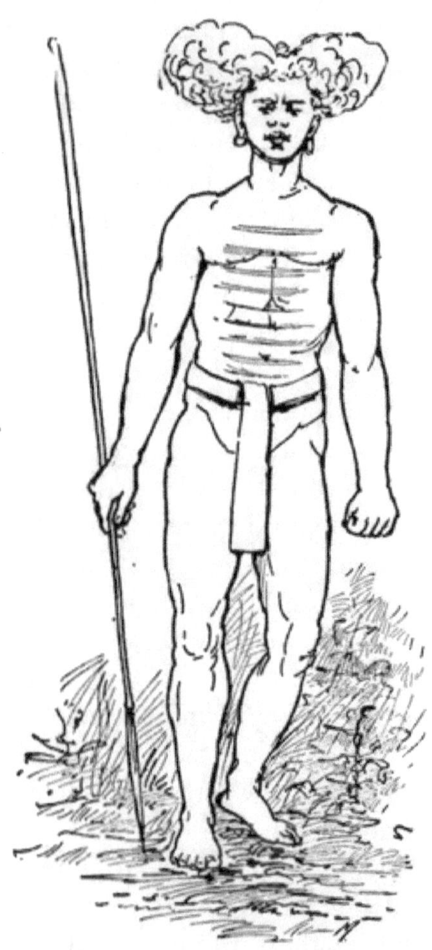

NATIVE LOW CHIEF OF THE FIJI ISLANDS.

marks of distinction. The big chief, or *turonger lib*, as they call him, allows his hair to grow very long. Their hair curls, and in the lower class is quite kinky; but the nobility comb their hair with a strip of tortoise shell, which is about three eighths of an inch wide and about twelve inches long, and pointed at one end. This they run through the hair, which makes it stand out in all directions in the same manner as that of the Circassians. The *turonger lib*, or big chief, will take two or three yards of the thin tapper cloth and wind it lightly over his already big head, and secure it by tucking it in under the lower parts near the neck. This dressing gives his head the appearance of being about the size of a four-bushel basket. The *turonger lili*, who stands next in rank lower, allows his hair to grow long like the big chief. Instead of the tapper covering, he will have a strip about two inches wide shaved to the scalp, from the forehead to the back down to the neck, which leaves two bushy tufts of hair standing out over each shoulder. The next in rank has the big head of hair with about two thirds of it shaved entirely off one side and over the poll some two inches; it makes him look lopsided. The chiefs sometimes wear a wrap over their shoulders, but it is more common for them to wear simply a strip of tapper around their waist, tied behind them, with the ends brought up between their legs and tucked under the belt in front and the ends allowed to hang down half-way to the knee. The chiefs usually are very large men. One fellow whom I measured with my rule was seven feet in height, and weighed from two to three hundred pounds.

All natives under these three chiefs are what are called *abelee*, which means slaves. The chief can sell or eat them, as suits his pleasure. One dollar was the market price for male or female, fat or lean. The females appeared to have ideas of modesty and to have had some regard for it long before the whites found them.

There is a little black root which they gather and work into a belt. When done, with its appendant, it is wrapped around the loins and secured behind. That is the covering they wear, and it appears to be a very ancient costume with them.

The women sometimes get together and dance. They have something like an inflated bladder, flattened somewhat, one in each hand. They form two lines near together, then sway backward and forward, singing, and at the same time slapping the two bladder-like bags together in their hands. As to their chastity I have nothing to say. They do not, however, adhere strictly to monogamy.

Some forty miles distant from the main group of the Fiji Islands is an island called *Tongaboo*. The natives on that island are quite civilized and much lighter in color than the Fiji proper; and they appear to be a different people. Their hair is straight. About twenty of their young converts came one day on a mission tour, with them being their native missionary. They came on board our ship. The young ladies were aged from sixteen to twenty; and they were all supposed to be virgins. They paraded along the deck, and on removing their head covering their hair was seen to be cut close to the scalp, excepting one lock of about the size of one's finger, which hung down on the right shoulder; this was their only ornament. Notwithstanding they were well civilized, yet they were unadorned, and a more perfect illustration of the human form is seldom seen. They were as comely in feature and figure as any people on earth, and were quite as modest and well behaved. They appeared to know no evil.

A root grows on the islands called *carver*, from which they make a liquor. The natives gather in a circle around the chief, and all squat down. The root is cut into slices or chips, and the slaves put them into their mouths and commence to chew. They continue to feed themselves with chips until their cheeks swell out as large as a man's fist, when they grind away with their molars until they reduce the mass to a pulp. Their mouths get so dry sometimes that they have to take a little water to enable them to chew the cud. When it is ground fine enough, it is taken out and put into a large wooden bowl. If there are four or five slaves chewing, one cud apiece will be sufficient. They fill the bowl two thirds full of water, then with the fibres of the cocoanut husk they stir the contents of the bowl and draw this strainer through it, taking the fine material out. They continue this until the liquid is completely free from any signs of the root; it is then ready for use. With a cocoanut shell they dip out a full cup and hand it to the chief. He takes the bowl in his hand, and as he raises it to his lips the circle of slaves around him begin a sort of chant and continue it until he has drained the cup, when they end with a whoop, and the next in rank takes his drink. After the chief and his followers have satisfied themselves, if any is left the chewers finish it.

There does not appear to be much wild game on these islands, other than wild hogs. They are quite plenty. There is a large variety of fruit, but not many vegetables. The fruits consist of breadfruit, bananas, oranges, lemons, limes, and what the whites call custard apple, a fruit of delicious quality. There is an abundance of cocoanuts. The vegetables are yams and *taro* and some other small varieties.

The breadfruit grows something like a citron, and is about the same size. When the breadfruit is ripe, the natives pick and roast it; the whites, after picking, allow it to lay in the sun two or three days, then cut them open. The inside is like buckwheat batter sweetened a little. The whites either put it into a hot oven and bake it, or dip it out as one would batter and fry it. Fried bananas taste very much like fried breadfruit.

There is a large fruit called *shaddock*, which is nothing more than an overgrown orange, sometimes being the size of a man's head. The meat is very coarse and of somewhat reddish color, with a mixture of sweet and sour. There is some little cotton growing wild. There is quite a variety of small fish and turtle.

It would appear, with the abundance of fruit and other eatables, that the natives would have no occasion to eat each other, and surely hunger would not drive them to it. Possibly they eat their enemies from spite, thinking that to be the quickest and best way to permanently be rid of them. In the islands a hog that would weigh three hundred pounds could be bought for as much vermilion paint as I could hold on the point of a knife, or for three fish hooks. They were underselling the people at Melbourne, who sold beef, pork, and mutton at a penny a pound, while these fellows were selling at the remunerative price of a penny a hog. To cook their meat and vegetables they will dig a hole in the ground, lining the bottom and sides with cobblestones, then build a fire in the hole. While the fire is burning they kill the hog, and when the fire has all burned to coals, they throw on a lot of boughs and lay the hog on the funeral pile; the steam that arises loosens the bristles, so they scrape them off easily. Then he is removed, and his entrails removed with the boughs. The hole being cleaned, they lay the hog in the hot hole and stuff it with hot stones, put yams and *taro* around, put more hot stones around and over it, then cover it with boughs; they then leave it for a few hours. When roasted they remove boughs and stones, and the creature is ready to be served from a primitive platter, the place in which he was baked.

One of our sailors ran away, and the captain offered the chief some calico if he would hunt him up. In a day or two the chief sent word to the captain that he had the fellow. The captain went ashore, taking me with him. When we found the chief, he was about to dine. He was so happy over his find and his promised reward, that he invited the captain and crew to partake of the royal feast. The old chief had a carpet about ten feet square, made of tapper cloth, spread out on the floor of his bamboo palace. We gathered around the carpet, but there was nothing on it, and there we sat squatting on the ground. Soon, however, four or more young women with powdered hair came tripping in with rush plates loaded down with roast pork and yams. Each gave a squatter around the board a plate, and soon after they brought on the dessert, which consisted of fruit and nuts; the fruit was good, but for the nuts I had no appetite; they were cocoanuts that had been buried in the ground until the meat had rotted, which made a black oily mass.

Soon after finishing our repast we heard a commotion outside, and soon saw two natives coming out of the bushes with a pole between them, the ends of which were resting on their shoulders. On the pole hung the body of the sailor who had run away, head down. They had tied his hands and feet together, and run the pole through in the manner that pigs are carried. The poor fellow was half dead, and we soon eased his position by placing him on board the ship. Had I desired I could have run away and not have been captured. The natives had many old English pistols and muskets taken in exchange for their products by way of trade; and when these got dirty or the locks out of repair, they did not know how to fix them. I sometimes cleaned them and repaired the locks. When they found me handy at that work, they wanted me to run away. They said that they would hide me so that the big *turonger* chief, meaning the captain, could not find me. I might have made money by so doing; they would give me for repairing one lock one head of tortoise shell, about four pounds in weight, which at that time was worth, in Sydney, four dollars a pound; but the inducement was too small, and I was not in the mood to venture.

I did not then know but that there was more truth than poetry about eating their dead. When they thought me fat enough, they might hide me, after the manner of poor Jonah of ancient writ, and I might not be so fortunate in getting out in three days. I therefore declined their urgent wishes, although afterward regretting not remaining with them. Had I escaped their jaws, I might now have been one of the honored kings of the cannibal islands.

The natives went to war while we were there, and it took them three months to get their weapons together, and when ready for the fray they fought with spears and clubs.

They did not dare to trust to their muskets, as they had found that they did not always shoot when they wanted them to, but the spears and clubs never missed fire. Their battle lasted half a day. Nine were killed on one side, and thirteen on the other. That battle ended the trouble. Had two white hostile armies fought, they would have fought until the last man was killed or taken prisoner. The savages are much easier convinced than the white men, and so there is less slaughter.

All were very anxious to get back to their own island. They could not get away rapidly enough in their double canoes, so they hired the captain to take some three hundred of them home.

There double canoes are made of planks about fifteen

or twenty inches wide and from twenty to thirty feet long, sewed together. Everything they wish to join together is either sewed or lashed with the fibres of the cocoanut husk plattened into *sinnet*. They can do it as neatly as an old sailor. These double canoes are from fifty to seventy-five feet long and six feet wide, pointed at both ends. Two are placed about eight feet apart, and beams are lashed from one to the other. Then a platform is laid over, leaving a few feet at each end of the boats clear. A mast is stuck up in the middle, with a mutton-leg sail. A few holes are cut through the deck, so that when there is no wind they put paddles through these holes, and scull the craft along by swaying sideways, singing at the same time a song like sailors when heaving up anchor.

There was one chief called King Philip, the only one I saw who had any signs of civilization about him. He had his hair cut like a white man, and wore trousers and a coat. There was another old chief called Old Snuff, who said that when he could see a ship go through the water without sails and without oars, he would become a Christian. Some one had told him about steamers. I think he has seen one by this time, if alive. Whether he has become a Christian yet is more his affair than another's.

One of the most beautiful sights in the world is to be seen in the water about these islands. They appear to have been originally volcanic many ages ago, and at a later period the coral insect wrought so diligently and so beautifully that the harbor is filled with reefs; and to sit in a boat and look down upon the forest of coral of every hue of the rainbow, and to see the fishes of every color, presents a sight worth a long journey and which is seldom seen, and once seen is never to be forgotten.

I read not long ago a story which reminded me of my experience,—the story of a reporter who made himself king. Apropos of that, one day a canoe came to the ship. A native was at each end. A white man squatted in the middle. The white man was dressed in gold-lace from head to foot. His cocked hat was covered with tassels and gold-lace. The canoe came alongside, and the visitors were soon on deck. I recognized the white man at the first glance. He was my old friend, the American consul of the brig " Falco," of Lynn, Massachusetts, whom I left at King George's Sound two years before. He had run into those islands some six months before, to trade with the natives. His brig struck on one of the coral reefs which abound in those waters, where she stayed. The crew had all gotten away from the islands, leaving his excellency the consul. Perhaps he thought that the great American Republic should have some one there to represent the country and to look after cast-away Americans, so remained on the islands.

He looked over the ship a little, to see if we had any stowaways on board, since he had learned that we were about ready to leave the islands. Finally he went ashore with his body guard, thinking, no doubt, he had done a stroke of duty for his country.

It was a mystery to me then, as now, how he kept his regalia so well. He had to sleep on the ground, and likely with his trappings on ; or should he take them off, he would have to hang them on the limb of a tree and roll himself in a native tapper carpet. For a pillow he might use his cocked hat. The natives use a little stick, which stands up on legs about four inches high, on which they rest their heads. The chiefs use that kind of a pillow, for by that method they do not rumple their hair. Since the consul was so great a chief among them, he certainly would have to raise his head somehow, or lose caste and be rated as a little chief. I never saw the consul or heard of him after we left the islands. Possibly he became a king and exchanged his regalia for the native costume.

The islanders come very near being spiritualists. They build a cabin of bamboo, and make it tight with but one opening, that is the door. Then they carve out a human figure roughly. They then make a lot of rope from cocoanut fibre, and lash the image to the outer side of the shanty. The rope is made fast to the head of the image and strung around the cabin. The rope represents hair.

When they wish to consult the spirits, the old medium will go inside with one or two others and close the door, when all squat in the middle of the floor with clasped hands, and while in this circle they call up the spirits and consult them, for weal or for woe.

There is one token of honor among the higher order of natives. They pierce their ears with a pointed bone, and insert therein a narrow strip of bamboo bent in the form of a hoop. They change the hoop frequently, and with every change a larger hoop is inserted. They continue this process until the hole is of the desired size, which is according to their rank or station. These holes are sometimes so large that I could run my closed hand through them without touching the sides. When the hoops are taken out, the loops will hang down and rest on the shoulders.

The season for whales was over at these islands. We had remained there five months without taking a whale. We therefore weighed anchor and started out for a short cruise. We sighted no whales, and finally ran into Sydney, where we lay some three months, as the ship needed some repairs.

A piece of gold which weighed about one ounce was

found somewhere in the interior of the country, and brought into Sydney while we lay there, which was in 1845. No one knew enough about gold to look for more where that piece came from. While I was cook at Hobartstown on the " Governor Phillips," the coal came from Port Arthur, and was what might be called slate coal, and I frequently found pieces of it that were gilded with fine gold. I called the attention of several parties to it, and it was pronounced to be gold.

After the ship's repairs were completed we left Sydney for another short cruise. About five hundred miles from Sydney we came to Lord Howe's Island, and some of us went ashore. There was one man with his family on the island, and he was the governor. The English early had the habit of planting their flag on newly discovered lands, and having one man to keep it flying, and by that method claiming the island. They took possession of this island in this way, and Norfolk also, as well as many other islands. Norfolk Island produces a large variety of fruit, with oranges predominating and being native to the island. There is as much difference between the oranges of that country and the ones we see as there is between a potato and an apple. The oranges of the islands are the most delicious fruit I ever tasted. At Lord Howe's Island we found plenty of peppers, of which we gathered an abundance. On this island there is a remarkable tree called the banyan-tree, that covers several acres of land. When the first tree started and had grown some twenty-five or thirty feet, with its branches spread out in all directions, shoots ran down from the limbs to the ground, where they took root and grew into another trunk, from which other branches grew out, which extended itself after the fashion of the parent tree until a small forest had grown up that covered many acres of land. Were the branches that rise above those horizontal arms of wood that connect the perpendicular ones together trimmed down, one could wheel a barrow over the entire forest with ease and safety.

We soon left the island and, after a cruise of a few months, chasing many whales and catching none, we went into Hobartstown again, where I had shipped some fifteen months before, thinking that I was going home, but I could not quarrel with fate, so renewed my acquaintance with my old friends, who were much pleased to see me back again.

I was set at work coopering casks with the third mate. It took about three weeks to set up what casks we wanted. Having been on shore a number of times, and mixing with my old associates, I began to hanker for the land again. I felt rather sore toward the captain, because he did not promote me when he had opportunity. One of our boat steerers ran away at Sydney, and when we were out at sea the captain put one of the forward hands in to fill his place, — a position which I thought should have been given me. The reason why we did not catch more whales was because the boat steerers could not hit the whales, or were afraid and would not strike them. I believed that I could hit them every time, if put near enough.

I wished to get something that would bring me in a little money, so when we got to Hobartstown I concluded that there was no money in whales for me, no matter what ship I was in, therefore left the ship. One of the boat steerers quitted with me.

A man on shore with whom I was acquainted agreed to stow us away in his house. Accordingly, when we thought the ship about ready to sail, we went ashore and to my friend's house, where we were soon tucked away in his loft. There were no stairs, but a hole cut in the ceiling overhead reached by a ladder. It was removed

when we were in the loft, and we put some loose boards
over the hole. No one thought of looking aloft for us.
Through a hole in the roof, between the shingles, we
could see the ship, and thus we watched day by day for
three weeks until the ship left the bay. We wanted for
nothing, my friend providing plenty to eat and drink.
The first and second mates came into the house one day,
and we knew their voices, but we kept very still. Little
did they suspect the men they wanted were hiding above
their heads.

After three weeks of watching, one morning we
found the ship was under way. This was about ten
o'clock, but we kept in hiding until the next morning,
and it was lucky for us that we did. When we went out
the following morning, we learned the captain went down
the harbor about twenty miles and dropped anchor, and
then sent a boat to town, thinking that we would, after
seeing the ship go down the bay and out of sight behind
a point that made out into the harbor, come out and
show ourselves; but I was not to be caught in such a
simple manner. The captain, finding he could not catch
us, before leaving went to a merchant, who kept a store
near the wharf, and who also owned a number of vessels
sailing out of Hobartstown, and told him that he did not
want to lose me, but, since he was obliged to leave me,
he advised him to get me to join one of his vessels when
I appeared out, and gave me one of the best of recom-
mendations.

The morning when we went down to the wharf I was
met by a man who told me that Mr. Johnson, which was
the merchant's name, wanted to see me. Going to him
at once, he informed me what the captain had said, and
wanted me to ship then and there in a schooner which
he owned. This schooner at that time was the smallest
vessel that had ever been around Cape Horn, being only

about fifty tons' burden. She was going on a four-months' cruise along the coast after whales.

I did not take very kindly to the project, but told him I would let him know in a few days. Thinking the matter over for a while, I concluded four months would soon slip away, and if we only got one whale, I would have quite a stake on our return, and I shipped and we were soon out of the harbor.

We went around to the farther side of the island and dropped anchor in a little bay not far from one of the penal settlements. We were not allowed in there, but the captain made things all right with the officers in charge of the convicts. We used to go ashore and look off from the high rocks. There was a small island to which I used to go, and which was not more than half a mile from the mainland. There were plenty of penguins there. There were holes in the ground near the water, and I found they contained from two to six eggs, and from many of the holes the bird would rush out and dive into the water. I gathered a bucketful of the eggs and carried them to the ship, where the cook fried them, but they were not very good. They were about all yolk and very dry, but being eggs we ate them. By visiting their nests I found that they laid about as regularly as a hen does. Notwithstanding we had robbed them, we would always find newly laid eggs. One day while we lay in the bay, the "Governor Phillips" dropped anchor near us. The captain came on board, the same that was in her when I was cook.

He was surprised to see me, and said he expected that I was at home by that time. I gave him a short sketch of my experience. He told me that he wanted to see me privately. Just before he left he called me aside. He wished me to go with him, and said he would give me a good chance if I would go in the brig. Answering, I replied that I would like to be with him again, but as the schooner would only be out four months, thought it best to remain with her and finish the voyage.

"Well," said he, "you can do so if you prefer, but I would like to have you with me, and if you will say the word, I will send a boat alongside about nine this evening, and all you will have to do will be to get into her and come aboard."

I thanked him for his kindly consideration, but thought he had better not send the boat, and that when I came back to Hobartstown I might ship with him, and with that understanding he left us. I never saw him or his brig afterward.

We saw one whale a few days after the brig left the bay. We gave chase with two boats for about ten miles, but he went like a race horse, and we could not catch him and had to give him up. We thought that perhaps he was not worth the trouble of catching, since he must have run all the fat out of him through making such wonderful speed, so called him a dry shin, and let him go like a bunch of sour grapes.

We found there were no whales in the bay, so we ran into a little bay farther down the coast, where we dropped anchor and sent the boats on shore to look out for whales. Out about two months, we had seen one whale in the distance. By that time I concluded there was no money in whales for me. I began to feel homesick, and made up my mind to run away. I had become quite proficient at that, so I broached the subject one day to a young fellow who was as sick of the business as myself. He readily entered into my plans, so, one morning when the boats went ashore, we filled our pockets with bread and meat and went ashore likewise.

When boats are sent ashore in this manner, the crew all land except one man, who remains in a boat. After the men are landed, the boat is hauled off a little and anchored, yet near enough to the shore, when swung around, to allow the crew to get in at the stern end, so that, if whales are discovered, the crew can get on board quickly and start on the chase. We agreed to remain in the boats that morning. The crew well out of sight, we pulled the two boats upon the rocks, jumped out, and started by land around the little bay. We were soon in the thick forest, and after a few hours of travel we came to a clearing of some ten acres. Near one side of the clearing was a farmhouse. We skirted the clearing, and getting about half-way around it, came to a road which led away into the country. We concluded that the road led to Hobartstown, so we took to it at once, and pushed forward at a good speed.

In the middle of the afternoon we heard a noise behind us, and looking back in the distance through the forest we saw two men on horseback. We thought, naturally, that they were after us, so we sprang into the forest, and coming to a log we quickly hid behind it, and were soon hugging the ground as closely as we could. I felt quite safe, for I had found in a former emergency that the friendly protection of a log was quite ample for a short time. The men rode by without halting and were soon out of sight. We concluded we were not the game they were hunting, and we were soon on the road again. My companion, much younger than I, was not used to such a tramp and could not keep up with me, and we each had quite a bundle of clothing that we had smuggled ashore when we left the schooner. My friend lagged behind, which I knew would not do, so I took his load upon my back, which gave me a double load to carry, but I was equal to the task. We pushed on until sundown, and then camped away from the road far enough to hide ourselves should there be any nocturnal travellers on the road.

The next day we passed through a little hamlet, but spoke to no one, having no time to form new acquaintances. We passed that day and the next without trouble. On the third day we came to a river at sundown, about three miles from Hobartstown. The river was a half-mile wide, and was crossed by a ferryboat. When we applied for passage, we found we were to be interviewed by officers. They thought us escaped prisoners. My friend had come from England but a short time before, and had got his discharge from the ship, which he happened to have in his pocket. He showed his papers to the officers, and then they wanted to see my proof. I told them I had belonged to the same vessel, but had lost my discharge. After using much persuasion they let us over, and we were soon in town and well housed with one of my old friends.

The vessel, the keel of which was laid some eighteen months before, was finished and launched, and nearly ready for sailing. She was going to Melbourne, and from thence to Geelong, a little town on one side of the harbor at Port Philip. Melbourne lies at the upper end of the same harbor. She was to take a cargo of wool and tallow for London. When I heard that she was soon going to England, I made up my mind that I would ship in her and perhaps get away from the country. Starting out to find the captain or owners, I soon learned that they wanted more hands. They asked if I was an able seaman; I told them that I was, and they put my name down at once at two pounds ten a month. I received one month's pay in advance; and as the vessel was to sail in a week, I took my money and began to get together an outfit, such as blankets and other clothing which I would need for the voyage.

There was at that time many small tradesfolk who kept blankets and other small articles, which they bought of the convicts who had finished their terms, and on leaving the country sold the blankets, being allowed to do so. All such goods have the government mark, such as the crowfoot or broad R, as it is commonly called, and B. O. for *bond of ordinance*, besides many other marks and figures. In my hunt I found a woman who had some of those blankets. They were just what I wanted, for the English government blankets are the best in the world, thick, heavy, and durable. I bought two at half a crown each. It was very fortunate for me that the woman knew all the marks and figures that were on the blankets. I had seen so many of the articles with the government mark on them that I paid no particular attention to them. On my way down the street I came to a little store that was kept by a woman whose husband was book-keeper for Mr. Johnson, the merchant who owned the schooner I had left a few days since. I wanted a few small articles, so put my blankets on a bench near the door. A few blankets belonging to the store were piled on one end of the bench. I thought nothing of that; there was plenty of room on the other end and some two feet distant from the woman's blankets. I went in, bought what I wanted, and paid her what she said they came to, and then betook myself and my blankets to the ship, which lay at the wharf nearly opposite the store where the woman's husband worked.

I went on board, put my blankets into my berth, and then went up to my boarding-house. In the afternoon that book-keeper came in and accused me of stealing a pair of his blankets. He said that his wife saw me take them from the bench. Furthermore, he had been on board, looked the blankets over, and could swear to the marks on them. I saw at a glance that the fellow had the thing all his own way, if the woman of whom I bought the blankets could not identify them or describe their marks, I would, perhaps, have to stay seven years longer in the country whether I wanted to or not, and sleep every night under the same kind of blankets, and also wear a garb with the same marks on them. I learned that when he went to dinner his wife told him that I had stolen a pair of her blankets, and that she saw me take them from the bench and carry them off under my arm.

I had told the woman what ship I belonged to, with the result that after dinner the fellow went to the ship and found out by some of the men where my berth was and had taken down the numbers and other marks on them. No two blankets are marked alike, every one being a little different. I had not noticed the numbers or marks, while he could swear to all of them. So sure was he that I had stolen them, because his wife saw me take them, I thought my chances slim, but was not ready to give up without a struggle for liberty. I explained about purchasing them, but he would not believe me. Finally I proposed we go with my friend, the man with whom I boarded, to the woman's house that he might interview her, to which he agreed. Upon arriving at the house, he would not allow me to go in, thinking I would give the woman a hint. So he and my friend went in. While they were inside, which was for about twenty minutes, I prayed hard for that woman's memory. When they came out the fellow looked crestfallen, and I knew the woman's memory had saved me. My friend said that she proved beyond a doubt I had bought the blankets of her, for she described every mark that was on them, at which he very reluctantly gave in. Then thinking he must say something, he declared I had not paid for the things bought in the store. I replied I had paid all his wife asked. He insisted that I had cheated her out of something. I replied if he could prove that I owed either him or his wife, I was ready to pay. He finally left us rather abruptly and went on to his store, which was the last I saw of him.

Two or three days after we sailed for Melbourne, where we stopped a few hours and then went around to Geelong, where we dropped anchor and lay four months taking in wool and tallow. Sheep and cattle in that part of Australia were slaughtered simply for the hides, wool, and tallow. Beef and mutton were a penny a pound, take your cut where you pleased.

We had been there some four weeks when a strange-looking craft came in and dropped anchor near us. We could not tell whether she was a Dutch galley yacht, Chinese junk, or Noah's ark, until, catching sight of her figurehead, I knew in a moment what the craft was. It proved to be the old brig which I helped build on the west side of the island, whose designer and builder was the man I performed the surgical operation on. She had afterwards been finished and was in the coasting trade. The carpenter who built her belonged in the northern part of England, where he had been used to building vessels square at both ends, and this craft was of that model. She had a native model for a figurehead, which I remembered seeing when it was being carved.

I went ashore but once during the four months' stay and then for a half-hour only. I determined to stay by the ship until she hauled into the dock in London. I had been disappointed too many times to take any chances of being left again. It appears very strange to me now as I think of it; it was fate, seemingly, that pursued me. Then, above all others, was the time when I should have run away. Had I done so, I might have been the first man to discover gold on a large scale in Australia. I made it a point always when I ran away from a vessel to get back into the forest as far as I could;

and had I run away at Geelong, I would have gone inland where the sheep ranches were, near Ballarat, and which is about sixty miles from Geelong.

Every one knows the history of the Ballarat gold mines. I always had a desire to look into things, and to examine rocks and other objects in different countries in which I happened to be, and am quite certain that I would have found gold, when it is considered how easily it was discovered. It appeared to be scattered everywhere on the surface of the ground as well as in it. At Ballarat there was one gulch that was quite shallow, out of which fifteen hundred pounds weight were taken. It ran into a flat where the depth, from surface to bed rock, was over one hundred feet. Seven sailors sank a shaft into that flat, which shaft had to be timbered. They went below salt water. The first tub of dirt from the bottom yielded them twelve pounds of gold.

It used to be law among the miners that if one man drifted on to another man's claim, to fine him five pounds sterling. It was found that law would not do. A man might take out several hundred dollars and only have to pay about twenty-five. The law was changed. Out of a pan of dirt, obtained by an act of trespass, the trespasser was fined as much as the dirt would pay upon washing. One man worked over his line and one foot on his neighbor's claim. He took out one pan of dirt and washed it. It paid one thousand pounds sterling to the foot. The fellow paid a thousand pounds fine, and then offered to pay another thousand pounds for another foot of the same ground, but the neighbor would not sell. This shows what might have been had I left the ship at that place.

My gold hunting in Australia happened a few years later on. This was early in 1847. Our cargo on board and stowed snugly away in the ship's hold, there was nothing to keep us longer, so we up anchor and were soon out to sea again. The ship's head was turned toward Cape Horn, and arrived near the Cape ere many weeks passed. We had a fair wind until we got quite around the Horn. It is well known among nautical men that in doubling Cape Horn from the Pacific to the Atlantic, the wind is generally fair, and oppositely true going from the Atlantic to the Pacific.

The captain thought he shipped twenty able seamen and six boy apprentices; but when we got out to sea it was found that only about one half of the crew could steer the ship when in a heavy sea and before the wind. I was one of the few who could handle her in any sea or weather. She steered very hard, and off Cape Horn among the heavy seas, which I believe are much higher than elsewhere, we had to have a man at the lee ·wheel to help to turn it. Stationed at the wheel one night, the rain falling fast, I had a big Dutchman at the lee wheel; and we were running with lower studding sails. The captain thought the weather might be too severe in the night, and he ordered them taken in. I could not see forward very well, it was so dark and raining quite hard, so had to steer altogether by the compass. When I could see the ship's head or the stars, I used them as much as the compass, although running on a set course. The binnacle glass under which the compass was located was so wet that I could not see the compass. I therefore told the Dutchman to hold her steady a moment. I let go, and one step took me to the binnacle. I had given it one wipe, looked at the compass, whirled around and caught the wheel just in time to keep the Dutchman from going over my head. At the same time there was music ahead. It appeared that the vessel had got nearly aback forward, and the sails were slapping furiously. The studding sail had got aback and nearly thrown three men overboard.

The captain was on the poop deck in a trice and wanted to know what I was trying to do. I told him that I could not see the compass and did not want too long to steer by the wind; and had told the lee helmsman to hold her steady a moment while I wiped the water from the binnacle light, and he had nearly allowed her to broach to.

The captain took the Dutchman in hand and dressed him down handsomely for about ten minutes.

" You came on board," said he, " as an able seaman, and you cannot stand at the lee wheel alone for a moment without endangering our lives or sinking the ship !"

All sailors know where we would have gone had the ship got all aback forward under a ten or twelve knot wind, with the ship in a trough of the sea, with waves ahead one hundred feet high and rising up from the ship at an angle of forty-five degrees. It has been said that waves seldom rise over forty feet. Any one who has doubled Cape Horn knows better. When one has to look upward at an angle of forty-five degrees to see a vessel that is a mile off, and one can see nearly her entire keel, as I have, one knows the waves can sometimes reach a higher altitude than forty feet.

When I let go the wheel, it threw all of the water on to the Dutchman, and he began to ease a little; and the ship swung a little near the wind. As a consequence she would crowd the man at the wheel a little harder, and he, not knowing how to check her, would at once have been all in the wind, and all hands would have gone down with the ship stern first. Had I not checked her, in five minutes more we would have all been buried a hundred feet beneath the ocean.

I was taken ill soon after we rounded the Cape, and was sick for a week. A day or two before I got about, while in a very rough sea, the ship rolling and pitching a good deal, I lay in my berth in the topgallant forecastle where I could look out on to the deck, through a hole over the windlass. About four in the afternoon I heard a terrible snapping on deck, and the men were running in all directions. I saw the third mate run a little way up the main rigging with a yard or two of small rope in his hand; he stopped climbing and began to sing out for some one to go up ahead of him and lash the spars that were hanging aloft and swinging every way, and likely to break away at any moment and come down on deck or go overboard. A number of the ship's crew stood on the deck looking up at him, but no one cared to try to lash the spars. I could not quite see what was the matter, but knew it must be something serious. I had on but my shirt and drawers. I did not mind that. Out I went through the hole, over the windlass and over to the main rigging. I saw at once the trouble; the fore-topmast was broken off just above the cap, and, when that went, the main topgallant mast just above the loops of the fore and aft stays which run from the top of the foremast-head and then looped around the top of the main topmast, which was broken also, it will readily be seen that the main topgallant mast broken close down to those loops, there was nothing to prevent the loops slipping off at any moment with the ship pitching and rolling heavily, while the topgallant mast and yard with sail furled swung away to come back with a furious blow against the stay.

The mate wanted some one to go up, and then down that stay some six feet, and when the yard and mast swung in to catch them and lash them to the stay, also to lash the fore and aft stays more securely to the top of the mast.

I started up at once over the man's head and caught the rope in his hand. Up I went, then down to the stay head first with my feet clinched around it behind me. I caught the yard and mast as they came in and lashed them and came down.

The mate told me to go into the cabin and get an extra glass of grog, but I went straight to my berth.

I was out and at work soon after that. We had no further trouble during the voyage, and arrived in London about the first of March, 1848. We hauled into Saint Catharine's dock and made fast, and the ship was soon full of boarding-house keepers hunting for boarders. Three of us were soon picked up by one of them, and we started up the wharf and were soon out on to the street.

I was extremely happy to get my feet on land again north of the line, and then it was a step nearer home, or toward it.

We soon were domiciled in the boarding-house, and the next day I went with my boarding-house keeper and bought a suit of fashionable clothing, from a beaver hat down. I found after about seven years of experience at the antipodes that my head had got its growth, and there was more in it than when I left Canada. In about three days we were paid off. I received eighteen pounds for my eight months on the ship.

There was a young fellow on board who knew my old friend S. whom I left at Murray River. My friend S. told me if I ever came to London to look him up, and that I would find him at the London Stock Exchange. His father was a member of the Exchange, and he intended on his return to enter into the same business. I felt a hesitancy about hunting him up, knowing his social standing at home, while I was only a common sailor. This young man had come to England after a fortune that had been left him by friends in Liverpool. I told him where Mr. S. was, and that he might say to him that I was in London and stopping at —— Hotel, on Radcliffe Highway. He said that he would call on him after his return from Liverpool.

I never saw him afterward, but he delivered my message.

I knocked about the city sight-seeing, and went to some of the theatres, museums, a celebrated museum of wax figures, and many other places of interest, such as Stepping Fair, Rag Fair, Petticoat Lane, Whitechapel, the Tower, and Newgate. I was not able to get inside of this latter massive structure, the granite walls of which are black with age.

London proper looks like a city that was built about four thousand years back, and had perhaps been buried beneath their accumulated rubbish, to be finally brought to the light of day, like Pompeii.

The city has not yet cast off her winding sheets, since she is forever wrapped in fog or smoke, so that the sun seldom has a chance to look down the streets.

The famous dwarf, Tom Thumb, had left London some two weeks before I arrived. I found that he had left something for the cockneys to remember him by. While at Madam Tussaud's Wax Figures, I saw Queen Victoria and Prince Albert in wax, life size, and by their side stood Tom Thumb dressed *à la* Napoleon. The queen presented Tom Thumb with a pair of ponies and a carriage to match; the whole outfit, with Tom in the carriage, was put on to a platform mounted on wheels, and with four horses were drawn through the principal streets.

After I had been in the city about a month, I found that my money was getting painfully short. I finally had spent my last shilling, and in order to hold over a little longer, exchanged my nice suit of store clothing and beaver hat for something cheaper, and received a few shillings to boot. I then began to hunt for a ship to go to the United States. I could find no American ships in need of help, so I went to an English vessel and found that I could not ship until I had a registered ticket.

Similar to the American protection, it entitles the holder
to protection by the country that issues the ticket. After
obtaining one, I was rated as a British seaman and could
get a British ship any time, and wanted to ship very
badly just then. I found one that was going to New
York, shipped at once and received one month's advance
of two pounds ten. I was "flush" again, for a few days.
The vessel lay at a place called Black Wall, some three
miles from the city proper.

My money was soon pretty low. London, like all cities,
has abundant opportunties where one can lose a deal of
money in a very short time, unless one sews his pockets
up tightly. I took the elevated cars across the city. At
Black Wall I found the ship, and was told she would not
be ready to sail for two weeks. My lip hung low when
I heard that. Before returning to London I decided
to look the place over a little. I sauntered down
the dock. I saw some men building a fence across the
end of the wharf. When I came to them I saw the cause
of the fence. A few rods from the wharf, riding at
anchor, was a Chinese junk just from Boston, Mass.,
where she had been on exhibition. The men said that
the queen was coming down at ten o'clock to see the
junk. I looked the strange craft over, and took the half
past nine train to the city.

I would have had a chance to see the queen had I
waited a half-hour, but I did not somehow care to see
her. I thought it strange for people, who had always
lived in London, to rally to see a woman on horseback
or in a carriage; but they did it by the tens of thousands,
and I suppose always will.

In the city again, I could not stand it long without
money, so began to look for a ship that would sail in a
day or two. I soon found the New York packet, of
Greenock, Scotland, and shipped in her to sail the next

day for New York with passengers, thence to St. John's, New Brunswick, and back to London again. I had to ship for the voyage, and take my chances of getting away at New York. If I could only get sight of Yankee-land, I should be happy. My past experience in getting clear of vessels had not been forgotten.

I got my advance, and went to the man who had shipped me in the other, and paid him the money that I had from him. The change gave me no more money, but a chance to get out of the country at once. I thought I had seen London, both above ground and under ground, as I had been through the Thames tuunel several times. About half-way through the tunnel a place was boxed up and the water was trickling down a little. When the tunnel was being constructed a brig dropped her anchor over it and the bottom of the river dropped out at the same time and filled the tunnel with water.

A few years later I met the man who stopped that hole. A large canvas tarpaulin was made and sunk, with weights at each corner, over the hole. Then bags of sand were piled on and kept drawing in toward the centre until the hole was finally stopped, the water being pumped at the shaft at the end of the tunnel. This man had made money enough to take him to Chili, and from there to California, where I met him.

One day before my money gave out I fell in with the keeper of the queen's park, and he was a royal good fellow. We went over a number of streets sight-seeing. The English people who are above the ordinary class of people drink much gin and brandy, while the laboring class take along to their work a lunch of bread and cheese, and at dinner-time go to a tap-room, of which there are many, for a pot of half-and-half, which with bread and cheese make their mid-day meal.

I noticed the keeper of the royal park would stop at

about all the tap-rooms that we came to and call for gin. Although not caring for liquor, yet I could take a glass with a friend. I could not very well refuse to drink with my new friend, so, out of deference, would take a sip, and when his back was turned I would pour the liquor on the floor. After one or two hours I found that my head was getting pretty heavy, and things began to look rather dizzy, but my legs were steady enough. I made some excuse about the boarding-house and bade him good day, starting on a blind hunt for my boarding-house. I somehow found that haven of rest, and made for bed. I thought the whole city was having a dance. Everything was going around like a top, — chairs, tables, water-pots, and bowls alike; the house seemed to be bringing up the rear. I grasped the bed to keep myself from being thrown out, and finally lost myself in the whirl. After sleeping about four hours, I came to life again with something of a headache. I took good care after that not to sip again, no matter with whom I might be.

Saturday, the 8th of April, 1848, the day that I was to sail, had arrived. We were to haul out of the dock that afternoon at four o'clock. I was at a hotel 'on Radcliffe Highway at about ten, when some one opened the door and stepped in.

He was a man dressed in the height of London fashion. He carried that never-to-be-left-behind umbrella, which every Englishman takes when he goes on the street. I turned partly around facing him. The moment I caught his eye I knew him, and he recognized me.

He exclaimed, " Why, Jack! " as he always called me, " I have found you at last."

"Why," said I, " is it possible that this is Mr. S. ?"

"Yes," said he, and then told me about looking for me since seven o'clock that morning. He said my young friend told him I was in London only a day or two since, and also what ship I came in. He said Saturdays were his days off, and he had started on a hunt for me.

Living on the opposite side of the river Thames, he had taken a groom and two horses and rode down to the ferry, and then sent his groom back with the horses and taken the boat over to London. He went first to the ship in which I had come to London. There he was told what ship I was in, which was down at Black Wall, and down there he went and learned that I had since shipped in the New York packet to sail that day. Back to London again, and down to the vessel, he learned I was at a hotel on Radcliffe Highway, where he found me.

When he learnrd I was to sail that afternoon, he advised me to go home and see my friends. He also had known what it was to be absent from home a long time.

He told me that I ought to have come to him at once, as I knew where to find him; that I could have seen a great deal more of London, and it would not have cost me anything; and that when I was ready to go home he would have paid my passage to any part of the United States. Finding I had no money, he pulled out his wallet and divided the contents with me, and further assured me, had he known or thought of finding me hard up, he would have brought me forty or fifty sovereigns. He said it would have been nothing out of his pocket.

I thanked him for his great kindness.

He intended on finding me to take me to his home, but since I had shipped and was going to sail that afternoon, he said that I had better go on home. We went out on to the street for a short walk, during which he told me what had transpired at Murray River after I left. Mr. Morris, who was building the brig that I worked on, had failed, and the brig was sold while on the stocks; and that Mr. Peel, who owned the land from which we cut the mahogany to build the brig with, had found his land so sterile that it was not fit for a sheep or cattle ranch, although it was said that it cost him but sixpence an acre, gave the land back to the government, sent his two daughters home to be educated, and what became of him my friend did not say. His brother was premier at that time, Sir Robert Peel, and I believe one of the best that England ever had. My friend said that shortly after the brig was sold his mother had sent him out one thousand pounds and requested him to pay his debts and come home at once, which he did, as he was as anxious to leave the country as I had been.

When he arrived home his father gave him a thousand pounds and one month's time to make up his mind which of two offers he would accept. One was that he would buy and give to him a ship and he might go to sea, or he would retire from the Stock Exchange, and the son might take his seat. My friend said that he had a royal good time while that one thousand pounds lasted, and at the end of the month he concluded to take his father's seat in the Exchange. When he met me he had then been nine months in the business and had cleared nine thousand pounds sterling and was in a fair way to soon accumulate a handsome fortune, which I have no doubt he succeeded in doing. While on the street we saw a few of the London upper circle. One was Lord John Russell ; my friend said when we saw him ahead with that proverbial umbrella in his hand, which he was using for a cane, " Look ! I think he has found some good brandy this morning."

I thought that the umbrella was convenient even in a clear day, since it might hide now and then a moral defection.

The time grew near when I had to go on board. My friend said before parting that I must write him when I got home and let him know how I found my friends, etc.

" Now, Jack, don't go home and say that you never saw one true-hearted Englishman."

My friend was one of the best young men I ever met in any part of this wide world, nor do I expect to meet his equal again. Such men are few and far between, now as then.

To show what stock he came from, I will relate an incident which happened a short time before he went to Australia. His father had a friend, whom we will call Jones. Jones had an only son. It is well known that a man in England can cut his children off with what is called " the shilling " ; that is to say, leave them but one shilling in their will. Jones, Jr., had disgraced his sire's gray hairs, and when Jones made his will he left his large fortune to my friend, who was the son of Mr. Jones's friend. The father of Mr. S. was the custodian of the will of Mr. Jones. It was locked up in a safe, and when Mr. Jones died, Mr. S., Sen., took out the will and found that Mr. Jones had left his entire fortune to his son, amounting to one million pounds sterling, and but one shilling to Jones, Jr. Mr. S., Sen., threw the will into the fire, remarking that he had enough for his son and he would not see young Jones robbed of his fortune in that way.

There are not many men who would have burned the will; they would not only have taken it, but burned the man's bones because he did not have double that amount to leave them ; such is the difference in men.

My friend and I parted after a hearty shake of hands, he to go back over the river, and I to go over the great pond to my home across the Atlantic Ocean. I was soon on board. We hauled out and ran down the river Thames and out into the channel. Soon out of that, we were on the broad ocean, headed for New York. I found the food on that vessel the worst that I had ever seen, excepting none. The meat was bad and the bread also. About once a week we got a bit of fresh meat stewed up with Scotch barley groats, such as they say Scotchmen get fat on, but I think that I would starve to death on such diet. As I was going home, I did not grumble.

CHAPTER V.

ON our voyage nothing happened of note until we
arrived on the coast off New York, where it is often very
foggy. On the 6th of July we came on to the coast. I
was at the wheel from six to eight, the dog watch. The
wheel was on the poop deck. It was very foggy, and I
could not see more than a ship's length ahead. A lookout was stationed on the topgallant forecastle. All at
once I discovered a large ship straight ahead. The
lookout shouted, but I saw the danger quite as soon as he.
The law for the guidance of nautical men in such cases
is, for each vessel to put the wheel " up," as it is called ;
that is, to the side of the ship the wind is blowing from,
so the ship will pay off farther from the wind. When
both vessels do this, they are supposed to swing clear of
each other. I was steering about two points from the
wind ; in other words, to bring her up two points
would cause her sails to be shivering in the wind and
caught aback. I at once ran the wheel hard down, while
the mate was singing at the top of his voice, " Hard up !
hard up !" I paid no attention to him ; but pushed it
hard down, and at the same time kept my eyes on the

A CLOSE SHAVE ON THE COAST OFF NEW YORK.

ship ahead and the sails, so as not to get aback forward. Our vessel came up so that the fore topgallant sail began to tremble a little, and the ship that was ahead shot alongside our lee.   I righted the wheel and kept the ship steady until the other one was past.

She was within an arm's length of us, but not a word was spoken on either side until she was past; then they sang out on the other ship, "Well done, John Bull!"

She was a whaler.   Her quarter boat just grazed our bumkin, a spar about four feet long, secured to the ship's quarter with a block on the outer end, through which the main brace runs and which is more commonly used when running with a fair wind.   This method makes the brace less oblique when hauled taut.

Had I put the wheel "up" according to the law, and had they done the same, we might have fallen off about one point, and the other ship the same. With each vessel going about nine miles an hour, we would have crashed together, and both ships would have sunk.

The mate said nothing, but when the captain came on deck at eight o'clock, he wanted to know why I did not obey the mate's orders.   I told him that I could see the position of both ships, and I did the only thing that would save us.

"Well," said he, "if anything had happened it would have been your fault."

He said nothing further, and I thought it was my fault that prevented something from happening.   I seemed to be forced, in spite of myself, by some outside power, to do as I did.   I thought so at another time when I saved a brig from total destruction, with about a hundred lives.   I then felt there was some invisibe force directed me for the welfare of others.

The second incident happened just one year later to a day. The first was the 6th of July, 1848, between the hours of six and eight in the morning, and the second was the 6th of July, 1849, between four and five in the afternoon.

We soon dropped anchor at Staten Island, where the passengers had to be examined by the doctors, and were then sent ashore.

I found that the ship was not going any nearer the city, therefore began to plan how to escape. There were seven of us who wanted to leave the ship, so we watched our chance and soon got it. With the exception of four or five cabin passengers, all were landed. The captain was ashore with one boat, and one small boat was towing astern, and the third boat was on the skids overhead, where it would take some time to get her down. While the officers were at dinner in the cabin, one man managed to haul the boat from astern alongside pretty well forward, and we seven were quickly in the boat, and with oars out we were soon on our way to the city. About one hundred yards from the vessel, the mate came running forward and sang out for us to come back. We shouted back if he wanted the boat, he would have to come ashore for her. We pulled on until we ran into a dock where there was a flight of steps that led up to the wharf. We landed, found a dray on which we piled our luggage, and, when ready to start, who should come along but the second mate, who had got the boat down from overhead and had managed to get ashore!

He wanted to know where the boat was. We pointed to her, and off we started after the dray that had by that time got well away from the wharf with our kits. We were all soon snugly hidden in a boarding-house.

I was ashore at last in my own country, but without money, but I did not much mind that. I had been through many a tight place without money, and thought I could get to Boston somehow.

The boarding mistress was willing to keep me until I could pay her. The second night ashore, while I stood on the sidewalk in front of my boarding place, the captain and one of the cabin passengers came by. He asked why I had run away.

I told him that I had been away seven years, and that this was the first time that I had landed on American soil, and that I wished to go home to Boston. He said that he would like to have me go back with him.

I told the woman I was afraid the captain would come back and take me to the ship. She gave me a quarter to go to the theatre, which I did, but the captain did not call again. It was at this boarding-house that I met my old friend, the fifer, and leader of the band, whom I left at the Rosemary Islands. He had gone into business in New York, and was doing well and was happy.

After being around the boarding-house a few days, I concluded to walk to Boston. A man who boarded at the same house also wanted to get to Boston. He had about two dollars, so we started together one morning to walk to Boston by way of one of the two rivers, but did not get far. I found that my travelling companion would stop whenever we came to a place where he could get liquor. He had taken on board more cargo than he could carry with safety. Soon he could neither tell where he was nor where he wanted to go. I finally left him on his beam ends by the roadside, and turned back for New York, where I arrived about noon. I never saw my heavy-laden friend again.

On returning to my boarding-house I found one of the boarders was going to ship in the United States service. He knew I wanted to go to Boston, and that I had no money. He said I could ship in the service, get three months' advance, and would be put on board of the receiving ship. If we were not drafted to go to sea, after the three months had expired I could get my discharge, and then I would have money enough to get home with.

I thought it a good idea, so shipped with him for three years, and was soon on board of the " North Carolina," which was then the receiving ship, anchored near the navy yard at Brooklyn. On board, I was told my outfit would be sent to me in a few days. I began to look the situation over, and did not like the appearance of things; but I was on board and could not get ashore again. I was told to go down into the doctor's room, for examination. I found the doctor waiting for me, and was told to " strip." He made me hop around like a savage in a war dance. I hoped he would not pass me, having by that time got sick of my venture. The doctor stamped me " O. K.," and sent me on deck. The next day my outfit came on board, which consisted of a blue jacket and pants of the same material, two pairs of duck pants, two white frocks with wide collars, one blue shirt, tarpaulin hat and hammock, and one blanket. My three months' advance came to thirty dollars, and the outfit to twenty-eight dollars. I thought if I got my discharge in three months, I would be no better off than before I had shipped. My outfit could have been bought for half that sum at any store; but I suppose the man who shipped me and furnished the outfit, like the fellow in Boston, thought he would need a pretty margin, considering the risk he was running. The New-Yorker, however, ran no risk, as he got his money the day after the doctor passed me.

Is it any wonder that sailors run away, when they are robbed in that manner? I began there and then to lay plans to get away. I saw a number of the sailors try to swim ashore at night, but all were caught and brought back. I dared not try that method, and knew that with my experience, if I was patient, I would succeed. I was soon undeceived about getting my discharge after three months, which would have paid for my advance. I would have to stay the three years unless discharged through disability; and when I came to think that I was only a few hours' ride from home, and yet could not get there and was likely soon to sail again for three years without seeing any of my friends or knowing whether they were alive or not, my thoughts made me very miserable. Finally, seeing no opportunity to get away, I wrote a letter to one of my brothers in Boston and told him where I was, and that I expected to go to sea again soon. I did not write to him before because I had been away seven years, and yet in all that time could not raise money enough to take me from New York to Boston. It would not speak well for my ability as a financier, nor did I want to be beholden to any one, even for the small amount that would take me to Boston. I wrote the letter, but did not know whether any of my relatives were alive or not. When enlisting I had not given my middle name. It was then my week to prepare the mess for the cook, such as peeling potatoes and getting other things ready, carrying them to the cook, and setting the table for the men.

The following day after the letter was sent, about ten o'clock, I was in the mess-room peeling potatoes when I heard the boatswain sing out on deck above my name with the middle letter in its proper place as given in the letter. I knew at once that some of my folks were on deck above. I dropped my potatoes at once and ran up. There was my brother, whom I had left at the store in Boston seven years before. I knew him at a glance. He recognized me because he was expecting to see me; but I think had he met me in the street he would not have known me. I had grown from a lad of seventeen to a man of twenty-four, and was near six feet tall and had grown a beard. I was glad to learn that all of my folks were well, father, mother, brothers, and an only sister.

Before my brother left for home again he offered the lieutenant in charge forty dollars for my discharge; but the lieutenant said that the only way that he could get my discharge would be to write to the Secretary of the Navy at Washington. Before my brother left I told him privately that he need not try to get my discharge. I would take what sailors call "French leave." After my brother's visit my mind was much easier.

About three days later a draft came from Washington for three hundred men to man a new frigate, which was at Norfolk, Va. She was going to the Straits of Gibraltar or up the Mediterranean to remain three years. The frigate's name was the "St. Lawrence." I was one of the victims drafted. We were sent to Norfolk in two schoonors, one half in each, and were soon on our way. The schooner I was in, while beating out of the harbor against a head wind on the New York side, would run so near to the wharf that, when she swung around in tacking, her jib-boom would pass over the wharf. I thought this might be a chance to watch for my opportunity and run out along the boom and drop to the wharf. When she swung her boom over it, I got forward and watched the occurrence, which was repeated several times. I thought the chances were about ten to one against dropping to the wharf. If I missed the wharf I should be in a pickle and well salted, with a slim chance of finding a place to land; while if picked up I would be put on board again, to be constantly watched, which would lessen any future chance that might occur, so finally let that idea pass out of my mind. We were soon headed for Norfolk. On the way, the smallpox broke out on board. Quite a number were taken with it, so that when we arrived at Norfolk, instead of putting us on the receiving ship " Pennsylvania," where there were one thousand men, they put us into an old hulk under quarantine, not far from the hospital on shore. Every day one or more would be taken down with the disease and would be carried ashore to the hospital. Having learned by that time all of the first symptoms of the disease, I thought that by feigning sickness I could get ashore and might get away. One morning I did not turn out of my hammock with the rest. Presently the lieutenant in charge came along and said, " What is the matter with you ? "

I told him that I had pain in my head and back.

" Man the boat at once," said he, " and take this man to the hospital."

He told me to get up and get into the boat. It is needless to say that he did not have to repeat that order. I was only too ready to get out of that old hulk. After I arose my hammock was taken down and my effects lashed up in it, and that soon followed me into the boat. I was landed about two hundred yards from the hospital. While going up the gravel walk which led from the landing, one of the men wanted to know how I felt. I replied that I felt badly ; at the same time I could hardly keep from indulging in a good hearty laugh.

I was marched into the front door, and had hardly got inside when along came one of the doctors. He took my nose with one hand and chin with the other, and opened my mouth as a jockey would a horse's mouth to see how old he was. He looked into my mouth, then said, " I don't see anything the matter with you."

I thought to myself, you have guessed right the first time, doctor.

" Take him up to the upper hall," said he ; and I was marched up three long flights of stairs into a large hall.

My hammock was put into a room at the end of the hall, and the door was locked.

It will be necessary, to be understood, to give a diagram of this upper hall, since it was to be my prison for a brief time, and also of the room from which I was to make my escape to liberty again.

On arriving at the room I was shown an iron cot, and was told to occupy it. I soon got into my humble couch, and was very sick, apparently. My nurse offered to bring me some broth, and wanted to know if I thought I could eat anything. Prepared for that, I told him that I cared for nothing but to be let alone. He left me and went below, not long after returning with a bowl of nice broth, which he set on the stand, telling me that if I felt like eating to do so when I desired. He said he would be up again at twelve, and retired at once.

After his footsteps had died away in the distance, I raised my head from under the coverlet and took in the situation. Before me was the steaming bowl of broth, looking very tempting, but I dare not so much as taste of it, lest the nurse notice it and report to the doctors. It was my desire to remain pretty sick for a few days, and when I did get well, to get out into the fresh air very speedily, without help from the doctors or nurses. The hall was about fifty feet long and twenty-five or thirty wide, with a number of iron cot bedsteads on each side, with windows some ten feet apart on each side. The building was in the neighborhood of seventy feet long and thirty feet wide. The upper floor was partitioned off twenty feet from each end, with a passageway from the large hall running down to each end of the building. The part at the end of the hall, thus partitioned off, was divided again into four small rooms, two on each side of the narrow passageway, and had doors leading into them from it. There was one window in each room.

The other end of the building was similarly arranged, and were called "dead rooms," where patients who had died were laid out for burial. My hammock was put into one of those little rooms and locked up.

Apparently I was pretty sick the first day, when any one was near. I learned that if the patients on my floor were not very sick, the doctors only came at nine in the morning and at nine at night. I sipped a little of my broth for supper and stirred about a little, that the doctor might think I had suffered a slight pain at least, otherwise he might think me resting too quietly for a sick man. He came at nine and asked a few questions, and of course I was feeling badly. I found he did not order any medicines, for which I felt very grateful.

After he left me I dropped asleep and dreamt of the exploits of Jack Shepard, whose daring escape from New York was related to me while in London. I kept my couch the next morning until after nine, after which I arose and began investigations. The hall contained two other victims, by their appearance about as sick as myself. I went to a window and found the upper part was sashes with glass, while the lower part was little panel doors. Each quarter panel swung into the hall, and when shut could not be opened from the outside, as there was neither thumb-catch nor knob. A piazza ran the length of the building, and there were two piazzas below, and the floor of the lower one was about twelve feet from the ground. The courtyard enclosed about one quarter of an acre of land. The wall around it was fully twelve feet high. It ran under the end of the piazza and against the building, then commenced at the other corner and went on around. In this court were some tents which were used for crazy folks. I took particular notice of a fig-tree that stood near the wall on the opposite side of the court. I measured it carefully with my eye and believed that one could climb the tree, and its limbs would support him until he got high enough to reach the top of the wall. After this I retired to my couch to think over matters at my leisure. I concluded to eat a little that day, thinking I would need strength to help me over the wall. I had played the sick man so fine that I began to think perhaps I was sick, and did not know it. At all events, I did not wish to starve amid plenty.

After dinner I again began investigations. I found it would be necessary to have a line of some kind, and my hammock lashing would be just the thing, could I get it. With that, the way was clear. How was I to get it? It was locked in one of the little rooms.

It is said that where there is a will there is a way, and it was evident I did not lack the will. Out on the piazza I crept along until opposite the window of the room containing my luggage. I could plainly see my hammock with others, but the doors in the window had no thumb-latch. I returned to the door out of which I came on to the piazza and looked the matter over. I found that they were only about one inch thick, and the latch that held them together was one of the old-fashioned kind without the thumb-piece through the door. I took my pocket knife, measured down from the bottom of the glass to the bottom of the latch, and then went around and along to the little room and measured the outside from the glass down the required distance, ran my knife through and used my knife handle for a thumb-piece. I raised the latch and walked in without being challenged. I found my hammock, stripped off its lashing, taking what things were needed, rolled it up, and threw a bundle over it to cover my tracks, should any one enter the room before my departure. I returned to the piazza, closed the door behind me and reached my cot undiscovered. I stowed my hammock lashing and extra suit along with myself under the coverlet in less time than it takes to record it.

When the nurse came again I was so far convalescent I could sit up a little. He thought I was getting along nicely and would soon be out. I thought there was likely to be more truth than poetry in his remarks.

There was an invalid who had a cot not far from me with whom I became acquainted during my *rational* spells. I found that he also wished to get away. When I found he was on the same sick list as myself and afflicted with the same malady, my heart went out to him. I told him I had a plan about completed whereby we could get outside of the high wall, if he wanted to make the venture. He said he would be willing to face anything or any danger to get away, and I unfolded my plans and he readily joined me. I told him how to get his things out of the little room, and that I was going to start that night. He went after his clothing, and I kept pretty well under my blankets, while he was picking the lock of the little room. If he was caught in the act and I was found lounging about, I might be taken as an accomplice, yet I would help him as far as possible without endangering my own chances of escape. He got what he wanted without trouble and stowed them under his quilts. We arranged that we would go to bed that night and keep pretty quiet until the doctor had been around at nine, and then, after all was quiet, we would steal out. All he had to do was to follow me, and I would lead him outside of the wall. Once outside, he must depend on his own resources. My course would depend on circumstances, for I had explored no farther than the outside of the court.

The night came and our regular broth with it. I left nothing on the plate, but ate heartily and cleared the plate for the first time during my illness. I was soon after in bed clad in two pairs of pants, three shirts, and two pairs of socks. I did not intend to go to sleep; but I did, however, and when I awoke it was three o'clock in the morning. When the doctor came and found me sleeping so quietly, he thought he would not disturb my slumbers. I jumped up at once and went to my friend's cot and shook him a little and told him that it was three o'clock. He turned over to whisper that some one had just gone through the hall, and we would be detected. I said no more, but went to my bed, took my hammock lashing and shoes, went out to the corner of the piazza, climbed over, and slid to the next below, then down the next post, and so to the last floor, where I tied my little rope to the post, stepped over and lowered myself down to the yard. I some expected the crazy fellows who were camping in those tents would make a racket, but they did not; they were asleep. I went straight to the tree. In the gloom of the night I mounted the frail limbs until I could reach the top of the wall, then pulled myself up, swinging first my legs and then my body over. Suspended at arm's length I let go noiselessly, to pull myself together in a potato patch. I hurried along by the wall and turned the corner. A few rods farther took me to the beach. I sat down, put on my shoes, and found myself none the worse for my venture. Had any one given me a thousand dollars, I would have not felt better pleased than I did while sitting on that sandy beach. The cool morning breeze across the water seemed to be burdened with freedom; but alas! I am ashamed to acknowledge that there was no patriotism in me that morning, and yet I sat nearly under the folds of that emblem of liberty and freedom, the star spangled banner. I was patriotic enough, but that flag had held me in durance for the last two months, so near my

friends and home and yet so far, and I could not have
the privilege of going home for one short week. If my
adventures had been in the sixties instead of the forties,
my real patriotism would have prompted me to fight
until all the rebel rams that sailed were sunk or driven
from the seas. I consoled myself with the knowledge
that the country was at peace and resting on its laurels,
having just finished taming down Mexico. I had a desire myself about that time to be at peace with all mankind, and only wanted to be let alone.

I do not speak of these little episodes of running
away from ships because I feel proud of such exploits,
since I confess I feel heartily ashamed to relate them :
but I started to give a correct and truthful account of
my experience during those seven years of my absence
from home, and my narrative would be incomplete without them.

From the start I was beguiled and stuffed with stories
of big fortunes that seldom come to a foremast hand,
with only a chance of getting one dollar out of one
hundred and sixty, and one whale out of fifty seen, or
chased, and a big bill for outfit awaiting to be paid at
home along with a sailor's board. When I realized all
these things I thought it more than human flesh could
bear. But all the ships, barks, and schooners I had
left were deserted with the sole idea of getting a step
toward home.

Although some of the steps might seem rather wild
and far from the mark, while others overreached it, I
found it necessary to keep stepping, until finally, after
leaving the antipodes, it took me just fifteen months to
get home. I do not approve of sailors running away if
they are treated as they should be, but if badly treated
do not blame them. It was my good fortune to get into
good ships with good officers on board ; and as I was

always ready and willing to do my duty, had no trouble, and never left a vessel on account of any dislike of ship, officers, or crew.

As I sat on the sand beach I saw the gray dawn in the east, which reminded me that I had no time to spend in reveries. I started up the beach; not far away I came to a small creek that ran landward into the marsh. I followed it to come to a footbridge, which I passed over and passed on up the beach. I soon came to another creek, over which was another footbridge like the first, only much longer; it was about two hundred yards across. Crossing this I came to the little town of Portsmouth, it then being broad daylight. A large flock of geese sat on the bank, and it is needless for me to say what they did. It was a cackling goose that saved Rome once on a time. Disturbed so suddenly while taking their early nap, they all together set up a great ado at once. There was danger of their arousing the town. I hurried past my tormentors, to find myself on the main street.

About half-way through the town an old colored man came into the middle of the street. I spoke to him gruffly to disarm him of suspicion, if he had any. A transport lay a little way out in the harbor opposite the town, lately arrived from Mexico, where I supposed she was used during the Mexican War. I could see the tops of the vessel's masts.

I asked the darky if there had been a boat on shore that morning. I told him I belonged to that vessel, and came ashore the night before on "liberty."

"No, massa," said he, "no boat come ashore this morning yet."

"Well," said I, " I want to get aboard at once."

I pushed on through the town. The street ended at a little jetty, where the passengers landed from a small ferryboat which plied between Norfolk and Portsmouth. She ran from one side to the other about every ten minutes from daylight until late at night. I had taken note of all that might be for or against me in my future movements while on the old hulk. As I neared the jetty I saw the boat about half-way over, and approaching. I hurried along, knowing it would stop but a minute or two before leaving for the other side.

As I came near the water, some three or four rods from the street at my right, I saw a beef cart loaded with beef; while on the water there loomed up before me, hardly a quarter of a mile from the shore, one of the largest ships Uncle Sam had built at that time, the "Pennsylvania," used at that time as a receiving ship, upon which I would have been put had I remained in the hospital a week or so longer. The boat was alongside and the sailors were getting into her. They were coming after the ship's daily supply of meat. I hurried along to the jetty as the ferryboat ran up against it. She had but one wagon on board, which drove off at once, and I passed on board at the same time. The boat pushed off, rapidly leaving the wharf, and I felt wonderfully relieved.

There was but one more guard to pass between myself and liberty, that liberty and freedom that I had so longed for. One can better imagine my feelings at that time than I can describe them. My heart was filled with joy, and hopes long deferred were now to be realized, as I felt that the outer picket would be easily passed. The only trouble I now feared was that some of the officers or men from the receiving ship might be ashore at Norfolk; and if I should happen to encounter them, in man-o'-warsman's clothing, I doubted my ability to make them believe what I might tell them. I was much gratified that no one awaited me. Not far from where I landed a steamboat lay alongside a wharf. I boarded her at once. I met the mate on deck, and I inquired if that boat was going to Richmond.

He said she was.

I then told him that I wanted to go to Richmond, but had no money, but I would do any kind of work on board to pay for my passage.

He said that he could not make any bargain of that sort, but I might wait until the captain came down.

I thanked him, and told him that I would do so.

While waiting, I observed the engineer at his engine getting up steam. I had a chat with him about getting to Richmond, and mentioned having spoken to the mate for a chance to work my passage, and that he had referred me to the captain. I never cast so much as a glance in the direction of the receiving ship. If danger lurked in that direction I did not want to see it, for fear I might be tempted to jump on to the dock and use my legs. I was aware to do so would attract attention, which I did not care to do.

Finally the captain came aboard, and walking boldly up to him, I said, "Captain, I understand that this boat is going to Richmond."

"Yes," said he, "she is. Do you want a passage?"

"Yes, Captain, I do, but have got no money to pay for a passage. I am willing to work my passage, if you will take me along."

He looked me over a little to remark, "We do not make a practice of doing business that way."

"No, Captain," said I, "I did not suppose that you did; but I am very anxious to go to Richmond, and thought perhaps you might make an exception in my case, as I am a seafaring man."

"I don't know about that," said he. He turned and went into his cabin.

I could see a twinkle in his eye as he so abruptly left me. I concluded my clothing had betrayed me, and that he was possibly afraid that if I was found on his boat with his consent, he would be held liable for aiding me to escape from the service.

I had determined to be a passenger on that boat, with or without the captain's consent; and it made but little difference whether deck or cabin passage. It would have taken more than the captain's eloquence or moral suasion to deter me. I went along to the engineer.

He wanted to know what the captain had said. I told him.

"Well," said he, "you go into that coal bin below and shovel coal up toward the furnace; I guess it will be all right."

Down I went, like McGinty, and was right glad to get below decks out of sight, stripped off my jacket and went at that coal pile like an old miner.

I was not particular about the quantity of dust I got on my hands or face; the more the better; if any one came along and was inquisitive enough to look down the hatch, he would think me one of the black coal heavers or firemen.

I had been at work about half an hour when the engine began to work. By the motion of the boat I knew we were leaving the wharf. A few minutes later it stopped. I knew by the stamping on deck that she had run over to Portsmouth to take on passengers. I kept up a tremendous racket in the coal bin. The boat started again and moved down the river. I kept at work about twenty minutes longer, when, thinking by the appearance of things, that she was not going to land again, I went on deck and looked toward the shore. About a quarter of a mile off was the hospital that I had so recently left; in fact, we were right opposite it, and around the place not a soul was stirring.

Musing to myself, I thought the early bird had got ahead of them that time, and it was evident enough had caught his liberty. I was beyond the lines of the enemy, and took no further pains to conceal myself, but walked boldly about the deck.

About nine o'clock the colored steward came around, ringing a bell and shouting at the same time for all the passengers to come aft to the captain's office and settle their bills. I watched each man as he went to the office, which was on deck, and finally saw the last man depart; then thinking it my turn, marched boldly aft to the office and presented myself. The captain looked up with a half-smile on his face, and I looked as pleasant as possible under the strained condition of things.

" Ah, you are here, are you ? "

" Yes, Captain, I am here and await your orders."

" Well, you have no money; I don't suppose that I can get any. Go forward and do what you can to help work the boat up to Richmond."

Thanking him, I obeyed and went forward.

All I did was to occasionally shift a box of chains to one side of the boat or the other in order to trim her when she turned the bend of the river, — a condition of things at that time entirely satisfactory. I was fast leaving my late friends behind.

All the passengers went into the dining-saloon at noon. The engineer, before going into his mess-room, said he would see that I had some dinner.

The passengers had returned to the deck, when the mate came to me and said, " Come, go down into the saloon and get some dinner."

I thanked him and went below with the dignity of a commodore and the gravity of a clergyman. I found a long table, with all the delicacies of the Southern market. Seeing so much food left after the passengers had dined,

I thought perhaps they had anticipated my advent among them and had made ample provision for a hungry uninvited guest. The waiters received me with much attention; they were all politeness, and appeared to be trying each to outdo the other. When I got through my dinner I left the cabin. On deck again, I went forward, and soon after up came the engineer with a plate heaped with beef, bread, and many different kinds of vegetables; indeed he brought more food for my dinner than I had seen during the entire week at my late boarding-house at Portsmouth.

"Why," said I, "who is all that food for?"

"For you," said he; "sit down now and pitch right in. Don't be bashful, if you do you will get left."

I thought to myself that it would be a cold day when I got left.

"Well, man," said I, "I have dined in the saloon with the captain."

"Is that so?"

"Yes, I have just returned from there."

"Well, if you want more, here it is in plenty."

"Yes, I see; but I thank you, I have had a plenty for one meal."

He took the food down-stairs with a disappointed look on his face.

I found the people in the South and Southern people generally very liberal and courteous in the manner in which they entertain their friends or guests, and it is all done in a very modest and unassuming manner, which affords much freedom and confidence of action. Under such conditions, strangers meeting for the first time soon become fast friends.

We went up the river and arrived in due time at our journey's end, and hauled in alongside of the wharf. I have forgotten the name of the place, at that time, 1848, a very small hamlet, located about three miles below Richmond. That place was as near as vessels could get to the city. All freight from Richmond down the river James was taken there in barges and then shipped on seagoing craft. Getting ashore very soon after the steamer was made fast, I noticed a schooner not far from where we landed, taking in flour and tobacco from a barge alongside. On her stern was her name, "The Rainbow," of Boston. She was just the boat I was looking for, and my arrival was most opportune. I went on board of her at once, and met the captain on deck. Without hesitating a moment or betraying any sign of weakness, knowing I was a long way from Norfolk and the old hulk, I addressed him, saying, "This is the captain, I believe."

"Yes."

"I see by the name of this craft that she belongs in Boston."

"Yes, she does."

I informed him that I belonged in Boston and had been absent a number of years, and wanted to get back home again, but having no money would like to work my passage. I would help load and unload, also to work the vessel during the trip.

"Well, all right, I will take you along."

Accordingly I went to work, and we finished loading the next day, and were soon towed down and out of the river. It was, however, nearly two weeks before we got out to sea on account of head winds, but we finally got out and were two weeks more getting to Boston.

On the way, I told the mate the story of my leaving the navy, believing as a brother sailor he would not expose me. We hauled in alongside of Long Wharf, Boston, about four in the afternoon. I was ashore again in Boston, and on the same wharf I had left seven years before nearly to a day, but without that three or four hundred dollars that Mr. Drake said I would bring home with me. I found myself in the same condition financially as when I had left Boston.

After a tramp of seven years, searching for a fortune which had not materialized, I recalled a remark I heard a Chinaman make, in Australia, who had lost his last shilling at fan-tan, " Gone, just like woodbine climbs."

I was in Boston again, which was some consolation. I looked around somewhat, thinking I might recognize some of my old creditors in the crowd that gathered around, but I failed to notice any faces I had seen before. It was too late in the day to take out any of the cargo, so I told the captain that I would return in the morning, and started out to find my uncle, and succeeded without much difficulty. The locality outwardly had not changed during my absence, neither had it faded from my memory.

I found my uncle's home with the name on the door, and rang the bell. He came to the door, but did not recognize me until I made myself known to him.

I was soon in the midst of his family, for he had married after I left the country, and had a lively young family growing up around him. I remained that night, and the next morning went with my uncle to see one of by brothers, a teamster, who kept a stand for his teams not far from the house.

After a few minutes with him, I went to the wharf to help unload, as agreed. All that day I worked hard, and at night my brother came down and took me on his team home with him to Charlestown. The next morning I went again to the wharf to work discharging the schooner. About four in the afternoon the cargo was out of the hold, but two or three boxes of tobacco, when along came a load of freight to be taken in. The captain stopped hoisting out tobacco, and began to get ready to take in the load of freight. Believing I had fulfilled my agreement, I stopped work and went on to the dock.

"Where are you going?" said the captain.

"I am going home," I replied.

"You come back here and help me take this freight in."

"No, I did not agree to help load here. I will help you take the tobacco out, but nothing further."

"I shall not do that until that freight is taken in."

"Well," said I, "if that is the case, you can go straight to h—l," and started up the wharf.

He sang out as I was leaving, "You runaway from a man-o'-war, I will have you arrested; I can get ten dollars for the job."

I was very soon out of sight of him and his schooner, nor did I ever see or hear of him after. The mate had told him my story. He was one of the kind of men who was not contented with all I had to give, but wanted a little more. It is that class of captains that make sailors run away. They get all the work out of the men they can, then abuse them because they cannot get more. Generally, when sailors find out these kind-hearted fellows, they keep clear of them unless they are compelled to ship. In the navy every man knows what he has to do; it is true, however, that there is a deal to do to keep the ship clean and in good condition, but there are plenty to do it, which makes it easy work when compared to the duties of sailors on merchantmen, where there are barely men enough to handle the large ships.

Into the "service" is where I would advise all young men to go who desire to go to sea. There one is sure to get his pay, with plenty of good food and good treatment. I have seen salts who had grown gray on the sea who had got to believe they owned the ship they

were in, and would cling to their berths until the third
and fourth call before they would turn out. I have no
sympathy for such, always considering that when sailors
ship and go to sea every man on board is part and parcel
of that ship, as much so as the masts, spars, ropes, etc.,
and the success of the voyage and the safety of the ship
and crew are dependent on each one. All hands are frequently called when the ship may be in danger, and perhaps the man who never hurried to get on deck until
after a number of calls might have been the one, had he
been more lively, who would have saved the ship or some
of her spars. Knowing the dangers of the sea, I was
always at my post when duty called. How little sailors
realize when they go out to sea in a ship that they take
their lives into their own hands, and that the welfare of
all hands and the life of the ship are in their keeping! It
has been said that a sailor's life is a dog's life. I deny
the assertion, for I have spent some of the happiest days
of my life while in mid-ocean with the seas rolling mountains high in all directions, and again when the heavens
were overcast with murky clouds from whose blackness
shot forth a thousand thunderbolts at one discharge.
At such times the vessel would be illuminated as with a
torch at the top of every spar and mast, seemingly to
add a last touch to this terrible yet sublime scene.
While the ocean would seem to battle with heaven's
artillery, amid the confusion and war of the elements I
was happy and contented. Nevertheless, a sailor's life is
not all a dream of paradise, having walks strewn with
roses. The sailor is sorely tried when on the coast in
winter, while in a rigorous climate there is less danger
and less work in mid-ocean than near land.

As I have found it on the sea, a sailor is like a rat
in a trap, while the officers are standing outside with a
red-hot poker in each hand. If the rat behaves himself

and don't squeal, he is unmolested ; if he squeals, he is all wrong, and will soon find himself very much tangled up with a rope's end. Thus it will be seen that there are thorns as well as roses in the path of the sailor ; if it were not so, the voyage would be too monotonous for human beings to endure.

Home again, safe and sound, without money, but in good health, and knowing more than when leaving. With no small opinion of myself, my head would, I think, fill the plug hat that I wore when starting out. I have seen many foreign lands, and also many big fishes in the ocean, and a few little sharks of the deep, but my experience with men leads me to believe the man who wrote that a whale swallowed Jonah made a mistake, and it should have said that Jonah swallowed the whale ; for I have seen some men whom I think could not only swallow a whale, but a good portion of the ocean thereafter to wash his whaleship down.

CHAPTER VI.

STARTS FROM BOSTON FOR THE GOLD FIELDS OF CALIFORNIA —
ONE DOLLAR A MONTH AND FOUND — SAVES THE SHIP
FROM THE BREAKERS — FRISCO IN THE EARLY DAYS OF
'49 — BECOMES A GOLD HUNTER — ILL LUCK IN FRE-
QUENTLY JUST MISSING GREAT FINDS — QUESTIONABLE
METHODS OF PROFIT MAKING BY EARLY TRADERS — MEET-
ING WITH OLD ACQUAINTANCES IN THE GOLD FIELDS —
LARGE TREES — STRIKING IT RICH — DEALING OUT CARDS
FOR OWNERSHIP OF A MINE.

ON the twelfth day of January, 1849, I went aboard
the old brig " Atilla," of Boston, which lay alongside
Long Wharf. She had been bought by a party of men
who wanted to go to California at the time the excitement raged in Boston, to go to the wonderful gold fields
of that far-off western country.

So many wanted to ship as sailors to go to California,
in order to get there without paying the large sum
charged for passage around Cape Horn or across the
isthmus, that we had to work for nothing, so to speak.
We were paid one dollar a month. The sailors had to
be paid something in order to evade the law, and I was
booked for a voyage of six months.

We soon pulled out into the srream. When the last
boat pushed alongside, who should appear in it but my
old friend and shipmate, Rufus Holmes, from Duxbury,
the mate of the whaleship I first went to sea in! I had
not seen him since running away from that bark at
Geograph Bay in Australia. He was one of the owners
of the " Atilla," and was going to California. There
were over a hundred souls on board. We soon weighed

anchor and pushed out to sea. We had bad weather until we got off the coast and into a warmer climate. The brig was commanded by a man named Baker, who had been running on some of the packets across the Atlantic. It was said he had killed two or three men before taking command of this brig. We soon crossed the line and were in a cooler climate again. We thought some of going through the Straits of Magellan, but the night before we reached the straits the captain said he dreamed a dream which caused him to change his mind. We could see the land, but after that dream, the captain bore off and ran for the Cape. We soon rounded a bluff that makes out from the Cape, and before we had got fairly around, a head wind struck us and we were driven off our course to the south full sixty degrees. After some two or three weeks, we got around the Cape. We had bad weather until we got into thirty or forty degrees south latitude, where we had some pretty good and some very warm weather, especially as we neared the line

It is strange but true, however, that it is several degrees warmer at from six to eight degrees from the line than it is on the line, or equator. We found the temperature on the line to be one hundred degrees, while ten degrees north it registered one hundred and ten degrees.

We stopped a few hours at the Galapagos Islands, which are located on and near the equator, and caught many good fish near the islands. We killed several sea lions on land. To see those animals on shore from the ships, they looked like tall nude savages or black men, climbing up from the water over the rough broken shore. In travelling they appear to raise their fore parts so that they will stand some five or six feet high, standing on their hinder parts and their flippers, then sway sideways, and at the same time throw forward one flipper, and then sway the other way and put the other flipper forward. They make a very canny appearance when travelling, while they get over the ground quite rapidly

The Galapagos Islands were the first land sighted after leaving Cape Horn. We got on as fast as the wind would permit. As we neared the coast of California it became very foggy ; the captain had not been able to get the sun, therefore did not know how near the coast he was. One afternoon about four o'clock, when all hands except the man at the wheel were below to get supper, having finished my supper a little ahead of the others I went on deck, and went forward and looked over ahead of the vessel and over the water. I saw long streams of kelp ; I knew at the first glance that it was a kind of kelp that grew from the bottom to the surface and trails many yards along on the water with the tides and currents. Farther ahead, not more than two or three hundred yards, the breakers were rolling up, scattering the white foam in all directions. I ran aft to the companionway which led to the cabin and sang out, " Breakers ahead ! "

All hands were on deck in a trice, and also many of the passengers.

The captain sang out to the man at the wheel, " Hard up ! hard up ! " and " Wear ship ! "

To " wear ship," as it is called, is to put the wheel up toward the side of the ship the wind comes from. The ship will pay off, while the yards are pulled in, so that the sails are kept full of wind until the vessel gets around to the other tack.

The captain thought to get her around far enough so that he could sail back on the track he had come over. We got around and started on the back track. We had

IN THE BREAKERS OFF THE COAST OF CALIFORNIA.

just started back, when the fog lifted, and hardly one hundred yards' away was a rock elevated above the water, and quite as large as a good-sized house.

We had to pull as close to the wind as possible to clear the rocks ahead. We had just cleared them, hidden by the fog, on our way in. Behind us was a bluff of land reaching high up and almost hanging over us, while between us and the land, not half a mile off, was a mass of breakers and foaming waters. Had the alarm been delayed a moment, we would have been inevitably wrecked. It was on the 6th of July, 1848, that I saved a ship in the fog on the coast of New York, and this was the 6th of July, 1849, that I saved the brig and all on board.

The captain, after looking over his charts, found that we were opposite Monterey, about forty miles below San Francisco. We ran along under easy sail that night, and the next day ran into the harbor, and anchored in front of the canvas town of San Francisco.

We made the trip in six months, less six days. The " Edward Everett " sailed from Lewis Wharf the 13th of January, 1849, and she dropped her anchor alongside us, one half hour later, on the 6th of July, 1849. The harbor was filled with vessels at that early date of the discovery of gold. Each was black with men ; they would all cheer when a new arrival passed in and dropped anchor. I soon got ashore. Mexican gold and silver appeared to be scattered everywhere awaiting to be picked up by any one who might happen to come along. Mexicans, with blankets spread out on the street or anywhere, had piles of gold and silver stacked high, while they, half naked, were sitting beside their coin with a pack of monte cards in their hands, making overtures for bets as people passed along.

Farther up among the tents, through the open end of

the large tents, a large space inside was filled with a
mixed lot of humanity, as thick as they could stand. In
the centre of this crowd was a table, made by driving
into the ground four short posts with rough boards nailed
on the top. Over that was thrown a blanket or cloth of
some kind. A man sat on each side, and between, on the
table, would be piled thousands of dollars in gold and
silver ; also many buckskin bags of different sizes and
shapes filled with gold dust. The favorite game played
at that time was a Mexican game called " monte."

The regular monte cards are marked differently from
the English ones. They throw out all spot cards over
the seven spot, thus the pack will contain only forty
instead of fifty-two. They shuffle the cards, then some
one cuts them, the dealer drawing two cards from the
bottom and laying them on the table some two feet apart,
one at his right and the other at his left, and calls for
bets on those two cards, — that one particular card of
those will appear first when the cards are turned face up
and drawn slowly off. When the bet is made, he pulls
out two more cards and places them right and left about
twelve inches from the others, to wait until some one
has bet on those cards. He turns up the cards and
begins to draw. Of course the card that comes first
which is like those laid out wins. That card is covered
over by some card that may have been drawn, or another
one is drawn from the deck ; the bets are made again.
Sometimes a card will lay on the table through the deal
without winning, since every card placed against it would
come first. It is a very fascinating game, and one by
which a fortune can be won or lost. It was common for
big gamblers to put down at one time as high as ten,
twenty, and sometimes fifty and one hundred thousand
dollars, which will be won or lost on the turn of the
cards. If the winning card happens to be the first card

in sight when the pack is turned up, whoever has the bet on that card is only paid one half unless he cuts the cards, when he gets paid in full.

There was but one framed house when I arrived in Frisco. That was called the Parker House. I believe this Parker was the same man who run the Boston Parker House at one time. I saw a pile of gold dust on the counter of its bar that would fill a half-bushel measure. Men, as they landed on the beach, just from the mines, carried bags of gold dust so heavy that two had to carry it on a pole between them. It was said that the Parker House was let for twenty-five thousand dollars a month, and that small tents were let for five thousand a month. Board was twenty-four dollars a week, and wages for any kind of a mechanic were twenty-five dollars a day. A man might board himself easily for three or four dollars a week. There was plenty to eat, but the cost was in preparing it. Anything in the shape of a man could get three hundred dollars a month and found. Every one appeared to be rich and happy, and did not appear to care what their fortune might be to-morrow.

A captain, whose crew had left him for the mines, came ashore one day for some one to go on board and cook for him. He saw a colored man who appeared to be loafing. The captain approached him and said, " My man, I want a cook to go aboard of that ship,"— pointing to the ship, — " and cook for me. I will be the only one beside yourself to cook for, so you see the work will not be much, and I will give you three hundred dollars a month."

The old darky looked at the captain with a broad grin on his face, " Why, Captain, if you will come ashore and cook for me, I will give you three hundred dollars a month."

Just so independent was everybody. Another case

was of an officer who had come ashore. He wanted a man near where he landed to carry his trunk to a tent not more than five or six rods. He offered the man an ounce of gold if he would carry the trunk.

The man said to the officer, "I will give you an ounce if you will shoulder your own trunk and carry it where you want it."

The officer picked up the trunk and was paid the ounce for it.

There was a man-o'-war laying in the harbor at that time. I think it was the "Ohio." I have forgotten the commodore who, it was said, used the government money that was on board to buy gold dust at eight dollars an ounce and ran down to some Mexican port and sold it for sixteen dollars an ounce. In that way he made a fortune speculating with Uncle Sam's money.

I have no doubt but it was true, as large amounts of gold were sold at that time for eight dollars an ounce, when its true value was from sixteen to eighteen dollars an ounce. At the same time when it was said the commodore was speculating with the ship's money, two sailors were rowing a middy ashore one night. They found everybody was getting rich, while they, the poor sailors, were not allowed ashore for fear they would run away. The paltry pay they were getting, probably not over twelve dollars a month, looked small indeed compared with what was being paid in other vessels sailing out of port, which was three hundred dollars a month. On their way ashore they threw the middy overboard and tried to escape, but were recaptured and hung at the yard-arm like dogs.

It was said that the site of the city of San Francisco could have been bought the year before gold was discovered for a bottle of rum. Commodore Stockton, as he was called, got hold of about all the land in that locality.   He also got control of a large tract of land where Stockton now stands.   Many others got control of large tracts of land, — land that is now worth many thousands of dollars.

John C. Fremont came pretty near getting a large lot of land in the mineral district, it was said, by shifting his boundaries.   I think the rumor was true, as I have seen the man who shifted the stakes in Mariposa County.

Many a California millionnaire got his start in that way. I know of many who were but miners when they began, who were not satisfied with their share in the claim, but got a large part of their partners' share.   When in a rich claim, they would tell their partners to go to camp and cook dinner, and they would remain and clear away the dirt so that they would have a good chance to take out a lot of gold in the afternoon.   Just as soon as the partner was out of sight, the fellow left behind would rob the claim of all of the rich spots that he could find.   Many a poor honest fellow has been robbed in that way by unprincipled scoundrels, who only needed the bristles to make them into hogs.

About all the sailing craft that came to San Francisco at that time were owned by those who came there in them.   The craft were sold for what they would bring, which was not much.   The " Edward Everett," which cost forty thousand dollars in Boston, was sold to the captain for thirteen thousand.   The old brig I went out in cost five thousand dollars, and sold for five hundred.   These two were fair samples of the sales.   It cost about thirty dollars to get to Stockton or Sacramento, so our captain and the owners found it cheaper to pay a pilot five hundred dollars to take the brig to Stockton. In this manner we got to Stockton for five hundred dollars, when to have paid on any other conveyance it would have cost two thousand dollars.   The brig was then sold at Stockton for five hundred dollars. At that place I was paid off with six dollars, but I did not mind that, as I was within seventy miles of El Dorado, and the balance of the way could be walked in a very short time. At Stockton there was one log-cabin and about a dozen tents. The day after my arrival I started with two ship-mates for the mines, going by the way of McKnight's Ferry on the Stanislaus River.

After two days' hard travelling over the hot sand with but little water, hardly enough for one swallow, we reached the river, I being about as near choked as I ever was. I quickly made for the water, laid myself down and quenched my thirst. We camped at the river that night. Lieut. U. S. Grant was stationed in that locality at that time, where it was said that he had a squaw for cook, which was much cheaper than paying three hundred dollars to men cooks as at Frisco.

The next morning we pushed on to soon reach what was called "Wood's Diggings." The day after we arrived I got an old pan and pick. I did not have money enough to buy anything decent in the shape of tools, and a good new pick was worth ten dollars; a crowbar three feet long sold for ten dollars; while a tin pan in which to wash out the dirt, which was about the same as an old-fashioned country milk pan, sold for twelve dollars.

It will be seen that after travelling seventy miles on my six dollars, there was not much left to pay for tools. I began picking around and found a little gold, but not much, being a novice at the business, and after working a day or two began to get discouraged. A man who knew something about mining came along and told me I was throwing all the gold away. He picked up a clod of clay and broke it apart. Sure enough there was the gold sticking in the clay which I had thrown away. I worked at that place about a week and made perhaps ten dollars.

Hearing that on the Mokalunme River, which was some twenty miles north, miners were making two and three hundred dollars a day, I started for that place and in two days arrived there. What I had heard was true, men were making all the way from one to five hundred dollars a day, but all of the good claims were taken up. However, I picked around until I got enough to get me an outfit of tools. One day I went on to a bar where I thought no one else had any stakes and took out one pan of dirt. While washing it out a man came along and after he saw what I had got, said that he and others claimed the bar, so was obliged to leave. I have my doubts whether he did or did not claim the bar until after he saw in my pan nearly twenty dollars of nice river gold about the size of wheat kernels, but I left at once.

The next day a man came in with a pack train of goods which he dumped down in a pile. He wanted me to build a rough shed over them. I consented to do it for sixty-four dollars, and he ordered me to go ahead. Hunting up a Scotch boy I knew, we built it in half a day. It was little else than a sunshade.

I went down the river one day about a mile, to a place where the banks were so steep and ragged one could not get farther down the stream without going around some distance. I found a long, narrow place in the river, and the banks were quite rich. To run a shovel into the water and dig up a shovelful of sand, then run the shovel through the water, the water would wash back the sand and leave a yellow rim of gold around the entire width of the shovel. At that particular point there was no chance to turn the river, so could only content myself with the knowledge that it was there and in plenty, and that was all the good it did me.

A stony gulch emptied into the river at that place, the bed of which was a ledge. A rod or two back a tree had

blown down and completely filled the gulch with brush.
No one thought it worth while to try to get through the
brush, as it appeared that there was no dirt in the gulch
to hold gold, if any had ever been there ; but I found by
getting down on my hands and knees I could crawl
under the limbs. By that means I soon got above the
tree. I found a little dirt in the crevices in the bed of
the gulch, and dug out about two quarts and went up
the gulch about a rod to a little spring of water and
washed out my dirt, finding about seven dollars in gold.
I picked up a little nugget by the spring, yet, strange as
it may seem, I did not sink a hole in the gulch. I went
back to the little camp and showed the gold that I had
washed out, and told the boys where it was from.

I soon left the camp, going up the river, never to go
there again. A year or two after, meeting a man who
was at that little camp when I left, he told me that parties went where I washed out that seven dollars, and that
they found the gulch immensely rich. They found gold
throughout the length of the gulch, which was several
hundred yards long. Had I known enough to have sunk
a hole, I would have struck it, and could have worked
the gulch out, blocking the passage under the old tree-
top, and by that means closed all signs of entrance. I
could have camped there with plenty of water to drink
and with which to pan out gold, come out at night for
food, and returned again under the shadow of darkness.
When thinking of that lost opportunity it fills me with
regret to think how hard I have worked for one dollar a
day in this part of the world, when in that little gulch,
quiet and alone, I could have made from one hundred to
one thousand dollars a day, and not overworked either.
But this was only one of many lost opportunities.

I have often thought the reason why I did not appreciate money when in those rich gold fields was because

of spending so many of my younger days in Australia, where we had no money, and therefore did not wish for it so long as I had enough to pay my bills.

I have seen men making one hundred dollars a day with plenty of provisions in camp, who would live on thin gruel rather than pay for something more substantial.

I met three men on what was called Big Bar on the Mokalunme River. They came out on the "Edward Everett." One was named Sargent; he was one of the Sargents who kept a hotel at the head of Lewis Wharf, and was known as Brad Sargent. One of the others was a negro cook, and the name of the third man I have forfotten. These three washed out eighteen hundred dollars on the banks of the river, which they divided, and then the other two went away and left Sargent.

About that time I concluded to go over to the Stanislaus. Sargent asked that if I found anything that was good to let him know and he would follow. After a week's prospecting, liking the place, I went back to the Mokalunme River. When I got within some two miles of the little camp, I met Sargent. He had bought a jack and was going to leave that part of the country. I continued on into camp and came to Sargent's old brush shanty, and entered to see what he had left behind, and found an empty candle box, as I supposed. When opened I found inside a stocking which was very heavy. Putting my hand inside, I found a yeast-powder box full of fine gold dust such as was to be found on the banks of the river. I knew at once that it was Sargent's share of the eighteen hundred dollars, it being about six hundred dollars' worth, and that he had forgotten it. Putting it back into the stocking and into the box, I went off a few rods to a tent which was used for a little bakery, sat down on a log and waited for Sargent's return. In about ten minutes Sargent came over the hill running like a race horse; going straight to the brush hut, he soon came out and was over the hill and away out of sight, never suspecting I had found his gold before his return.

In a day or two after I went to the Stanislaus River, overtaking on the way a party of five from New York, and bought into their outfit. They had a large tent and a lot of provisions. We camped on a large bar a little below the mouth of a stream called Coyote Creek. One of the party became my partner. Winter was just then setting in. In that part of California they get a good deal of rain in winter,—what we would call a very rainy summer in New England.

One day my partner and I went to a gulch and worked all day with little success. At night I thought we had better cross over into another little gulch that led down to the bar near our tent. When we arrived, we found that it had been worked a little. We started down toward home, and soon came to where the bed rock had been washed bare, with several rough points rising one or two feet above the banks of the gulch. I took my knife and began to pick out the dirt from the crevices, soon picking out a nugget of gold; and keeping on, in about ten minutes, had about one hundred dollars in six pieces of gold. We went home, and did not go back to the place again until quite a time later. We thought then that we had obtained all there was. Winter had set in, which gave the miners plenty of water in all the gulches. We worked around in different places, and made about a hundred dollars apiece a week. There was a ferry about a mile above our camp, run by an Englishman named Bolles. He kept a store also, and had a young native with him that he had taken along from some island that the ship stopped at in which he came from Australia to California.

To turn back a little, three men came into camp who were new arrivals in the country, and perfectly green. They built themselves a brush shanty about half-way between our camp and the ferry, five or six rods from the banks of the river. A few days after we noticed, as we passed, that they had a rocker, such as was used to wash gold at that time, placed near the river, from which they bailed water to wash the dirt from a little pile by the side of them. When any one asked them how their dirt was paying, they would say, "Not very well." Perhaps they would show a dollar or two, and say that that was all they had got out of a small mound of dirt that was by their side. Sometimes some fellow would try a pan of their dirt, in order to be more fully convinced than to take the man's word. He would always get very little gold, perhaps twenty-five cents, which at that time was considered next to nothing. These three men worked in the above manner for three weeks.

I noticed that the little pile of dirt appeared to look about the same every time that I passed it, and yet I thought nothing strange, nor did any of the others. One Sunday the native at the store happened to pass into a thick lot of underbrush, which resembled barberry-bushes, about five or six rods back of these three fellows' brush hut. The boy noticed that the ground was considerably dug up, and a good deal appeared to have been carried away. He began to pick around near the bed rock, which had been stripped bare, and very soon dug out two ounces of handsome coarse river gold. He then ran to the store as fast as his legs would carry him. The story that the fellow told and the gold that he had were convincing to all. The news spread like wildfire. All hands were soon on the run, and there were some very long steps taken to see who would get there first. Unfortunately for me, I was down at my own tent at the time. When I arrived the best claims were staked. At that early day miners were allowed only fifteen feet square for a claim. I finally got hold of ground and stuck down my stakes. Those three men had kept one man at the river washing out dirt that they knew had but very little gold in it. They kept this man working at that worthless stuff as a blind, while the others were concealed in those bushes taking out a fortune, which they succeeded in doing. I went into their brush hut the day after; and they were all making buckskin bags the size of a man's arm and some ten inches long. How many of those bags they made I do not know, but they sold their effects and left the country.

I bought a pair of common cowhide boots of them, and paid ten dollars for them. Boots at that time were worth one hundred dollars, but they only charged me ten. I took them to camp, knowing one of my camp-mates wanted a pair. The storekeeper offered me four ounces of gold for them, which was equal to sixty-four dollars, but I would not let him have them, but sold them to my camp-mate for sixteen dollars, thinking six dollars enough for me to make on them, having only carried them about half a mile. I knew that if my companion had to buy them of the storekeeper, he would have to pay one hundred dollars for them, which he could not afford to do.

A man called at our tent one day who had on a pair of long-legged boots, the heel of one of which was ripped off some four inches. I offered to mend them for him, and he said that if I would he would give me four dollars. Taking the boot I went to work with a common table fork and some twine, and in less than half an hour had the boot mended good as new and received my money.

On the bar where I was camped stood an old log-cabin built by a man named Murphy, who used to trade with the Indians. His stock in trade consisted of blankets and many small trinkets, and some provisions, such as flour, sugar, raisins, etc. His books at night would show many pounds of gold from the day's sales instead of ounces or dollars. It was said that an Indian came to him one day with a nugget of gold which was too heavy to be weighed with his gold scales; the Indian wanted raisins for it. Mr. Murphy was not long in devising a plan to weigh the gold. He put the gold into a water bucket and took a box of raisins and tied a string around it, and then balanced a crowbar across a log and hung the box of raisins to one end and the bucket with the gold to the other and made them balance. The Indian was satisfied that he had got good measure, and left the camp rejoicing.

The traders used always to take double weight in gold from the Indians, and quite often from the miners, as many of them at that time did not know a one-ounce from a two-ounce weight. Few had ever even seen a pair of gold scales until they came to California, so were easily imposed on.

The Indians, after mixing with the miners, began to catch on to Mr. Murphy's little game, so when they found a large lump of gold they would chip off a little piece and bring that in and sell it, and after they had used what it bought they would chip off another piece and sell it, and continue in that way until the piece was disposed of. Many a man who made a fortune in trading in those days in California got his start in that way. Not content with a good thing, they wanted the whole earth and thought they had a clear claim to it. This man Murphy made several fortunes and lost them playing monte.

It was said that at some of the little towns on the coast

he bet one hundred thousand dollars on one card. He was too drunk to look after his bet, and the gamblers drew the man's winning card, and kept on drawing until their card came, and then took the stakes. Parties looking on saw the cheat, but dared not mention it, since the gamblers had their six-shooters by their sides on the table, and would have used them freely at the first word against them. Murphy died later on, a poor man.

A man named Robinson started a store in our settlement. He used to cheat the Indians with double weights, as I have seen him do many a time. He made about sixty thousand dollars, and then went home to the South. He was formerly a Northern man, but settled in the South. I met a soldier of the late war who knew him. He said that Robinson bought negroes with the money that he got in California, and during the war kept a sutler's store and would take all the Southern script that he could get hold of; and it was said that our boys supplied him with a goodly lot. After the war he went back to California again, but I presume found it rather dry picking, with no Indians to help him to another fortune.

When in California the first time, Mr. Robinson built the first ferry across the river at that point, I having sawed the planks for the boat at twelve dollars a day and board. That ferry later on became the principal passage across the Stanislaus River.

Another man kept a store about a mile above this big bar, whose name I need not mention here, since a very recent wonderful discovery in that immediate neighborhood might connect him with an uncanny business; besides, it may be possible that he has good and respectable connections yet alive who would regret to know that he might have been connected with such unlawful business. According to his account of himself, he was an old pirate captain. He boasted of his deeds of daring, of the fights he used to have, and how many men he had slaughtered. He always had a rough lot around his place; he also traded with Indians in the same manner other traders did. After the mines began to fail he left the camp.

I left the camp in the early spring of 1852 to go to Australia in 1853, where I spent a year in the mines, and returned home by the way of South America, when, after four months' stay at home, I returned again to California. This time I took a brother along, and when we arrived at Stockton we started on foot for Angel's Camp. The camp was in the mining district about seventy miles away. We took a road that led up by Bear Mountain. The second night out brought us into the foothills at the extreme edge of the plains. There we found a rudely built cabin. I went to the door, opened it and looked in, and before me was the old pirate captain and two or three rough-looking fellows. He appeared pleased to see me and invited us in. I told him we were on our way to the mines, and he invited us to remain with him over night, and we concluded to do so. After dark we spread our blankets on the ground, for there were no bunks or bedsteads in the place. I did not feel just right, knowing what the man had been, and yet I knew that he must be aware that we could not have much money about us, as I told him that we had but one dollar when we landed in Stockton. We got to sleep after a while, tired with our long tramp over a hot and sandy road. We slept soundly until about midnight, when we were awakened by half a dozen rough-looking fellows who had just entered. They appeared to be at home, and when they espied an extra bed on the ground, they were more guarded. They had looked us over a little, and soon camped down on the ground. I felt a little nervous, but kept quiet and thought I would keep awake and see how things turned out. I did not mean to be caught napping if they meant us any harm. I waited and watched anxiously for daylight to shine through the one little window, and at the first glimpse of day we were up and ready for the road again. I told our host, whom I found also awake, that we wanted to reach Angel's Camp that day. We thanked him for his hospitality, and left to arrive safely at Angel's Camp that afternoon.

A number of years after this event there was discovered in California down in the foothills near the plains, and also near an old cabin, a well filled with human skeletons. Reading that, my mind went back in a moment to my old friend the pirate captain, and I saw the whole scene over again. I also read the account of finding naked skeletons in the marble cave in Toulumne County. According to the locality as reported, it could not have been much over one mile above this man's store. There were many men about that place from Australia who had been convicts, and had either made their escape or had served out their time and come to California. Now it seems to me that the two pits containing human bones and the pirate captain were somehow connected. To account for the absence of remnants of clothing in the marble cave is very easy, when we take in the situation of 1848 and 1849. Anything in the shape of boots or clothing, either old or new, was worth nearly its weight in gold, and no one would think of asking a man where he got his boots or clothing or whether they were old or new. Again, I have seen many Indians, some with a vest on and nothing else, and others with a pair of pants, while others had one boot on one foot and a hat on their head, not knowing, neither caring, where they came from. The Digger Indians in that part of the country did not appear to be a people who ever went to war among themselves, therefore I do not think those bones belonged to that tribe ; and yet, if they were remains of Indians, another theory would explain the cause of their bones being found in the cave. A few years ago the miners, who were working their claims under Table Mountain, which is about one mile from marble cave, dug up a human skull in a good state of preservation. Now Table Mountain stands on the bed of an ancient river which undoubtedly was the old course of the Stanislaus. The river had been driven from its course by a tremendous flow of matter which must have flowed from some volcanic source above ; the result being to dam the river and cause large lakes to be formed, which would eventually break their way through the walls which held them, and when once liberated the water would soon cut a new channel. It must have been very many centuries since, for the present channel of the river Stanislaus is some five hundred feet below the old bed under Table Mountain. The country being deluged with fire and water, the natives would think the world was to be burned up, and would flee for some place of shelter, and knowing of the cave would plunge into it, taking their chances of getting out again. It is evident there were Indians inhabited the land at the time of the filling of the old river bed. The finding of the skull beneath the mountain is evidence and proves that bones might preserve their general contour for an indefinite period in a dry cave.

But to return to my narrative. In company with another party I tried to turn a creek a little below, where rich diggings had been found and worked out, thinking the bed of the creek at that point must be rich. All the other miners had left the camp except us two. We worked about a week, when, finding that there was too much water to contend with, we gave it up. and I went to Sonora. Later I heard that others turned the creek at that point, and very soon took out thirty thousand dollars. Arriving at Sonora, I put up at a cabin kept by a man whom they called Josh Holden, and it was said that he was an old Southern steamboat gambler. The first man that I had occasion to speak to was the notorious Billy Mulligan, whom the vigilant committees had such a tussle with in later years in San Francisco; but he was an honest, law-abiding young man when I first met him, so much so that I often trusted all my gold with him, and he never betrayed my confidence. After a while he got into bad company and commenced gambling, going from bad to worse.

There was plenty of rich ground both in and near the town. Some parties struck it rich when digging their cellars; but strange to relate, I thought they were not rich enough for me. Every camp, if only a week old, looked to a new arrival as if it was all worked out. Everybody appeared to be unsatisfied unless he happened to be one of the first to stake a claim at a new discovery. If a man was seen sticking a stake or digging with a pick at any little distance away from the mines that were being worked, all hands would get out of their holes, catch up a pick and a shovel, and start on the run for the fellow. When they got up to him they would commence to mark out claims all around him, and after they had staked out a few hundred claims, and had the fellow completely hedged in, they would approach him and ask him how it panned out. After all, the man might only have been digging out a stone to put into his chimney or throw at a bird. I noticed that the miners got into the habit in Australia of running after all new finds; but there was less shooting in Australia, notwithstanding that it was full of old convicts. There were plenty of mounted police to look after matters, while in California each man was his own police, judge, and jury. Everybody wanted the richest claim, and would often leave a rich claim and stake out a worthless one, and some one else would take the abandoned claim and take out a fortune.

There were many in that country in the early days who wanted to stake out the whole country and would hold it if they could. I have seen many of them who were worse than any brigands that ever infested any country, and yet at that time there was plenty for all to be obtained for digging for it in an honest way. But no matter how refined and law abiding men may be at home, turn them loose in a new country like California in 1849, away from law and order, with no restraint over them, and they soon become devils incarnate. Although there were some noble exceptions, this was generally the case. I have been driven away from many a rich claim which legally belonged to me, but never carried a pistol, as the majority of the miners did. I thought it the better part of valor to take water when I had a good navy revolver stuck under my nose, and at the same time saw a large Texas dirk knife slowly slipping from a fellow's boot; but some of those fellows would sometimes meet with the wrong man, and get loaded with bullets. I think it well that I did not carry weapons, since I might have let daylight through a number that I met with. I did not go to that country on a hunting tour, so never had any serious trouble with any one. I found it quite as easy to keep out of trouble, as to get out after getting into it.

Sometimes two men would have a rough-and-tumble fight, which would start the whole camp on the run. Some of them would be shouting, " Hang him! " and when they came up would inquire what the fellow had done.

My first night in Sonora had something to do with my keeping away from wrangling crowds who used pistols freely. While in Mr. Holden's cabin a little after dark, we heard a riot going on not far away. A number of shots were fired. Young Mulligan said to me, " Come, let us go down and see what is up." We found the trouble was in a large gaming tent. Started in, I passed many who seemed to be in a great hurry to get out, and I noticed that several shots were cracking painfully near me, but I pushed on inside, which was packed with seething humanity, each trying to see who would be the first to get out. Jammed into the middle of the group was a savage-looking Mexican, with a large knife twenty inches long. He was shouting at the top of his voice in his own language. At the farther end of the tent was a table, and a man who held a candle beside it, bending over a young man who was laying on his back on the table. The young man was in great distress and pain. Pushing my way through the crowd to the table where the young man lay, I stumbled over the bodies of a few dead men who lay stretched on the floor. On reaching the table I learned that the young man had been shot in the lung, and that the man at his side was a doctor, and I held the candle while he probed the wound for the bullet, but the wounded man soon died. The gamblers had got into a dispute over their games, and had mounted the tables and opened fire right and left. I concluded that if gamblers were so very careless as to where they threw their lead, it was best to keep clear of them. This young man who lay on the table had nothing to do with the trouble, but got shot from being present. The Mexican with the long knife was his partner, and he was on the hunt for the man that shot him, and this caused the stampede. Each man thought himself liable to become the Mexican's victim.

A day or two later there was a party formed to go up into the mountains, and I joined them. About a dozen of us started with pack animals loaded with supplies and tools. We passed up through what was later known as

Columbia Mining Camp, which contained at that time gold enough to have made us all rich, but we did not know it was there. We finally came to a place called MacDonald's Flats, which was paying well. Going up to one tent where two or three men were standing, who should be standing there but my old shipmate, the second mate of the old bark "Kingston," of Fairhaven, from which I had run away at Hobartstown, Van Dieman's Land, in 1846? He had given up whaling and had taken to mining, and he advised me to stop with him, but being bound for the mountains nothing would stop me. We encountered snow which had lain on the ground apparently many years, and was as solid as the ground beneath it. We camped one night on the snow, and a big snowstorm came on before morning. After daylight we dug ourselves out and took the back track for a more congenial climate, which, in travelling through the country, we soon found. Below the snow line we saw some very large trees. One sugar pine which had blown down was quite twelve feet in diameter at the but. We tried to get on top of it, and to do so had to go about one hundred feet to the first limbs, and by mounting the limbs managed to get on top of the log. It was one of the handsomest logs that I ever saw, and would have made many thousand feet of clear lumber. It seemed wicked that it was destined to rot where it lay, or become food for the brush fires. I paced a small pine that was about two feet at the but which had been blown down and from the but to the top was seventy-three paces. I had lingered behind a little, and to catch up cut across by a near way to reach the party. I saw ahead of me what appeared to be a Mexican corral, which was made by driving posts into the ground in a large circle. On coming up to it I found on investigation that the posts were the pillars or ribs that are found on those big trees that were discovered standing two years later. Passing around the pillars or roots, it measured twenty paces, which would make the distance through twenty feet. I called the attention of our party to them when I overtook them, but they were so preoccupied with the object of our journey they did not think it worth while to investigate. I believe it to be a fact that I was the first white man that discovered that gigantic trees existed in those mountains, although a hunter who was hunting for the Union Water Company, who were putting water into Murphy's Camp, found two standing, two years after my find. Of the two trees found by Lorenzo Dow, that being the hunter's name, one was cut down and a ten-pin alley cut on the upper side of the trunk, and the stump was levelled off and used as a dance hall. The bark was taken off the other up to the first limb, one hundred feet, and at that height the trunk was twelve feet in diameter. The first limb was four feet through. It took several men six weeks to cut one of these trees down. They cut it down about three feet above the ground by boring it with a long auger. It took a week to fell it after it first began to lean and to crack. Every new hole would weaken it a little, until it finally went to the ground amid cheers and a tremendous crash, which resounded throughout the silent forest. The stump measured in solid wood twenty-seven feet, but when planed off, the ribs boarded over the total length across the stump, was thirty-three feet.

Capt. Hunford, the president of the Union Water Company, had the bark off to the height of a hundred feet. To accomplish it they bored holes in some twenty inches and drove in trunnels and continued up in a spiral form, thus passing several times around the tree in reaching the hundred feet. Then a tackle was attached to the big limb, and the bark taken off in sections. Thirty feet of the bark was sent to New York and set up, but people could not believe that it represented the size of one tree; they thought the bark had been taken from different trees. The bark was eighteen inches thick. A small section of the bark of that tree was to be seen in the old Scollay House in Scollay Square, before the old building was torn down. One man fell from the big limb to the ground, one hundred feet, but escaped with only a broken thigh, as there was about twenty inches of moss covered the ground, which broke his fall.

Leaving the mountains, we were again soon camped on MacDonald's Flat. The next morning, after our return, a lot of miners were gathered around a tent, and going over to see what was up, I looked inside, and there lay a man that was almost entirely covered with court-plaster. He had been attacked in his bed that night by two Mexicans whom he had taken in and befriended. They first threw a large stone on to his head, which aroused him; and as he sprang up they went at him with their knives. When they made a thrust at him, he would clinch the knives right and left, and of course they would draw back the knifes and make another stab; this work was continued until both hands were cut into a shapeless mass, and his body had hundreds of cuts on it. He finally broke away from them and got into camp nearly dead from the loss of blood, but none of his wounds proved fatal. This was a sample occurrence in the diggings at that time.

Most of the camp had gone down a mile or two below to new diggings that had been found while I was in the mountains, and following them down I soon met my shipmate, who had got a rich claim. He said that he was the second man who staked a claim in that camp, and if I had taken his advice I might have been a third to stake a claim by his side, out of which had been taken one nugget that weighed four pounds.

This camp was called Columbia, which became a celebrated one on account of its extensive mining industry. The first man who discovered gold in that camp was a Mexican, who struck in a little gulch that led down to the main flat. The news soon spread like a forest fire. The miners found later on that the little gulch had furnished the gold not only for that immediate camp, but many others farther below. The old channel of the Stanislaus was traced from Table Mountain up the whole length of Columbia Flat, which was very rich in gold. The pent-up waters in the old bed beneath Table Mountain had broken through the crust that held them and cut a channel down the sides and into many gulches, and from these into creeks which emptied into the river miles below. In this manner the gold was carried from the fountain head, which was near that little gulch, through many different channels, where thousands and tens of thousands of dollars' worth of gold had lodged in the beds and on the banks where it was found by the miners. Thus it will readily be seen how many camps were supplied from Columbia Gulch.

I soon left that camp, thinking that all the best claims were staked up, while it was later proven that there were many hundred claims unstaked, and that, too, right at our feet. In leaving the camp I travelled fully a mile over the old river bed, which run under Table Mountain. It might truly be said that I was walking on a pavement of gold while hunting for gold, and did not know enough to stoop and pick it up ; but I was not the only one who did not know when he had a good thing, for there were many who had the same experience.

I have known diggings to be discovered by seeing a nugget of several pounds' weight sticking out of the ground that a stage wheel had turned out, in a road that had been used as a public highway for three years.

That being a fact, there was some excuse for me and perhaps for others.

Next I found myself back at my old camp at the ferry, and found that things were wonderfully changed in a few months. The ground where I had camped, and over which I had many times tramped in search of gold, was completely worked over, and many claims had yielded fortunes to the owners. Here I picked around in different places, but could not make it pan out much, so went to work on a bar on the river, a little above where the old pirate captain's tent stood. A little above where I was working were a lot of what I first thought were Indians, but when I went in amongst them soon found there were no Indians among them. A white man, not far off, was sitting near a little tent about large enough to hold one man. Upon approaching him, I saw that he was an Englishman, and a man of some note. He had that dignified, aristrocratic look about him that one will always see in a well-bred English gentleman. He wanted to know what he could do for me. I replied nothing in particular, unless it was to tell me who those black, curly headed people were that were mining there, saying that I had seen people who very much resembled them before. He wanted to know where I had seen such natives, and I told him at the Fiji Islands. He said that they came from that place.

Learning that I had been at the Fiji Islands and had spent several years in Australia, he became quite communicative, and related to me why he had the natives mining for him. Possibly he thought I had heard about him when in Australia; and since there are always two sides to every story, I might have heard the bad side of his experience in that country. He stated that he went out to Australia with half a million pounds sterling. He snpposed that the people in the colonies were English, and it would be quite as easy to get along with them as it was in England; in other words, could be moulded at the will and pleasure of their masters, the rich.

He bought a large lot of land not far from Sydney, and built up quite a town which he called Boydstown, after his own name, but through some mistakes and the high price of labor he did not prosper, and finally his property got run down, while things went from bad to worse. About that time the California fever was raging in Australia. Having a yacht and a few hundred pounds, he thought he would run down to the Fiji Islands and take on board a few natives and go to California and try and regain his fortune at mining. On arriving at California he left his yacht in charge of a part of his crew, and came with the rest and some natives to the mining district, and located on that bar on the Stanislaus.

After that meeting I called quite often on him, at his earnest desire. He wanted to talk over the matter of his misfortunes in Australia, since I had a good deal of sympathy for him. On my visits he always reached for his bottle of good old English brandy, which he claimed was older than himself, and he was near about seventy years old.

Hearing of good diggings that had been discovered at Carson's Creek, I left my friend, Capt. Boyd, behind with his cannibals.

A few years later, when in Australia, the other side of the old man's story was related to me, as well as the fate that befell him after he left California on his way back to Sydney again.

He did build a town, as he said; but the reason why he did not prosper was because he tried to bring wages down to one sixpence a day for labor, and the working class would not stand such reduction in a country where there was as much freedom as in the United

States to all those who were not held under bond. The result was that the old man was boycotted. When he left California he had about thirty thousand dollars in gold. He landed his natives at the Fiji Islands and started for Sydney. On the way his crew murdered him, threw his body overboard, took the yacht and gold and left for parts unknown. Such was believed to be his fate from accounts learned later.

At Carson's Creek I found on my arrival a lively lot of miners putting in their best work at mining, some sinking shafts, while others were scooping out the rich gravel and clay from the bottom of their sunken shafts. As in other camps, many shafts had been sunk which had not struck pay dirt and were abandoned. I strolled about awhile, and finally went into one of the abandoned pits, and picked a little with my knife and found some gold, but not enough to pay, but noticed a quartz bowlder at one side of the shaft. At first I thought I would remove it, and could have done so after ten minutes' work, but changed my mind, and leaving the shaft went down below to where a party of miners had sunk a shaft and struck water, and were pumping the water out which flowed down below them and over some unoccupied ground. Here I began to stake a claim. Before getting my stakes down I concluded that the water from the claim above would give me much trouble, so gave up the idea and staked a claim at a place which was clear of water. About that time I met five men with whom I was acquainted, and they wanted me to stake six claims and all go in together. I staked six claims, each fifteen feet square, and staked them all in a line above the party who had struck water as before stated. We worked three at a time on one claim, while in the mean time the other three went where they pleased. When it was my day off I worked on the other claim I had staked when alone.

Two or three days after leaving that as I thought lean shaft where the quartz bowlder was, another man went into the shaft and in a very short time dug out the bowlder and scooped up three thousand dollars beneath it.

After a while I got my shaft down about four feet and struck a point of the bed rock, then dug down by the side of it and soon came to water. In a crevice on the slope I found a little nugget worth about one dollar.

Just then one of our company's men at the shaft came to me and said that they had struck bottom, and wanted me to try the dirt. I took out a pan of the gravel and took it to my shaft and washed it out, but found no gold; then returned, took another pan at the same place, but a little deeper, and washed it out and got about forty dollars. I left my wet hole at once, and all hands went to work in the shaft where there was gold apparently in plenty. To make a long story short, we took out five thousand dollars in a short time, and then taking a pack of cards, one was dealt to each with the understanding that whoever got the ace of hearts should have the claim. The man who won it sold it for one hundred dollars.

Later on there were three thousand dollars taken out of those claims.

About the time we quitted working the claims a blacksmith from San Francisco came into camp who had never seen a mine before. The party whose water I had been afraid of had ceased to pump the water, and the ground was dry below his claim. This blacksmith hired a man and stuck his stakes where I ought to have first stuck mine, on the ground that had been flowed over. The man and his helper put their shaft down in two days some eight feet deep. The blacksmith then discharged his man, and in less than two weeks from the time that he landed in camp he left it with ten thousand dollars, and having many nuggets as large as a man's fist. He took out one afternoon thirteen pounds of gold, and brought it up to his tent in his boot, having picked it all out, not washing a pan of dirt. One man washed one pan of gravel for him to see what it would pan out, and got one hundred dollars. After he got what he could pick out with his knife, he sold his claim for twelve hundred dollars, and left camp for Frisco. This claim was near the creek. Just above this claim and in the banks of the creek was a crevice which run back at right angle from the creek. This man's big strike set all the miners to crowding as near to him as they could. The result was they got into that crevice where they struck paying dirt to the tune of thirty thousand dollars, in about that number of feet along that crevice, and to my disgust right through that wet hole of mine. I had got to within one foot of thousands of dollars, which were scattered along that crevice like potatoes dug behind a farmer. I had reason to believe "I was not in it." Fate was against me, as was the case with many others. The lode from which all this gold came was located a little above the camp, which was worked later and paid its owners well; and I believe there were millions taken out of it. One nugget was taken out that was worth twelve thousand dollars, and later was sent to the World's Fair in London. I had many other experiences similar to that at Carson's Creek, with opportunities equally as good, but which were lost.

CHAPTER VII.

ANECDOTES ABOUT MINERS AND MINING — TURNS BRIDGE-
BUILDER — A GAMBLER WORSTED AT HIS OWN GAME —
MEETING WITH WAH-KEEN, THE NOTORIOUS MEXICAN OUT-
LAW AND THREE-FINGERED JACK — STARTS FOR FRISCO —
SAILS FOR AUSTRALIA — STOPS AT A VOLCANIC ISLAND —
A PARLEY WITH THE ISLANDERS — AN ISLAND VISITED
AND DEPOPULATED BY SMALLPOX — ARRIVAL IN AUSTRA-
LIA — BENDAGO AND THE GOLD MINERS OF AUSTRALIA —
STRIKING RICH DIGGINGS — THE MINERS TAX AGITATION
— STARTS FOR DONKEY WOMAN'S GULLY — LOST IN THE
FOREST — WONDERFUL DISCOVERY OF WATER WITH WHICH
TO QUENCH THIRST.

BEFORE concluding the narrative of my experience at
mining I will state some things which it taught me, that
may be of use to the novice who starts out in search of
the yellow metal.

Our party left camp and located at a little place a short
distance above Carson's, called Albany Flat. We built a
cabin for winter and laid in supplies. We soon, however, rallied to a new strike near Murphy's Camp, and
there made many slips again. I finally left the company
and wandered around to different camps, getting some
gold in some camps and none in others. It had got to
be difficult to find gold in every gulch. Many thousands
of people had arrived in the country, and they had dug
all that was easy to get at, and it required a good deal
of hard work to find a rich shaft. I went to work for a
company who were building a flume and ditch to carry
the water into Murphy's Camp for mining purposes, and
I was to receive one hundred dollars a month and board,

which appeared to be better than mining, although I had left many a claim that would have paid me one hundred dollars a week, had I have stuck to them. I was content with my hundred dollars, since it was paid to me in coin, whose value I could realize, while gold dust or nuggets did not appear to represent much value. It appeared like so much iron, and not like money. After a week or two, I found the work pretty hard, and told the president — who, by the way, was an old church builder from New York, named Hunford — that I would not stay with them any longer. The work was harder than I expected, and I, being a sailor, had to do a large amount of climbing, and sometimes pretty high climbing. Capt. Hunford said he did not want me to leave, since I was the best climber he had, and I must stay, and as an inducement said that the company would give me thirty dollars a month more, making my pay one hundred and thirty dollars. I accepted the offer and returned to work. I will relate one part of the work that I was called upon to do, and did without hesitation. We had to flume across one deep hollow or depression, which was thirteen hundred feet from ditch to ditch. Our fluming gradually gained in height as we receded from the verge until we had advanced about four hundred feet, when at that point it was quite seventy-five feet high. Our bents were twenty feet span at the bottom and four feet at the top, well tied and braced. The bents had forty feet span between them, with a stringer eight by twelve, framed about two feet from the top, with a short tie framed in between the two posts, the same distance from the top, which formed a sill on which the boarded flume rested. When the bents were raised and two stringers in position, the two stringers which crossed the span of forty feet were four feet apart. My work was to walk from the end of those stringers with a foothold of only eight inches, with nothing to reach for in case of a slip or a misstep but the other stringer, which was of the same size and four feet distant at one side. After I had reached the last span raised, I would walk along and dress off the stringer with the adze every two feet on each stringer, and then put on the ties, spike them and cover them with boards, after which any one could pass over them without danger.

One misstep would have sent me down from that giddy height of from seventy-five or eighty feet like a meteoric stone, and I would have been buried in the earth. That span of fluming was then considered the highest in the country. After working about four months I returned to Murphy's Camp and succeeded well at mining for a while, but soon concluded to go back to my old camp at Albany Flat.

Before leaving this camp I broke a gambler of the habit of continuously making overtures to me to bet at his game, having become tired of being teased to bet every time I went near his table. I boarded with a Chinaman, who kept a little dining-saloon opposite the gambler's tent. There was not much doing in the day-time at the gambler's tables, since the miners were at work, but at night things were all in full blast. The day before I was going to leave camp I gave this man a dose of his own medicine. Having a bag of gold dust, which contained about four hundred dollars, I went and bought another bag of the same size and lead in bulk to be about the size of the gold. I placed it in the sack and rolled it up into a round ball to look like my bag of gold, then I bought two silk handkerchiefs of the same pattern and wrapped one snugly around each bag of metal. Putting the bag of gold into my breast pocket and the bag of lead also, and taking care to get the lead to the bottom of the pocket, I went to my friend the

Chinaman and said, "Let us go over to the gambling tent and see what is going on."

"All right," said he, and we started.

My tormentor began asking me at once to bet.

He happened to be alone as I expected he would, which was the reason for taking my dusky friend along, for should I make a blunder and encounter trouble there would, no doubt, be some tall shooting, and I thought that the Chinaman might perhaps be able to tell where my scattered remains might be found. I always thought a gambler next in kin to a thief, and I felt no qualms in what I was about to do, knowing that he purposed cheating me if he could.

He laid out his cards and invited me to make a bet. Taking out my bag of gold I unrolled it, pouring into my hand some of the yellow dust, and asked him what he would give me an ounce for such gold. He said that if I lost, he would allow me sixteen dollars for it. Putting it back I rolled and tied it as before, and in returning it to my pocket got it to the bottom and the lead on top. It was quite common for miners betting, when they had no change, to put their bag of dust down; and if they lost, they were able to redeem the gold again if they wished to later on.

After the gambler's repeated invitations to bet, I pulled out my bag of lead and laid it down on the queen, which was out against some other card. I bet half an ounce on that card. He won, and I doubled the bet to one ounce, when I won. Returning my bag to my pocket again, I bet with his own money without fear. Soon losing that, I drew forth my sack of lead again and won. Hiding my sack again, I bet his money a second time. I soon saw that the queen appeared to come oftener than it ought to in a fair deal, so kept betting on the queen, which kept winning for me. By this time my little stake was up to seventy dollars, and my friend with the pig-tail nudged me and said, "Stop now, you have got enough." I took his advice and quit the game seventy dollars ahead.

The gambler showed considerable temper because I stopped betting, but I left the tent and was not long in putting the evidence of my duplicity far beyond his reach, knowing well that if he should learn the secret of the bag of bogus gold, he would be apt to use as much lead as that bag contained for my especial benefit.

I did not leave camp for a few days, since it was not urgent that I should, as would have been the case had I lost at the game. I intended to tell the fellow, had I lost, that I would redeem the gold in a day or two, and when the time arrived to redeem, would have been many a long mile from Murphy's Camp. Within a week I turned again to Albany Flat and went to work with two of my old camp-mates. Not many days afterward a man whom one of my old company was acquainted with came over from a camp called St. Andrays. He said that a big strike had just been made in that camp, so as a matter of course we went over. We found that the big strike had been made in the bed of an old creek whose waters had been crowded out by some ancient lava flow in the same manner Table Mountain had been formed. We found the gold in a bed of cement some four inches thick, and it had to be hammered to powder before we could get the gold, and to work it successfully it would require ma-chinery such as we were not able to furnish, and we gave up.

One experience at this time, had I been successful, would have put me on the top round of the ladder, be-sides netting me many thousand dollars, or it might have wiped me out of existence. It was my experience with that outlaw and desperado Wah-Keen, a Mexican whose

very name was a terror to every one, from the sheriff
down.

He was said to have been once a quiet, inoffensive
miner in a camp in the northern mines, where his wife
was with him. The camp, like all others, was filled with
ruffians. They kidnapped Wah-Keen's wife, and abused
her so badly that she died. Many of the Mexicans are
very revengeful, and Wah-Keen, after this outrage, swore
death to all whites; and it is proven in the archives of
California how well he kept his oath.

The day before my arrival at that camp was Sunday.
Wah-Keen had come into the outskirts of the town and had
entered a gambler's tent that was run by some half-breed
Mexicans. Wah-Keen had some eight or ten of his followers with him, and attempted to clean out the place at
one scoop. The result was some target practice wherein
Wah-Keen lost all but two companions, who fled to the
hills. The sheriff turned out with a *posse*, but could not
find him. He had tried several times before, but either
could not or would not take him when he came up with
him.

Wah-Keen had walked through the camp in mid-day
shooting right and left, while no one dared to take him or
even to follow unless they had a *posse* of a score or more
well-armed men. On Saturday afternoon my partners and
myself were at work on the trail that ran through the flat
and down to Carson's Creek. About four o'clock we saw
three Mexicans ride past. After they had passed, I said,
"Who knows but that was Wah-Keen and two of his gang?"
but thought no more of them. Sunday morning a man
came up from Carson's Creek and said that Wah-Keen had
been at a little store on the creek the night before and
bought some food. I told my partners that those three
men that we saw the night before were Wah-Keen and two
of his companions, and we had better go at once and see if

we could not catch them. They said Wah-Keen must be forty miles away before that time. Saying no more, I took my rifle and started to strike the trail where we last saw them, which I soon found. I followed it over the brow of the hill and down to Carson's Creek near its head, where the creek forked, one branch running to the right and the other straight ahead. Reaching the creek, I met a man who lived on the bank of the creek, and asked him if he had seen any Mexicans around that morning. He said that he had, and that one had passed up on the opposite side only about ten minutes since. I crossed over and soon struck the trail, and following the marks up found that they turned up the right-hand branch of the creek. Following on I got near the top, where the branch terminated in a narrow ravine, there losing the tracks. Going up on to the ridge about fifty feet higher, I began to look around to find the tracks again, and soon discovered a man with a rifle in his hands, who was hunting for small game.

I asked if he had seen any Mexicans that morning, to which he replied that he had seen one at the lower end of that ride but a short time before I met him. I then started in the direction he pointed, and had not gone many rods before I could see out and down on to a flat and open space of several acres in extent. There in plain view, and not more than ten rods away, were two Mexicans on horseback. I knew that they were Wah-Keen and Three-fingered Jack, as he was called, a half-breed who was about as great a desperado as Wah-Keen. I hurried down the trail, and when it was reached they had got through the open space and were out of my sight, but not far off. I pushed on into the thick bushes that lined both sides of the trail, and soon came to a little tent, at the entrance of which was a man sitting. Repeating my question to him about the Mexicans, he said that he had, not five minutes before. When told who they were, he jumped up and said he would go with me and help take them. He had been in the Mexican War and was not afraid of any greaser, as half Indian and half Mexicans were called. I told him that he might go if he wanted to, but that they were ugly fellows to handle.

"Well," said he, "I am not afraid of them"; and sticking a little single-barrel pistol in his belt, we started on.

After we had got some five or six rods, I found that through talking with him I had lost the tracks of the horses' feet. We left the trail and tried to find the tracks again. Not far from the trail we met a man with a shotgun who was hunting for quail, and while talking with this man, we saw a Mexican coming up through the flat. He had on a poncho blanket, which is a square cloth with a slit in the centre. This is thrown over the head, and will hang down and nearly cover the wearer to the knees. This Mexican had a slouch hat well down over his face, but we thought nothing of seeing him.

I said to my new friend, "Let us go back and hunt until we strike the tracks, and try and not lose them again." We did so, and soon found the horses' tracks again. We soon found where they left the trail, and followed them into a clump of bushes and a few small trees on a space not over one or two rods square. When we got up to this little clump of bushes, we saw only a few rods beyond Wah-Keen and his mate on horseback riding slowly up a little ravine. I said, "There they are, now we will have them!" and started after them. Approaching them I noticed they held their heads so that they could see sideways, and as I was gaining upon them from the side, soon got into the trail behind them, but found that they managed somehow to see behind as well as sideways. When they got to the upper end of the ravine, which was not more than five or six rods long, and where stood a pine-tree about twenty inches through, Wah-Keen got off his horse and stepped behind that tree, where he was completely hid from me. Three-fingered Jack remained sitting on his horse, with one hand holding the bridle and the other placed under the lapel of his coat. He had on a heavy coat buttoned down in front.

I well knew that his hand had a firm grasp on a navy revolver, and also knew that he would draw it at first sign of danger from me. Being a pretty good shot at that time, and able to strike the head from a bird about as far as able to see one either on the wing or at rest, I felt pretty sure of toppling over one of them, and would have trusted to luck and chance for my companion to deal with the other one. I walked fearlessly up to the tree behind which Wah-Keen was concealed, and stepped in front of him.

Wah-Keen straightened up from a stooping position, and speaking to him in Spanish, — since I could speak that language to some extent, — said, " How do you do, friend?"

" Very well," said he.

Stating that I had lost a horse and was out hunting for him, I described the animal as having a white star on his forehead, two white feet, a long tail and mane, and so on. He said that he was hunting for horses himself; which without doubt was true, since he stole all the horses that he wanted, but said he had not seen any horse such as I described.

The two horses he and his companion had then were stolen from the Green Stage Company, and were two of the best the company owned. Wah-Keen never took a poor horse, but always chose the best, since they were all the same price to him.

Turning my back to them several times, I cast my eyes

over the hills to see if that horse was to be seen, and by that means gave them a chance to fill me with bullets if they chose to, believing that my boldness would disarm them of suspicion. I noticed that my brave friend had stopped some ten yards behind, and I went down to him and said, "Now you take one and I will take the other." The brave veteran of the late Mexican War, who was so courageous a short time before, was so frightened he could hardly speak, and I saw that if there was to be a capture, I should have to do the work alone. Knowing that the time had passed to make the attempt alone, I decided quickly what to do, and concluded to get the fellow out of sight and into more congenial climate before he gave the outlaws a cue, which he seemed in a fair way to do. When I told him to take one while I did for the other, he managed to say that they were too well armed and that we could not do it. I therefore told him to go around to Albany Flat and notify the camp, where they would find me entertaining Wah-Keen and Three-fingered Jack. He started off without any urging, and took a large circuit around the objects that had made such a sudden change in his courage. Returning to where Wah-Keen was standing, he mounted his horse and they rode slowly along, while I walked along by their side, and we soon came to a clump of scrub oaks and underbrush which covered about an acre. Here the two desperadoes went to the right while I took to the left, walking slowly along, since I did not wish it to appear that I intended to keep too close company with them. It only took some four or five minutes to get around to where they were to be seen, and, to my surprise when I did see them, they were going as fast as their horses could carry them in a direct line toward Albany Camp, and were some two hundred yards in advance of me. I could have shot one of them down with my rifle, but hesitated to shoot one who had done

ENTERTAINING THE OUTLAWS, WAH-KEEN AND THREE-FINGERED JACK, IN CALIFORNIA.

me no harm, but undoubtedly I would have been justified in doing so. I very soon saw the object that had caused their hasty flight. There were eight or ten men coming across the flat from the direction of Los Mortes, a little camp which was located between Albany Flat and Angel's Camp. Hearing that Wah-Keen had been to Los Mortes for food, they started to hunt for him and had just caught sight of him as he was passing along by that clump of timber. As soon as they caught sight of him, they all began to halloo and run toward him, which started Wah-Keen and his mate on the gallop.

Going direct to Albany Flat, I found every one running hither and yon, some riding on jacks without saddle or bridle, others on mules destitute of trappings, while others were running about with pistols and rifles in their hands. My two partners had stayed at home, standing near our cabin with rifles in hand. Wah-Keen had passed within two rods of our camp, but went so fast that before they could get out with their guns, he was far away and out of sight over the ridge on a trail leading toward Bear Mountain.

The man I sent around to camp told the boys that he went up to Wah-Keen and shook hands with him, while I told them that he went too far into his boots to do that, since he hardly got near enough to see him, let alone shake hands with him.

It is needless to say that I felt very much disappointed with the manner in which my venture had terminated. Starting out with the determination to find the outlaws, and to capture them also, I believe I would have been successful but for my cowardly volunteer companion. I would not have lost the tracks, and would have been led by them to the little clump of bushes where Three-fingered Jack was with the two horses, while Wah-Keen was at the camp of Los Mortes after supplies. I could have made Jack hold up and have disarmed and gagged him, and then laid in hiding for Wah-Keen and served him in the same manner; then bound them together and hitched them to their horses and led them into camp, which was not an uncommon way of caring for captives.

There was a large reward offered for them, but that was no great incentive. The honor of taking them alone would have been something worth while, since the sheriff could not take them when he had a *posse* with him.

The next day a man was brought into camp whom they thought was Wah-Keen, and I was sent for to identify him. Seeing the prisoner, I told them that it might be Wah-Keen's brother, but it was not the man they wanted; but the next day the fellow was found hanging to the limb of a tree, it being thought that he was one of the gang, so he was disposed of. He was undoubtedly Wah-Keen's brother, more half foolish than otherwise, and ought not to have been hung.

A few years later on, Wah-Keen, in trying to leave the State, passed into a camp of United States soldiers, where one of the soldiers recognized him and sung out, "Wah-Keen!" when shooting began, and Wah-Keen was killed, and his head was put on exhibition for a while in San Francisco.

About three weeks later I started for Frisco, having heard a good deal about the wonderful gold fields in Australia. I concluded to go back to the country again which I had tried so hard to leave a few years previous, although I was doubtful of the fields being so very rich, as there was but one nugget found while I was in the country before, and apparently there were no more nuggets where that came from. I arrived in San Francisco in due time, and soon found a boat for Sydney and paid my passage to that city, leaving California for a time, to return again before two years passed by, after varying fortunes in the land of the antipodes.

We sailed out through the Golden Gate with flying colors, and after being out about three weeks the small-pox broke out on board, and some half-dozen or more were severely attacked by the disease. All recovered by the time we reached an island called Tanner or Tenna. We needed some fresh food and water, so the captain made a stop to get a supply of yams, fruit, and pigs. On the island a volcano was at that time in active operation, discharging a large amount of lava. We dropped anchor about three miles off coast, and a boat was sent ashore. We noticed that the natives took the boat as soon as we were all out, and dragged her high up on the beach. We wanted to know why they did so. Pointing to the water, they said, " Hot, hot." Putting my hand into the water, I found it too hot to bear my hand in it long.

After we had been ashore a short time the tide had ebbed, and we noticed a few rods above a large stream of water which was gushing out through a hole near a point of rocks. A large cloud of steam was rising above it. We found the stream to be a hot spring, which was covered several feet deep when the tide was in. The water from the spring and the heat along the shore at the base of that volcano heated the water so hot that nothing in the form of fish could live within three miles of shore.

It has been related of this locality by some writer that a man can stand at a certain point and catch fish on one side and throw them over into the hot water on the other side and cook them, without releasing them from the hook. Now if it were said that fish could be caught anywhere in the bay already cooked and ready for the table, I might perhaps have believed him, but the other story is beyond belief. The saying may be true of the Yellowstone Lake, near Yellowstone Park, but is not applicable at this island.

This is the only hot spring on the island. In the side of a cliff of rocks is another spring, which flows very slowly, requiring an hour or more to furnish enough water to give a man or dog a small drink. The water from this spring is very cold and pure, while the hot spring has a large amount of sulphur. We were obliged to take that or none to fill our casks with for the ship's use. Being anxious to know how long that water would keep hot, I filled a keg, took it on board, and put my tea into a pot, poured my hot water on to it, and made a good strong cup of tea without putting it near the fire. Some of the passengers took tubs ashore to wash some linen, and had to let the water stand in the tubs two hours before it was cool enough for them to put their hands into it. When we got to sea we found our water hardly fit to use. There were several places around the rocky shore of the island where the fire could be seen leaping through the crevices. We could light a pipe from them, and at other points large volumes of steam were issuing. The natives and the few whites on the island drank cocoanut milk when thirsty. The taste when the nut is about half ripe is something like ginger ale. The island appeared to have many old craters, then sealed up, and seen at a distance large beds and cliffs of shining lava were visible that apparently had cooled off at no very remote date. The vent that was in full blast was throwing out large quantities of material. I noticed one day while looking at it that we would first see a large volume of black smoke and hear a loud report, and after the smoke had arisen about a hundred feet above the top of the cone up would come streams of fire, lava, and stones, which shot up several hundred feet. The large rocks would return and come crashing down the sides of the cone. We saw one rock thrown high into the air that looked to be twenty feet long and five or six feet thick. We were about three miles distant at that time.

One day we came near having trouble with the natives. Three of our passengers went ashore to take a bath in the warm water that washed the beach. Stripping off their clothing, they plunged in, and after getting about a hundred yards from the shore, two natives slipped out of the bushes and gathered in the swimmers' clothing and scampered back into the thick entangled bushes. The swimmers paddled ashore as fast as they could, but the natives had got far away by that time. They found it was no use to follow the thieves in the condition that they were in, as, not being used to the bushes, they would have fared badly among the sharp thorns. They followed the beach until they could see the ship, and then began to halloo and beckon to us to come ashore. A boat was soon sent to them. The poor fellows had not so much as a leaf to protect them from the burning sun, but we soon had them on board and dressed. One of the bathers said that he had three hundred dollars in his pocket. The captain sent word ashore to the natives that he would come ashore and fight them if they did not give up the gold and clothing, to which they replied, " Come on!" The captain mustered about forty of the passengers and when ashore.

The beach at the landing was about a hundred yards wide, then a bluff or sand bank rose up nearly prependicular about twenty feet high, then the ground ran back eight or ten rods quite level and was clear of underbrush or any other material that would obstruct the natives' movements. A deep cut had been worn down through this sand bank by constant travel, which was the only accessible point to the flat above. It was not wide enough to admit two abreast; we would, therefore, have to pass up in single file. This spot had been chosen by the natives as their battle ground. The fine generalship of the natives in selecting this locality for the reception of the captain and his followers is readily seen, as they could pick us off one at a time at their leisure. After we landed, the captain asked who would go up there with him. He used to boast a good deal on the passage that he was an ancient Briton, and it would take a good deal to frighten him. I always admired a brave man, so considered it an honor to follow one, and, therefore, stepped out and said, " I will go with you, Captain."

" Come on then," he answered, and we started for the ravine, the captain leading up the trail, with me close to his heels. When we reached the top and could see over the flat, we found before us some five hundred savage natives armed and stripped of all robes except a breech-clout. They had seen us at the same time we discovered them. Some had spears, others bows, and still others old muskets, secured from a few Englishmen on the island, who were trading with the natives for sandalwood, sulphur, and cocoanut oil, the natives having taken the old flint-lock muskets in exchange for their products. The natives confronted us with these old guns as soon as we got high enough to view the situation, when the captain halted.

" Go ahead," said I. " Don't stop here!" But my bold Briton would not advance another step. I saw that the temperature around the captain was getting rather chilly, and his knees were beginning to shake, so I pushed by him on to the flat.

The captain said, " For heaven's sake don't go up there, they will surely kill us."

The natives were brandishing their weapons and going through all sorts of pantomimic performances, — a display which was enough to frighten any, except an ancient Briton, nearly to death, and they could not be scared whatever the danger. About that time the captain for-got something which he had left at the boat; possibly it was a little of that ancient Welsh courage.   He retreated rapidly, making three steps to the rod, while I went on and was soon surrounded with the natives.   Finding that some of them could talk a little English, I told them that all we wanted was the money, and that it was of no use to them, and if they would give it up we would give them some tobacco and some calico.   After much talk some four or five of the head ones returned with me to the boat, where the captain was about ready to shove off.   When he saw me yet alive and no spears or arrows sticking in me, he appeared much relieved.   Taking my dusky followers to the boat, I told the captain that if he would give the natives a little tobacco and some other truck, which the captain finally did, they would give back the clothing and some of the money, a part of which they stated that they had lost.   Thus ended the prospective great battle.

There were a few missionaries on the island, with whom our men mixed freely, as also with the natives and what few whites there were on the island.   There were also a few little schooners trading around the different islands.

Our visit to Tanner Island was a disastrous event for the natives.   Vessels that later stopped at Tanner Island found it almost depopulated.   The natives had taken the germs of the smallpox from our ship, and it had swept from the island nearly all of our late dusky friends.   Our visit at Tanner Island was in the year 1853.

Many years later, in 1892, I saw in a Boston paper that some captain while sailing in the Pacific Ocean discovered an island with many human skeletons scattered around, but not a living soul on the island.   After reading the article, I remembered the calamity on Tanner Island.   The paper said that it was thought the bones had lain bare for forty years, which would tally well with the time of the smallpox there.

It probably was the case that when it was found

disease was sweeping the inhabitants off at a frightful rate, the few whites on the island took to their boats and left, taking as many natives as they could convey in the small boats or schooners with them; and knowing of many small uninhabited islands, it is natural they should sail for some of them, and after such arrival the disease may have broken out and carried them off to a man. There are many islands in the Pacific Ocean located far from the track of ships, which are only seen by some chance vessel that has strayed from the usual course.

We obtained the supplies we required at Tanner Island and sailed for Sydney. When we arrived at the harbor of Sydney, the health department overhauled us; and when they learned that the smallpox had been aboard, we were ordered into quarantine, where we lay one month, all being as uneasy as fish out of water. We then had no smallpox aboard, but having had it, we were obliged to obey orders. We finally outlived our waiting time at the mouth of the harbor, and hove anchor and sailed into Sydney, where we were soon let loose, and each one went his way rejoicing.

The city seemed much the same place that I left it a few years before. Going up Pitt Street no change was visible, except that it took a little more money to get about with than when I was there before. Strange to relate, I had no more money to spend now than when leaving the country, although I had dug many thousand dollars' worth of gold in California, but it had rapidly passed out of my hands. The best part of the country for mining was at Bendago, a camp located about eighty miles inland from Melbourne, at Port Philip, and to get to Melbourne would cost from eight to ten dollars, — an amount which I did not possess. To raise that stake I shipped in a coaster which ran from Sydney to Newcastle for coal, hay, and other truck, my wages being twenty dollars a month.

Going aboard, I was soon afloat again. We ran down the coast and up into a river almost to the head of the stream, where we found the little town of Newcastle. We hauled alongside of a small wharf at about mid-day, and sat down on deck and ate our dinner. While thus occupied a man jumped on to our deck from the wharf and was crossing to a little craft which lay alongside of us. Looking steadily at him caused him to return the gaze. We were old friends, and the recognition was mutual. It was the third mate of the old bark " Kingston," of Fair Haven, from which I ran away while at Hobartstown in 1846, Capt. Ellis, commander. My old friend told me that soon after I left the captain sold what oil he had taken and gave the bark over to the first mate. The captain, with the money he received, then bought two small vessels, putting the third mate in charge of one, and taking charge of the other himself, and began trading between Sydney and the islands near by. On one trip to the islands Capt. Ellis, while running into Ongalon and going through a narrow passage which led through one of the coral reefs which abound among the islands, having got a little too much tanglefoot down, managed to tumble overboard and was drowned. The third mate, coming into possession of the other craft, thought he would keep her and do some trading on his own account. He had taken unto himself a wife, and had become a resident of Sydney and was happy.

We took in a load of coal and left for Sydney, where I was paid off and was soon on board of a brig bound for Melbourne, where we arrived in two weeks. After landing I was soon on my way afoot to the Bendago diggings, a distance of eighty miles over a very dry road. In about a week I arrived at a camp which appeared to be all worked out. The ground was turned up in all directions, pits were sunk in plenty and worked out in most cases. Picking around the abandoned claims I found a little gold, and stopped at that camp about a month.

The experiences of the miners at Bendago were novel and varied, as it is ever with miners.

At the upper end of the flat near which the camp was located was a narrow strip which widened as one goes down the flat, which was two or three miles long and in some parts half a mile wide. Gold was found at the upper end which was coarse and very much scattered, and many holes were sunk which struck nothing. When a miner, after digging for gold had failed to find it, he would call the pit a shyster. One day an Italian, having sunk his shaft to the bottom and striking nothing, came up and sang out, "Another shyster! who will buy my claim?"

A young fellow near by said, "I will give you half a crown for it."

"All right," said the Italian; and the fellow gave him a half-crown, and went to work on his own shaft again.

Towards night the man who had bought the claim thought he would go into the shaft and pick around a little, and the Italian came and looked on to see what the fellow would find, well pleased to think that he had a big half-crown, while the man at the bottom of the shaft would get only one more chance for a fruitless search in exchange for his money. But the scene quickly changes around that pit. The young man at the bottom picked out a nugget that weighed twenty pounds, and worth between four and five thousand dollars. The poor Italian fell on his knees and commenced praying and cursing in his own language until the air was freighted with his bewailings over his lost opportunity.

Throughout the mining belt in Australia there was a white clay beneath the gravel strata. How thick this clay strata is I never knew, but the gravel above it was of various depths from six to twenty feet. The gold would invariably be found on the top of the clay beneath the gravel strata. The gold would hold tenaciously to the clay, and in order to remove and separate the gold the clay had to be taken from the shaft and put into tubs, generally half-hogsheads, then four or five pails of water were poured in and with a shovel it was chopped and stirred until it became thick and muddy, then all was poured out except the gravel, when more water was added and the process repeated until all the clay was dissolved, when the gravel would be taken out and rocked out after the California style. The miners would often find when they struck this clay many gold-bearing chunks which would be, instead of clay and gold, better described as gold and clay, having a much larger amount of gold than clay.

Down toward the lower end of Bendago Flat and nearly in the middle were located three mounds which rose about a hundred feet above the surface of the flat. All about these mounds were rich finds, but the hills were composed of gravel and cobblestones cemented together so very firmly that a blow from a pick or bar would have little effect. The miners believed the ground under those hills must be rich, so they staked their claims on the surface and went to work with hammer and bar and picked their way to the bottom, spending three months in getting down, then they found gold in plenty. They sunk some three or four feet into the soft pipe clay, then ran drifts in all directions. They would work up into the clay until they could see a little gravel with a dark reddish stain, then go no higher until they had got their drift in some eight or ten feet, when they would take down the thin flake of pipe clay and three or four inches of gravel which would all contain gold.

All the placer mines which I saw were worked in this manner, with few exceptions.

Just before leaving this camp the miners made overtures to the government to require less taxes for the privilege of mining. The tax was thirty shillings a month. The miners wanted it placed at one shilling or nothing. They gathered on a certain day at the Bendago. Numberless flags of various nations were afloat, and the stars and stripes were high above all the others ; even the English flags were outnumbered by the stars and stripes.

This matter was agitated throughout the country, and came near forcing the country into a republic. Every one in the mining regions was well armed, and the miners used to discharge their weapons at night, loading anew, so that if they should have need to use them upon the troops they would be effective. They frequently began to discharge their weapons about four o'clock in the afternoon, and from that time until ten o'clock there would be continual reports from firearms. The shooting was to warn the soldiers in camp what they would have to meet should the government employ force in the collection of the tax.

The leader in this movement went to Melbourne to confer with the authorities regarding abatement of the tax. The miners had the horse which he rode into town shod with gold. The result of his mission was a reduction from thirty shillings to ten shillings.

The English government is something like some of our capitalists, — they will never grant just what the men ask for, but come down a little, just enough to take the curse off. They think that if they comply with the demand to the full extent it will encourage trying again, and then it would virtually be admitting that they were in the wrong, which England, in the treatment of her colonies, will never do.

A day or two before leaving the camp, when coming up through the flat, it began to rain, and seeing a man sheltered under a tree, I took a stand beside him until the shower should pass over. To my surprise, the man proved to be one of my old shipmates from Hobartstown to London. I had last seen him in London, nearly five years previous. He had taken the gold fever like many others and returned to Australia, and, having been one of the lucky ones, had made quite a pile.

Volumes might be written about that camp if the remarkable experiences of the miners could be described; but with all its attractions, not finding gold very plenty, my restless spirit hastened me onward, and I started for the new gold field at Donkey Woman's Gully.

Being told that I could take a short cut in going to Donkey Woman's Gully and save several miles if I would start from Bullock Gully at the head of the Bendago Flat and take a certain course which they gave me, I started that way. My informant said that by so doing I would strike a creek called Jones's Creek, and from there the road was plain through to Donkey Woman's Gully. On this trip I had one of the most wonderful experiences of my life,—an experience which set me thinking upon things and has kept me thinking upon unexplained things ever since. I started with a little bundle of provisions, pick, and shovel, and arrived at Bullock Gully about noon. I did not hurry, since it was my intention to reach Jones's Creek, a distance of fifteen miles, and camp there for the night. I started into the dark forest, whose foliage shut out the sunlight from overhead, which made things appear rather sombre, knowing that no water would be found until reaching the creek. Pushing on, as I thought, in the right direction, and getting a glimpse of the sun now and then, I saw that Old Sol was getting painfully low and yet no creek in sight. As the night drew near the forest became darker until the last glitter of sunlight disappeared, and I realized for the first time that I was lost in a dark forest. I knew by past experiences what that meant in Australia, where there are jungles and scrubs so thick and tangled that I have walked many hundred rods on the top of the scrub without seeing the ground.

There is one of those tangled masses of vines and shrubbery called the Molly shrub, into whose jungles white people have penetrated never to return, and the natives seldom enter them unless hard pressed for food.

These facts crowded themselves unbidden into my mind, and a feeling of terror swept over me from head to foot, and I never felt so utterly forlorn before in my life. Not a bird fluttered in the rich foliage above, neither was there a reptile to ruffle the leaves beneath my feet. A sound from either would have been most welcome. Moving forward a few steps, the cracking of the dry twigs beneath my feet was all that broke the stillness, and that sound sent another thrill of terror through my partly unstrung nerves. I was so completely turned around I could not tell which way I had come, and found myself in utter darkness soon after the sun had set. Stopping to gather a few dry fagots, I soon had a brisk fire, but took good care to scrape all the leaves and dry twigs several feet away from my fire, knowing that if I did not, the forest would soon be on fire, and I had no desire to add to my unpleasant situation. There need be no fear of wild animals, since there was nothing larger than a kangaroo in the country, but where I should find water troubled me not a little. The knowledge of being lost and without water seemed to make my situation seem much worse than it really was. I had enough food to last with care two days, besides, if that gave out, I could find roots; but water I could not extract from the trees, nor could I expect in that dry country and in summer to find it by digging. Water in Australia is one of the greatest deprivations of the people. In the winter the rivers overflow their banks, and in some parts of the country form quite large lakes. By the summer season it has all run off, evaporated, or soaked into the ground, with the exception of a few pools in the depressions along the beds of the stream. It is to these pools that the miners carts their dirt to be puddled out, and to them ranchmen bring herds of sheep and cattle to drink. The ground in summer also becomes dry and hard, and will crack open to many inches in depth.

After starting my fire I ate a little lunch, but my mouth was so dry that I could hardly swallow my food. After sitting by my fire two or three hours pondering over my sad plight and suffering untold agonies with thirst, I took my pipe and filled it to the brim and went to smoking. I thought a smoke would not only cleanse my mouth, but would bring to that locality all the moisture that was in my body. I continued smoking until quite stupefied, and then laid myself down by the fire and slept a little, and dreamt of marble halls and crystal fountains which all vanished on my awakening, leaving nothing but the sombre forest round about. Being awake considerable of the night, I decided to be ready to catch the first glimpses of daylight; and as it grew lighter I began to look around to look for a sunbeam, intending to follow the sun that day, and perhaps, after going the semicircle, I might escape from the forest.

Gazing a little distance into the deep forest, I espied a a large emu, a bird similar to the ostrich. He had seen me and was making off at a rapid gait. It relieved me somewhat to think that he was not lost, since he appeared to know where he was hurrying to. Presently a cow was heard mooing not far away. I had decided the direction before the sound died. Now, with the prospect of escape, rivers of water appeared in the air on every side. Shouldering my kit I made a bee line in the direction from whence came that welcome sound, and after travelling a quarter of a mile I could see out on to a broad meadow, near the middle of which were four or five head of cattle.

Pushing on until nearly at the middle of the meadow, I noticed that the grass was all dry and the ground cracked and parched up. In parts the dry grass was thick and covered the ground from sight, yet all was as dry as an ash bed. Taking my pick I dug into the ground, but could find no signs of moisture. I took one or two steps forward and looked off over the meadow and cried aloud, " Where in the name of God shall I find water ? "

All at once feeling moisture at my feet and looking down, I discovered I was standing in a little puddle of water which nearly covered my shoes. I dropped upon my knees and put out my hands one upon each side of the water, and was bending my head toward the water when, casting my eyes to the right, saw I had put my right hand within six inches of a serpent, which was as large round as my arm and was several feet long. His head, which was as large as my outstretched hand, was partly under water. I did not disturb him, but lay down and took a drink with my head not ten inches from his snakeship, thinking that if he would let me alone I would let him severely alone also. He paid no attention to me, lying perfectly quiet.

After my thirst was quenched, I arose and turned about and started in a direction at a right angle to that which I entered the meadow, crossed the flat and passing over a dry crack at the edge of the flat climbed up a steep bank some ten feet high to the tableland. Soon I saw two men on horseback riding up through the forest, and hailed them. They were on a well-beaten trail. They said that the trail would take me direct to Jones's Creek, which was some four miles distant. Thanking them I continued on, nor did I tell them about being lost, as I felt crestfallen to think I had been making up my mind to spend a few months if not years in the jungle, while so near a well-travelled trail.

It has ever remained a mystery to me how that little puddle of water came to be there, not more than would fill a washtub. The little hollow was full, although there had been no rain for months, and the meadow was dry as all other parts of the country. The ground was so broken with cracks with the heat of the sun that it looked as if it might have been caused by a little earthquake.

I have had a better opinion of snakes since taking that drink with one than I had before. The snake appeared to be ready and willing to share and share alike his cup with me.

Why the water should be at that particular spot and nowhere else, why I came to go in a straight line to it, and, in fact, why I did not discover the water until after I had cried aloud, " Where in the name of God can I find water ? " is beyond my comprehension. Who can tell ?

CHAPTER VIII.

ARRIVAL AT DONKEY WOMAN'S GULLY — RICH DIGGINGS —
A VISIT FROM BUSHRANGERS — A LAZY PARTNER — WHILE
GETTING GOLD PLENTEOUSLY, YET MISSES MANY GREAT
OPPORTUNITIES — BECOMES DISGUSTED AND QUITS THE
CAMP — CONDITIONS IN CALIFORNIAN AND AUSTRALIAN
MINING CAMPS COMPARED — GOES ON A WILD-GOOSE
CHASE FOR GOLD TO CALLAO — RETURNS TO BOSTON —
AGAIN EMBARKS FOR THE GOLDEN GATE OF CALIFORNIA.

ARRIVED at Jones's Creek in the early part of the day,
I met two men who were on their way to Donkey
Woman's Gully. Jones's Creek diggings had been pretty
well worked out. The gold was in large nuggets, as was
the case at Bullock Gully.

Soon after the camp was opened a team loaded with
provisions was being driven along on the banks of the
creek. It being in the early spring and the ground soft,
the cart got stuck, and the driver went back to give a lift
on the wheel, when there he discovered beside the cart
rut a nugget weighing several pounds. The driver soon
got his cart out of the way, and staked out his claim, from
which he took many thousand dollars' worth of gold,
mostly in large nuggets.

We started for Donkey Woman's Gully, arriving in
due time. We camped at the head of the gully, at about
sundown. We built a good fire, and while standing
around it two men on horseback rode up and wanted to
know if we could direct them to Burnt Creek, which
was the name of a camp about two miles from this one.

Stepping out I said, " Yes," and started toward the
trail, one of them riding along by my side. After we

had got some five or six rods from the fire, the one who was with me stopped, and looking back I saw that the other one had got off his horse. The one with me then started back, and that move started me back in double-quick time. In a moment I knew they were bushrangers, or road agents as they are called in this country, mounted highwaymen. On arriving at the fire the fellow that had stopped behind got on to his horse again, and I said, " Now you know where the trail is as well as we do, and you had better be going as quick as you can."

They started in a hurry and galloped up the trail they appeared so anxious to find. Evidently they intended to get me so far away from my two companions that I could not get back before the one with me could with his horse. Then the two could hold up my two friends, rob them, and handle me at their leisure; but my return foiled them in their plans. We learned the next day that two bushrangers had passed up through the camp the day before, and our two nocturnal friends were the same outlaws undoubtedly.

One of the men that came into camp with me joined me as a partner, and at first we went to work in some of the old claims that appeared to be worked out. We found a little new ground and took out some gold. In some of the pits what appeared to be bed rock had been struck. Digging into the bottom a little, I found that it was not the bed rock, but a thin strata of gravel cemented together which made it appear like solid rock, and getting through this cement beneath it found considerable gold. My partner set to work in a claim near me, but I soon found that he did not know gold when he saw it. Going into a hole that he had worked in all day and found nothing, I would pick out nuggets that he had worked over without seeing them. I therefore set him to sinking a shaft, thinking that when he got to the bottom I would work it out while he was sinking another one. While he was sinking the shaft, I went into a little hole that had been sunk through the cement crust which covered the surface in that locality, and which was about eighteen inches deep, before coming to the pipe clay. Here quite a large chamber was excavated, and I found on the bottom a wooden match box and in it a dollar or two in gold. Concluding that the party who had abandoned the claim must have found something, I picked out a cartload of dirt.

We had to cart the dirt from that camp about three miles to one of the water holes to wash it. Getting my dirt carted down and going to work at it, the yield proved three hundred dollars, or fifteen ounces, the gold being worth twenty dollars per ounce. It was twenty three and five eighths carats fine. Upon my return to our claim I found my partner had got his hole down to bottom, and had struck a point of bed rock which appeared to be pitching down into a crevice. I thought of following it down, and yet dared not trust my partner to work in the hole where I had struck gold so rich, knowing that he would throw away more gold than he would take out, so I left the new shaft and called it a shyster. We then went to work at the place where I had struck the metal. A few days later another party went into the shaft that we abandoned and followed the slope at the bottom down a foot or two and struck gold to the tune of two hundred dollars to the cartload; but we were not troubled at our loss, being content with the two or three hundred a day that we were getting.

About half a mile down the flat below where we were at work and at the side of the road that we used to cart our dirt over I had noticed a shaft that had been sunk about ten feet and had gone a few feet into the pipe clay. The shaft had been abandoned, and on several occasions as I passed it I had a desire to enter it and look it over a little, but I did not do so. A large portion of the ground between the shaft and where we were at work was coated over with the cement mentioned. Many had tried to get through it, but found it too hard, and yet it was known that the lode run through the flat. One day a man went into that old and abandoned shaft and with his knife picked out about fifteen hundred dollars in a very short time. When it became known, the miners of the camp all rushed in and staked out claims. I got one, but it proved a shyster. Returning to the old claim I went to work, but did not feel contented with my partner, having to find all the gold and divide equally with him, so interviewed him one day to find out what he had done for a living before coming to the mines. He belonged in Canada, and was sent to the Kaffir war at the Cape of Good Hope and had become lame through the hardships which they had contended with, and on that account was discharged at the Cape. From the Cape he had made his way to the United States in an American man-o'-war, commanded by one Lieut. Hernden. I found that part of his story true later, upon my arrival at Aspinwall on my way home, since Lieut. Hernden was at that time in charge of the steamer "Central America," which plied between Aspinwall and New York. This steamer went down a few years later with Lieut. Hernden and about all on board.

I had got thoroughly worked up over my partner, whom I concluded was a very lazy man rather than a sick one. He grumbled around several days with a tooth-ache, until I told him to go down to the water hole and get the doctor who was camped there to pull it out. He went, and in a day or two afterward said the doctor had pulled out the wrong tooth. I believed he had not seen the doctor at all.

Finally I told him one day that I would take the load of dirt I was getting then down and puddle it out, and then leave the country. He replied that he would go with me. I took the dirt down and in the last hopper of dirt washed out one nugget worth one hundred and fifty dollars, and in all of that load about three hundred dollars. I gave away our tools and claim, and the next morning started for Melbourne. The man to whom I gave the claim said that he did not think he should work it, since he was getting two hundred dollars to the cartload where he was. There was fully two hundred claims unoccupied that would average two hundred dollars to the cartload which I left behind because of a lazy partner. I might have bought him out for twenty-five dollars ; but, knowing that the ground was rich, could not find it in my heart to deceive him or lead him to think I was dissatisfied with him, as he was thoroughly honest and simple-hearted; but I always did hate a lazy man or laziness in any of its many forms.

I turned my face from the claim as we passed by it on leaving camp. Two days later we passed within three miles of a new camp where the miners were taking out fortunes. Old women were making forty and fifty dollars a day picking up gold from the surface of the ground, and many others by hammering the quartz rock and breaking it up and picking out the gold thus liberated ; but all that rich camp did not move me in the least from my resolve. I should have kept on if I had waded to my knees in gold to get out of the mines, so thoroughly disgusted had I become with all mankind and all that was golden. We reached Melbourne.

Many things which I saw and heard while in the wonderful Australian mining country are well worth narrating. Everybody has heard of that celebrated mining camp called Ballarat. Ballarat is sixty miles from Geelong, a little town on the border of the bay of Port Philip. Port Philip is a very large bay or harbor, too wide to see across it in places. The entrance to the bay is not wider than the Golden Gate at San Francisco Harbor. Passing through this passageway and keeping right straight ahead will take you to Melbourne, but to turn to the left a few points will take you to Geelong, which is several miles distant from Melbourne. The coast in nearly all parts of Australia I have visited is very level from the shore back for several miles; hence the country from Geelong to Ballarat and much farther back into the country is very level. These facts are mentioned in order to explain why miners at Ballarat sank their shafts many times below salt water, and again to show how near I was, while lying at Geelong for four months in 1847, taking in wool and tallow for London, and how careful I was not to go ashore lest I be attacked by disease so chronic at that time, and run away.

Only once did I go ashore during the four months that we lay there, and then remained but half an hour. That was the place where I should have run away above all others, for I would probably have gone back into the country far enough to be beyond capture and fell to herding sheep, whose feet were travelling over millions in gold, much of it on the surface. Having a geological tendency, I undoubtedly would have known the difference between a pebble and a nugget of pure gold, and I might have been the man to first start the wandering gold hunters instead of the man at Suttler's Creek, California.

When gold was first struck at Ballarat, there was found a little gully not many hundred yards long which yielded fifteen hundred pounds weight in gold, much of it in large nuggets. This gully ran down into a lengthy flat. Several shafts were run down into the flat, but were abandoned on account of water and the great depth that one had to sink them, as at that time there were plenty of rich claims to be found that were shallow and easily sunk and worked. One day seven English sailors came into camp, and after hearing how rich that little gully had been, they staked out claims on the flat and began sinking their shafts. The commissioners gave them licenses free to encourage them in what was considered a risky undertaking. The sailors put the shaft down something over one hundred feet, and timbered it from the top down as they went, going through salt water. When they struck bottom they took out one tub of dirt, sent it to the surface and puddled it out. They were rewarded with twelve pounds weight of gold. Then the whole flat was soon staked off and alive with miners working like beavers to see who would get down to the rich lode first, which proved to be about three feet wide, running a serpentine course down through the flat, and containing more gold than dirt. There was one nugget taken out of that lode weighing seventy pounds. It was shipped to London in a vessel called the "Alexander," and she foundered off Cape Horn, and is now probably lying at the bottom of the ocean partially held down by that nugget of gold.

After the flat had been about all worked out, there was still one spot on the lode that had not been worked and no one in particular could claim it, but it was for the one who could get to it first, by drifting from their shafts underground, which could be done quicker than by sinking. There were a party of Americans who had a shaft quite near the rich spot that had not been worked. They started to drift in common with many others. They pushed on night and day, and after thirty-six hours of hard work reached the rich spot, finding it as rich as expected. But one poor fellow who had worked thirty-six hours, one hundred and sixty feet under ground, without coming to the surface, came up out of the shaft and going into his tent died in less than a half-hour.

In the early days of the mining excitement the miners would cart a load of dirt and puddle out one tub, and if it did not yield one pound in weight, they would dump the whole load into the water hole and go after another load. In later years parties went into these water holes and cleaned them out, making large fortunes in so doing.

About all of the gullies that were rich had what the miners called surface diggings. The gold in the flats and gullies could be traced out of the gullies where it could be found from the bottom to the surface. After a little rain, I have seen gold laying around on the top of the ground as thick as sowed corn, and much of it quite as large.

The government established an escort with mounted guards, who would carry the miners' gold to town for a certain per cent per ounce. There was also a private escort whose guards were paid by the month, but they were not obliged to defend the treasure to the death, as were the other escorts. The result was that the private escort was held up one day by five masked road agents. The guards fled, and the robbers got six thousand ounces. The robbers were all caught a few months later, and four of them were hung. There was a steamboat laying at the wharf at Melbourne, with passengers aboard for some foreign port. One of the passengers lost a pistol which he thought was stolen, and a search was instituted and the pistol found in a fellow-passenger's berth, and also in the same berth was found a large amount of gold, much of it being identified as the stolen gold from the escort. The passenger was taken ashore and soon confessed, turned queen's evidence, and told who the other four robbers were. They were caught and hung, while the informer went scot-free.

The discovery of gold in Australia did not have the same effect on prices that it did in California in 1848 and 1849. In California dry jerked beef was worth four dollars a pound; flour, one and two dollars a pound; butter, potatoes, and other such food, three dollars a pound; and other things in proportion. One pinch of gold between the thumb and finger was counted one dollar. In Australia in 1847 the best beef and mutton could be bought for one penny a pound, and everything in the country proportionately cheap, labor included. After gold was discovered beef and mutton went up only to sixpence a pound, and labor to five to seven dollars per day, while in California labor was ten to twenty-five dollars per day. The miners in either country did not appear to realize the value of gold when in nuggets or dust, and were reckless in spending it.

One instance which happened in Melbourne shows what effect gold coined and uncoined will produce on some people. A miner came down from the mines to Melbourne, having about five thousand dollars in gold dust, and going into Alvin Adams's express office, — which is a branch of the Adams Express Company, — sold his gold to the company. In payment they counted out sovereigns on the counter, and the pile contained something over one thousand bright round gold pieces. The man was told to take his money. He looked at it, stepped back a little, threw up his arms, and fell dead to the floor. When he realized the value of his gold in the form of money, the surprise was too much for him. The miner looked at gold more as a mercantile commodity than in any other way.

On arrival at Melbourne I met an old California partner who had come to Australia a year previous to my arrival in the country. He had just returned from the mines, where he had not been very successful, and was going to leave the country, and was about to sail for Callao, South America. He said that they had recently made some great discoveries in that country in gold, and the report was that no one who worked in the mines was making less than one thousand dollars a day. He believed these big stories, and I was simple enough to believe them also, and made up my mind to go with him. My partner, my old friend, and myself went aboard of a ship the next day that was going direct to Callao, and we were soon booming away from the land where I had been through gold nearly knee deep to get out of the country. Now I was going to a country where, it afterwards turned out, had been worked almost entirely out nearly a hundred years earlier, and where what few miners were at work were only making two and three dollars a day. We pushed on as fast as wind and water would carry us, without anything serious to record until we had been about three weeks out on our voyage, when, by a painful accident, two men lost their lives.

We were running under a stiff and fair wind, and had been carrying studding sails forward; the sail had been taken in, and two men were on the foreyard arm rigging in, as it is called, the studding-sail boom; casting off the lashing that held it to the yard, the boom tipped up — caused by the heavy roll of the ship — and threw the two men off. One fell on to the anchor, and then fell overboard and sank to rise no more. The other man went overboard apparently unhurt. The ship was immediately hove to, and a life buoy was thrown to the man at the same time. By the time that we got the ship to the wind, she had taken quite a long circuit, which left the man many rods distant from the ship. A boat was lowered and an hour was spent in hunting for him, but without finding him. He was near the life buoy when last seen and must have gotten into it, but we had to square away and leave without him. He was a Scotchman, and weighed nearly two hundred pounds, and was possessed of all the vigorous traits that the Scotch are known to possess. He had one brother on board, and I have often thought about what must have been the brother's feeling when our ship sailed rapidly away, unsuccessful in saving the unfortunate sailor.

Just before we reached our destination we learned that the fever that was supposed to be raging in Callao over the big gold find was really a myth hatched in the fertile brain of the captain and agents of the ship. The ship had brought immigrants to Melbourne and was going to Callao, there to load with wheat for home; and since there was no freight at Melbourne for him, the captain thought it a good idea to fill up the ship with fools, which they did to their entire satisfaction and to the disgust of their dupes. Had we known it soon enough, we might perhaps have baited some big fish, using the captain for the bait.

In good time we arrived in the harbor of Callao. I had when in California learned a little Spanish or Mexican, — a language spoken in almost all parts of South America, — and my knowledge of the language was ever useful to me. After we had dropped anchor the boats from shore came alongside filled with natives, offering fruit and other edibles for sale. I asked them if there was plenty of gold in the country. They shrugged their shoulders, as about all of the Spanish-speaking races do when they have any doubts or wish to evade a direct answer. After being pressed for an answer, one fellow answered that there was a little.

"Well," said I, "how much a day do the miners make?"

"Two and three dollars," said he.

I told my shipmates that was enough for me, and that

I should continue the voyage a little farther. We were soon all ashore and began at once a still hunt for some kind of a place which would be half civilized. After wandering around awhile and tumbling over a lot of buzzards, which appeared to be the scavengers of the place, — and I thought by the appearance of the streets there ought to be a large increase in their numbers, — we found a little place kept by Americans. We put up there for the night, and soon learned there was fever raging at that place so fiercely that it was carrying hundreds to their graves. It was the yellow fever and black vomit. Quite a number of my shipmates succumbed to the dreadful plague.

Feeling rather squeamish one day, I went into a saloon and drank half a tumbler of brandy, and had no further trouble after that dose.

A young American doctor was meeting with much success in his practice. He used nothing but tamarind water; but he, too, at last took the fever, and his skill could not save him, and he was laid away with many others.

Much rain was falling at that time, which caused the fever, it being the first rainy spell for three years. In dry weather the country is very healthy. We were told that there had been a time during which no rain fell for thirty years. There are many rivers flowing down to the coast from the snow mountains of the interior of the country which supply water, and fogs rising from the rivers kept the air in a good and healthy condition.

Callao was in a very dilapidated state. The people had not done much toward rebuilding the city since old Callao was sunken, many years since. Along the beach the tops of many of the old stone houses rose out of the sand, and the present inhabitants were digging out the stones to rebuild again. In the middle of the town was an old tomb, the sides of which were open to hogs, dogs, and buzzards alike, and exposing hundreds of human bones to view. Having some curiosity to see the inside, I got down on my hands and knees and went in, being received amid profound silence. There were no curiosities I cared to take away with me. The bones were very dry, and no doubt many of them had been entombed a hundred years or much longer.

Going up to Lima, the capital of Peru, I found that place much worse than Callao, with narrow and very filthy streets. I did not remain there long enough to take in the sights, only staying half an hour, but in that short time saw enough, but little of interest to relate. Returning to Callao, the following day the English steamer came in from Chili, and I took passage on her for Panama. Finding my money getting low, I worked my passage to Panama, and arrived at that place in good time. Before going ashore, I helped to take out of the steamer's hold one million dollars' worth of gold and silver, which was brought down from Chili. After that I told the captain my contract was at an end, and he let me go ashore. There I learned that we would either have to wait a week at Panama or at Aspinwall, or Colon, the proper name of the place. At Panama we could get nothing to eat except fried bananas, so we started for Colon. We walked a part of the way until reaching the railroad, which was then in process of construction at that time. We reached the railroad about three o'clock, A. M., and took the train. The railroad officials saw us long before we got to the railroad, and they waited nearly half an hour for us to arrive. They made up for lost time, however, when we got aboard, and we reached Aspinwall in a very short time.

In Aspinwall I soon found a good boarding-house, run by an American, who also ran a little vessel, trading among the islands, and he was therefore able to furnish his table with all that a hungry man could wish for, at seven dollars per week.   About a week after, the steamer from New York came in, and the boat from San Francisco arrived at Panama ; the passengers from San Francisco soon arrived at Aspinwall and were soon on board the New York steamer.   The steamer from New York was the old " George Law," and she was afterwards altered over a little, and her name changed to the " Central America."   She was a very old boat and hardly fit for the sea in heavy weather, knowing which her owners caused the reconstruction and the change of name, in order to renew her youth.   My Australian partner found in command the old friend and captain with whom he came to the United States from Capetown, Lieut. Hernden, and, through old acquaintance, got a free passage to New York.   It may be remembered that I stated this boat foundered at sea a few years later, and about all on board, including Lieut. Hernden, were lost.

My fare was eighty dollars from Aspinwall to New York, where we arrived in good time.   Taking ten dollars, I left my gold dust with my partner to be assayed in New York and exchanged into coin, and started for Boston, arriving there safe, sound, and right side up.

Having told my partner where he could find my uncle in Boston, two days later I met him with my uncle on the streets hunting for me.   He had with him my coin and the assay certificate which showed that the gold was twenty-three and five eighths carats fine, and worth $20.01 per ounce.   Twenty-four carats fine is pure gold.

I remained at home about four months, ample time for me to spend what few hundred dollars I had brought home with me.   What became of my partner I knew not and cared very little, since but for him I might have been at that time at Donkey Woman's Gully taking out hundreds of dollars daily, since the few miners left behind could not work the camp out under two years.

I was at my brother's office in Boston one day, and taking up the morning paper noticed an item which stated that the fare from Boston for San Francisco was thirty dollars, and going at once down to the office, bought a ticket and engaged one for one of my brothers. I returned home and notified my brother, and the next day we started for New York. We learned the next morning after buying my ticket that the opposition steamer at Panama had been bought off, and the fare raised to sixty dollars, but we got ours for thirty dollars.

CHAPTER IX.

TAKES PASSAGE FOR CALIFORNIA WITH BROTHER JIM — SEA-
SICKNESS — INFATUATION WITH FAIR VOYAGERS — VARY-
ING PASSIONS CAUSED BY LOVE AND JEALOUSY — POLLY,
FRANCES, AND MARY JANE — ARRIVAL AT SAN FRANCISCO
— FINAL LEAVETAKINGS AND DISILLUSIONS.

ON arrival in New York my brother and I were not
long in finding the boat which was to take us to Aspinwall. We soon got aboard, and as our tickets bore the
numbers of our berths we were not long in finding them.
We found that each section contained four double
berths, two occupants to each berth. Our numbers
called for an upper double berth. They were supplied
with a mattress, a pillow, and a cotton quilt. The partition board that divided the upper berth was about six
inches wide. I felt a little anxious about who was to
occupy the berth by our side, since it would be nearly
equal to the old fashion of bundling all in one bed. My
brother was somewhat dissatisfied when he found that the
accommodations were not the same as they were on the
Sound steamer. He called the berths rough pine boxes,
and hardly fit for a dog to sleep in. He had not
travelled far in this wide world, and therefore was not
very well posted. I told him that he had better occupy
the outside of the berth, and he readily assented to the
arrangement.

I thought, since the occupant of the other berth would
be near neighbors, we must be either friends or enemies;
and that if my next-door neighbor should be inclined to
cause trouble, I had better be the one it should be with,
rather than my brother. We had not as yet met the

party who was to occupy the next berth, so could not tell what might happen on the other side of the house.

Soon after leaving the wharf the vessel began to tremble and roll, and my brother began to look pale. He was beginning to inhale Neptune's bracing air, and I knew that he soon would be on his beam ends, where he would stay until he got what sailors call sea legs.

Presently I saw two moving objects on the opposite side of our section. One of them scanned the number of the berth and nodded her head. I had seen enough to convince me that one was a woman, and being curious about her companion, I stepped out where both could be seen, and discovered that both wore petticoats. Much relieved, I yet thought there might be a big brother somewhere about, so hesitated about letting them know who their neighbors were. Just then a low groan came from my brother, who sat on a box that some one had placed in front of our berth. His elbows were resting on his knees and he held his head in his hands.

"Hulloa, Jim," said I, "what is up? Is anything the matter with you?"

He cast a sorrowful look at me and said, —

"O Jack, matter is no name for it. Did you ever see a fox skinned?"

"Yes," said I, "they pull the body through the mouth."

"Well," said he, "that is just the way I feel"; and the next development in his case proved that he spoke truthfully.

"Come," said I, "I guess you had better go up above"; and by dragging and carrying him got him on deck, but his legs were sort of tangled and twisted, and refused to carry him. I therefore pulled him along to a settee, where he fell into a shapeless heap.

"Come, Jim," said I, "pull yourself together and take a

view of this beautiful landscape. It will be some time before you have an opportunity to look upon it again."

He cast his eyes toward the shore which we were fast leaving behind, and I left him awhile to drink in the beauties of the scene so lavishly spread out before him.

I went down directly to our berth, and noticed that the other party had got their side of the berth pretty well piled up with a mixed lot of feminine articles, consisting of bandboxes, bundles, and carpetbags. They were piled so high that one of them had fallen over the narrow board partition on to my side. Reaching out, I picked the bundle up, and was just about to push it back over the fence, when one of the ladies who claimed the berth arose. As she stood head and shoulders above the things in the berth, in full view, I was spellbound. Such a head of hair, black as a raven, which hung in luxuriant ringlets over her well-rounded shoulders, with a few little curls over a high, broad forehead. Her eyes, shaded with dark lashes, seemed aflame, with every movement bringing out a hidden lustre from those dark orbs to reveal the emotions of the soul at every flash, while her brow looked like a beautiful cloud above a setting sun. A goddess might wish for her nose, and her lips were like a June rose just putting forth its beauty to the world. All these attractions completed by a dimpled chin just double enough to give a little fulness, and you have the face complete.

She reached out her hand, which was a marvel of beauty, with slender fingers bedecked with jewels, and gracefully received the bundle, saying, " Me bundy, me bundy."

Thinking she was trying to tell me that we would have to bundle, I blared out something like, "Yes, yes, me too."

She smiled in return and said, " Mon Dieu."

Again thinking she was trying to find out how many were to occupy my berth, and had put the cart before the horse, as many foreigners do who cannot speak English well, saying instead of two men, man two, so I blurted out, hardly knowing what I said, —

"Yes, two of us. One is on deck nearly dead; and if you say so I will go up at once and throw him overboard, if you have any objections to the third party."

She smiled and said, "Vous nous parlez Français."

I concluded she meant Polly and Frances, meaning presumably that her name was Polly and her companion's Frances.

I said, "Yes, Polly, and if you want me too, I will soon fix the other fellow, although he is my brother."

She sprang up a little higher and said, "Oui, oui, me brother, me brother." And I thought after all she might have a big brother on board and that to be met later, but not wishing to be kept in suspense, asked if she had a brother on board.

She answered, "Me brother, Frisco."

I concluded after she had repeated this several times that she wished me to be her brother until we reached San Francisco, so I answered, "Yes, certainly I will be that and more, or I am a Dutchman."

"Bon bon," she said as she felt of the mattress.

I thought she was trying to tell me how hard the mattress was, and that our bones would ache.

"Yes, indeed, it will be hard on our bones ere we get to the end of our trip, but I can stand it if you can," I said.

She smiled and sank out of sight behind the berth, while I silently offered up thanks that kind fate had brought the star of my destiny to view.

I had travelled over many rough seas and foreign lands, had met some of Britain's four hundred, and had danced and frolicked with titled dames on the islands, had dined with kings and queens, but never before had I met a star of sufficient magnitude to entrance my soul. Now I could shout, " Eureka."

Finally I pulled myself together, and then wondered what my poor brother on deck, sick enough to die, would think of me for so long neglecting him.

I hurried on deck, thinking now the ice was broken, content to trust to time and circumstances to reveal the hidden future.   My brother was looking much better.

" Hulloa, Jim," said I, " how do you feel now ? "

" Oh, much better, Jack ! "

" That is good, you will soon be well again.   Come, let us go below, the steward will soon ring his bell for dinner."

" Don't say dinner to me.   It makes me sick to think of food, let alone eat it.   I have got rid of all that I have eaten for the last month."

" Well," said I, " you have plenty of room to accommodate a good hearty dinner."

He thought he would have to feel better than he was then before he could care for food.

" Why, you said that you felt better, and I thought that meant nearly well ; but never mind, old boy, let us go below, and I'll tell you about our next-door neighbors."

" Have you seen them ? " he asked.

" Yes, and do you believe it, they are young ladies."

" Is that so ? " he asked.

" Yes, and one of them is an angel."

" Well, and the other one ; you have seen both of them, have you not ? "

" No and yes ; that is, I have seen the face of one of them and caught a glimpse of the other, but the one that has the inside of the berth is a beauty, that is, if I observed her aright, and I think I did."

"Think!" he interrupted, "don't you know whether you did or not?"

"Well, no; you see they are French, at least the one I talked with or tried to talk with is."

I went on: "If you can engage the attention of the other one, why things will be quite pleasant you know, something to relieve the monotony of the voyage. Again, you will have some one to help you on deck when you feel a little sick."

"Ah, you mean to forsaké me!" he said, "and turn me over to a strange woman, one who cannot understand a word of English or speak a word either. What kind of a fellow do you take me for? Has your angel turned your head?"

"No," I replied, "but French is easy to learn."

"How do you know that it is?" asked he.

"Why, I have learned some already. You know we descended from the Corbins, and they were French, so you see that it is the French blood that is in our veins that makes it easy for us to. learn the French language. You would soon be able to understand her."

"Well, you seem to take it for granted that I am sure to please and be pleased with her, and yet we never set eyes on each other. Perhaps, since you know so much, you will act as interpreter."

"Yes, Jim, I will do all that I can to help you."

"How do you know that I would care for her?"

"Because one is so handsome, the other must be also."

"Well, you know roses grow amidst thorns and hedges; but I will take a look at her anyway, since we have got to be neighbors for a week or two."

At that moment the bell rang for dinner.

"Now," said I, "let us go below, but I want no love-making from you or anybody else, since there is but one brother mixed up with Polly, unless she happens to have one in California, then things might be a little different. If there is to be a fight, I would rather it would be at the other end of the journey."

We hurried along, and soon got on the steps that led to the mess deck. When about half-way down, where we could look over the heads of those below, who were crowding toward the table, I saw Polly's black head and flowing ringlets. Just then she stepped out of the jam.

"There," I cried, "there she is ! "

"There is who ? " said Jim.

"Why, Polly."

"What, the one with the black hair?"

"Yes," I replied.

"Well, she has a very pretty face, that is a fact, but I should think that she must have come over in the 'Great Eastern,' since no other boat could accommodate her."

Pretending to look the other way, I yet saw enough to convince me that what my brother said was true.

"Oh, well," said I, " she can't help her great growth."

"Growth," said he, " she is built up. Nature could not work such a miracle ; she is built up, I say."

She certainly did look a little that way I must confess. Being all one size from her shoulders to her feet, one could not tell where her waist was.

We found the tables well filled. "Well," said I, "there is no chance for us at these tables, let us go over to our berth and wait for the next table."

In getting to our berth, we passed by Polly's section, and as we came opposite it, saw her companion looking out of the ventilator in the side of the boat.

" Now, Jim," said I, " here is your chance, while Polly is at dinner. You know that it would be ungallant not to get acquainted with your neighbor."

Having aroused his curiosity, and knowing his fond

ness for female company when at home, I believed he would not need much urging. Not believing in eavesdropping, I slipped around to our berth and sat down. I was too far away to be one of the party, and yet too near not to hear what was said, and my curiosity being a little aroused to know how he got along, I listened and heard my brother say,—

"Good morning, madam."

Then there was a rustling of feminine furbelows, and a squeaking voice said, —

"Me Frances, no speak English."

Upon hearing which, my brother answered,—

"Oh, excuse me, I think I have made a mistake and come to the wrong berth!"

He quickly dodged around the corner to where I sat.

"Why," said I, "it did not take you long to break the ice."

"Ice indeed," said he, "straight from the north pole." ·

"For goodness' sake, tell me what she said," said I.

"She said enough to condemn her in my eyes if she had been an angel in other respects; she called me a speckled Englishman."

"Why," answered I, "you must be mistaken, she surely did not say that."

"But she did. I never want to set eyes on her again."

"Bah! I understand the whole plot now. You have met her on board before, and have told her that you were an Englishman and were going to California to speculate; and of all your fine story the only thing that she could remember, was 'speculate' and 'Englishman.'"

"Jack, you know better than that. I never laid eyes on her before, and never want to again."

"Well, then, tell me how she looks in the face; can't you describe her a little?"

"Great Scot," said he, "it would take a better mathematician than I to figure out that face. If you are so very anxious to know how she looks, go around and have a look at her."

Just then Polly returned from dinner, and seeing me gave me a pretty little nod which set those pretty curls romping over her beautiful shoulders. My heart gave a leap in response, as Polly passed into the slip between the sections.

Soon after the bell rang again for the next table. As we came out of our slip, Franky was a little in advance of us. Pushing on after her, I urged my brother to hurry, since if we missed that table we would not get much to eat at the third.

When we reached the table there were but three plates not taken. Franky took one, and I pushed my brother up to the one next her, I taking the remaining one. After helping the lady next to me, I looked to see how my brother got on. He stood with knife and fork in hand and a vacant stare in his eyes.

"Come, Jim," said I, "ain't you going to help the lady?"

He paid no attention to me, but drove his fork into a large piece of meat that had a great bone in it and placed it on her plate, piled on two large potatoes and slid a piece of bread alongside of her plate; then he cast his eyes over the table to see if there was anything else he could help her to, but failing to find anything more, laid down his knife and fork, and with one look at me, at the same time pointing to the deck above, vanished from the table.

The one look he gave me was long enough for me to see fire in his eye, and forebode trouble. Since my brother's departure was so abrupt, I turned to learn the cause; and as Franky was so near, I could inspect her at short range. My brother had not overdrawn the picture, had not even told all the truth. Her head was smaller than the average, and was covered with a thin growth of grizzly gray hair. She had a low rusty forehead, with two holes sunk deep beneath shaggy eyebrows. Two little round black spots at the bottom of those caverns might be seen, which shone like cats' eyes at night. Below was a long nose with numerous bends and curves, and the end turning up abruptly ; and a mouth that looked like a chasm. Her form I am unable to describe, for I, too, was content to turn away as he had done. I soon drew out of the fight for mush and molasses, leaving Franky still at the table wrestling with what my brother had given her. I went on deck at once and found my brother sitting on one of the settees, looking out over the blue waters, with his thoughts probably turned far away to the happy home he had left behind.

"Hulloa, Jim, what is the matter? Are you dreaming of the sweet by and by? Come, stir around a little and settle your dinner so that you will have an appetite for supper."

"Dinner did you say?" said he ; "well, I am glad you have found a name for it ; I should call it the remains of a butcher's graveyard."

"How is that, Jim, was there not a plenty?"

"Yes, plenty of bones."

"Well," said I, "you disposed of one large bone, and if you had remained a little longer you might have disposed of a lot more in the same manner."

"Look here, Jack, this thing has gone far enough ; you have steered me long enough. I propose not only to paddle my own canoe, but to steer it after this, and don't you forget it."

"Well, Jim, I will try awful hard not to forget it."

I came to the conclusion that he was getting bravely

over his seasickness, and perhaps I had gone far enough with my jokes. We had been on deck then about two hours and had got pretty well aired, so I said, —

"All right, Jim, but remember, if you run against a snag you must not blame me."

"You need not trouble yourself," said he; "if I am not old enough to look after myself, I will hire some one to take care of me."

"Well," said I, "let us go below."

We started at once for the berth deck, and on passing our neighbors found that Franky had returned from dinner, and she and Polly were having a lively argument in their own language. On catching sight of us, Polly nudged her companion and pointing to us said, "Brother, brother."

"Yes," said I, "brothers and two of us."

Then she pointed to herself and said, "Me brother, Frisco, me brother, Frisco."

"Yes, yes," said I, "glad to hear that."

Following my brother, who had got around the corner to our berths, I asked, "What do you think, Jim, that Polly says?"

"What the deuce do you think or suppose I care what your poll parrot says?"

"Why, Jim, she says that she has a brother in Frisco that is a millionnaire."

"Well, what of that, what do you suppose I care if he owns the whole State of California?"

"Well, you know we might not have to go to the mines."

"Do you know, Jack, that I don't think I shall go to the mines anyway; for if I ever get to the country alive, I shall leave at once to get back home, even if I have to walk the whole distance across the continent barefoot and alone."

"Oh, no, Jim, I would not allow you to do that."

"And pray what would you do about it?" asked he.

"I would not be so mean as to allow you to walk a journey of three thousand miles, if I had a million dollars behind me."

"Yes, I think it is behind you and a long way behind you, and likely to remain there."

"Well, Jim, I don't know about that. Polly and I are pretty good friends, and she wanted me to be her brother until we reached Frisco, and you know something might happen so that I would be more than her brother."

"Yes, I have no doubt she will want a coachman, and of course you will then want a tall plug hat; be careful and not get one that is too large for you; if you did, it might slip down over your eyes and blind you, and you are blind enough now. I think you may well say that something might happen if she has a big brother in Frisco."

"Oh, well, Jim, you know that is my lookout."

"Well, Jack, since you have such lofty ideas and hopes, what do you intend to do with that companion of your Polly? You would not want her hanging on to your coat tails, would you?"

"Well, no, but you see I have got that all planned out long ago. You see there are not many women in California, and there are plenty of rich men who would like to get married if they could find any one who would marry them, and you know that a drowning man will catch at a straw."

"A straw indeed! If they take her for a straw they will think that they have got the devil's reaper thrown in, in order to give good measure."

"Oh, no, Jim, you are too hard on the poor lady; she isn't to blame for her bad looks any more than you are for yours."

"Do you think there is any comparison between us?" he asked; "because if I thought there was a particle, I would jump overboard this minute."

"Oh, no, Jim, I did not mean that; I meant that she was not to blame for her looks any more than you or anybody else are."

"Well," said he, "I am glad that you chose the side of the berth you did, and I only wish that my side was a mile farther away than it is."

"Why, Jim, you will not be very near them long."

"I would sooner sleep on a bed of thorns than to sleep where you will have to for the next two weeks, and perhaps longer, if the berths are arranged the same on the steamer the other side of the isthmus."

"Well, Jim, you know that the most beautiful roses bloom amongst thorns and hedges."

"Rose indeed! I should call it a cauliflower, with a hamper of greens thrown in."

"Well, you know, Jim, that it is quite natural for mankind to want to get all that they can for the money invested. Now as to Franky, Polly can fix her up a little. You know that the French are skilled with the brush and paint."

"Yes, Jack, you may well say paint, and you might add a few pounds of putty. I think that they would find room for it on her face, and I also think that your Polly has a good supply of both articles now."

"I hope you don't mean to insinuate that there is anything artificial about Polly, do you?"

"Well, you may have a chance to find that out before morning, especially after she has made her toilet."

"Well, Jim, I think that we had better go on deck, since it is quite bedtime, and you know that gentlemen ought not to be present when ladies are making their toilets, especially the first night at all events. I mean not so soon after an introduction, but things might be different later on you know."

We soon went on deck and left the ladies to themselves to arrange their toilet after their own fashion, undisturbed by us.

After we had found a seat I began to quiz my brother, as he had scared me a little. He was much better posted in the ways of women than I, notwithstanding I had seen more of the world than he.

"Oh, Jim," I began, "what makes you think there is anything wrong with Polly?"

"I don't say there is anything wrong about her, but I think that those curls that you so much admire are a little too fresh for one of her age."

"Indeed, Jim, why, she told me that she was twenty-five."

"Come now, I think you have got the figures a little mixed; I think to reverse them would be a little nearer the mark."

"What," said I, "you do not mean to say that she is fifty-two?"

"Well, that is about right. You say that the French are skilled with the brush and paint, and perhaps you know what that lot of little boxes and bottles and other notions Polly took out of her bag contained. Well, they might contain paint enough to paint the White House at Washington."

"Well, you know, Jim, that when ladies are travelling on a long journey they carry a lot of cologne and other articles which are necessary for their toilet, and it is not supposed that men will know all about such things."

"Well, Jack, it would perhaps be better if they did know more about such feminine truck; if they did there would not be quite so many men making asses of themselves, as you have done, when they see a pretty face."

I felt the blood leap into my face, but it was too dark for him to notice it. He turned that moment and put his head over the rail and gazed over into the dark blue waters. As his last words left his lips a thousand demons seemed to hold me in their grasp, and my first impulse was to catch him by the legs and suddenly hurl him headlong into the ocean. I knew that it was too dark for any one to see me, and also that the wheels were cutting and slashing the water into a white foam but a little way behind where he would strike the water, and when they reached him they would soon grind him up. I bent over and grasped him by the legs, but in doing so my head came in contact with some one who had just come along. I sprang up, and there in the twilight stood Polly. She recognized me at once, and held out that pretty jewelled hand. I grasped it and she said, " Brother."

I said, " Yes, Polly, and you are an angel. You have saved my brother from a watery grave and myself from the gallows."

It was quite late, so we all soon went below.

I found that Polly did not hesitate to make her toilet in our presence. She simply threw off her shawl and retired. I soon thereafter threw off my coat and vest and took to my berth, not more than six inches on the weather side of Polly, but there was a board six feet long and six inches wide between us. Overhead I noticed there were some strips of boards nailed from beam to beam, which formed a temporary rack to hold passengers' baggage. Polly had the rack well filled, and in the lot was a little sunshade nicely wrapped in its case. Thinking of nothing in particular, yet being uneasy, I became absorbed in gazing on that article. I tossed and rolled over some fifty times, troubled not a little to think how near I came to becoming a murderer. After a while I fell into a broken slumber and was soon dreaming. In my dream I was on deck leaning over the ship's side with a long pole in my hands; there below me was my brother in the water grasping at everything he could see, while I was pushing him with the pole trying to keep him under water, and telling him to go below and see what he could find there, but, like Hamlet's ghost, he would not down. Finally he made one desperate struggle and grasped the pole and jerked it out of my hands. The shock was so great that it nearly pulled me overboard, and I jumped to save myself, and in so doing awoke.

I glared around with a vacant stare, and there sat Polly bolt upright in bed. She looked as if she thought she was being murdered in cold blood. She pointed at the sunshade, then at me, and then at herself. I discovered at once I had got her sunshade down and was punching her in the ribs with it instead of my brother.

I explained to her that it was all a mistake and a dream.

She said, " Mon Dieu!" and curled down under the coverlet again.

My brother woke up and wanted to know what in thunder I was trying to do. I told him I was dreaming, and thought we had landed in Frisco, and that we were out with a party for a few days of sport and fishing. In my dream I had just hooked a large salmon and was trying to land him, but that he was too much for me and had pulled the pole out of my hands, and I supposed that I had got Polly's sunshade for a pole.

" Yes, I think it is more likely that you were fishing for angel fish and hooked a whale," said my brother.

" Oh, well, it is all right now!" said I, and hid myself under the quilt and was quiet again.

I managed to get a few cat naps, but did not try to keep my brother down or to catch any more fish.

In the morning I was up and dressed at the break of day and went on deck at once.   Not caring to see Venus rise that morning, I remained on deck until the third table was rung for breakfast, which consisted of water and corn meal well mixed.   After partaking sparingly of my frugal repast, I went below and found everything serene as if nothing had happened to disturb them from their slumbers.   Things passed off that day and the night also without any mishaps.

One day when we had been out about a week and I considered myself Polly's best friend, I saw her go to the table with a large dark-looking fellow.   He seemed to be pouring his soft talk into her ears, and she appeared to be a willing listener, and was all smiles.   The green-eyed monster, jealousy, had me by the ear at once. Crouching along toward the table, I nearly broke my neck as I tumbled over one of the colored waiters.

" Take care, massa," said he.

" Get out of my way," I replied, passing on.

Polly and her companion soon reached the table, when the only vacant place was the third beyond them, and there were five men after that, but I gave an extra leap and came in ahead.

Polly and her friend had a good deal to say, but it was all in French.   How I wished that in my younger days I had learned French in my leisure hours, instead of playing marbles !   Finishing my dinner, I went directly on deck, thirsting for French blood.

On reaching the deck I met a young lady face to face whose uncle was taking her to California, thinking, perhaps, that she might marry there or get work.   I had spoken to her a few times before, but not often.   On those occasions she appeared to want to prolong the interview, and I would linger, since she was a very pretty girl and entertaining; but when Polly appeared, I would gracefully draw away, not wishing to see any hair pulling on my account.

On seeing her, I thought of a plan whereby Polly might be won back. Not knowing her name, I called her Mary Jane.

"Good morning, Mary Jane," said I.

"Why, Australia, how do you do?"

She had learned that I had been in Australia, so used to call me by that name.

"Oh, I am pretty well!" I replied, and then asked her how she was.

"Oh, splendid!"

"That is good. I have not seen much of you lately, Miss Mary."

"No, I have kept below a good deal of late; but the weather is so delightful now that I thought I would spend more time on deck."

I led her along to a settee and said, —

"Come, be seated."

She sat down, and I took a seat beside her.

"Now, Australia, I want to ask you a question," said she.

"Well, ask away, I am all attention."

"Well, who is that black-eyed girl whom I have seen you so much with, and at the table you are always by her side?"

My cunning did not leave me at this critical time.

"Well," said I, "it is a long story to tell you before you will understand the situation."

"Oh, do tell, it must be quite a romance, and with such a charming heroine too!"

"Not much of a romance, but quite singular that we should meet as we did. You see, I was born in France, and at the age of nine my mother died. I had one sister who was five years younger than myself. Well, we had an old servant who used to boss father a good deal, and after mother died she wanted to get what property father had into her own hands, so she made father marry her."

"Why, I should not think that your father need to have married her if he did not want to."

"But you see, she was boss, and so she made father marry her. She always took to my sister, I suppose because she was so handsome, but father and I had to catch it. One day she was dressing down father, and I knew that my turn would come next, so tucking my cap under my arm, slipped out of the back door and started down the street that led to a wharf. There was a large ship laying alongside, and a lot of people on the wharf, some of them going on board. Well, when I got there I went aboard with the rest, and pretty soon found that we were going down the river and I could not get ashore, so sat down on a box and began to cry."

"Poor boy, you must have felt bad."

"Yes, but I was to blame for going aboard."

"Yes, but you did not know."

"No, I did not know, but I soon found out to my sorrow. Presently an old sailor came along and said, 'What is the matter?' I told him that I wanted to go home. 'Where is your home?' said he. When I told him, he said that I should have thought of that before, and that it would be a long while before I saw home again; that they were not going to stop to put a kid like me ashore. He then told me they were going to Australia, and that I would have to go with them. I saw him go to the mate, and pretty soon the mate came to me and put his hand on my head and said, 'Look up here, little man, and tell me how you came aboard of this ship.' I told him as I had done the sailor. 'Well, don't cry,' said he, and he led me aft to the captain. The captain looked me over and said something to the mate. Turning to me the mate said, ' You will have to stay with us. Now go forward and be a good boy.' I went forward and was a good boy until we reached Swan River in Australia, and then I was a bad boy and ran away."

" Why, what made you run away in that wild country?"

" Well, because I liked the shore better than I did the ship."

" I have been told that the people in that country are wild. Is that so?"

" Yes."

" And that they don't wear any clothing in that country either. Is that so?"

" Oh, no; it is only the natives who don't wear any clothing."

" Do the white folks let them come around to their houses?"

" Oh, yes, the natives have access to all of the settlers' houses, and sometimes they are allowed to sit at the same table."

" Oh, I should not like that, although I should not want to hurt the poor creatures."

" Many of our best artists go out there to study the natives."

" Why, what do they do that for?"

" Well you see the nude in art is a microcosm in the eye of the artist. You see, when they get this world down to a minimum they can study their subject much better, and out there they find plenty of subjects to pose for them."

" I suppose that you learned to talk native."

" Oh, no, I spent most of my time learning English, and, do you believe it, soon forgot all of my French, so that when I left the country I could not speak a word of French."

" Wasn't that too bad?"

" Yes, indeed, since it would be of much value to me now. Well, after being in the country several years, I began to long for home, so one day seeing a ship that was going to London, I shipped in her."

"Wasn't you sorry to leave that country where you had lived so long?"

"Yes, but I wanted to see my father and sister, but I did not care about seeing my step-mother."

"No, I should not think you would."

"Well, I shipped and went to London and got there all right. You see London is like all other large cities, a good place to spend money in. After getting paid off, I had more money than I had ever seen before."

" Didn't they have any money in Australia?"

" No, not any to speak of. Well, I soon spent what I had in sight-seeing, and when I got ready to go home I did not have money enough to take me there, so thought I would ship and go to the United States, and landed in Boston. Somehow after getting ashore I got lost."

" Yes, I have heard that strangers get lost in Boston very often."

" Yes, I did, and night came on and found me wandering around, when all at once a policeman had me by the collar and wanted to know what I was loafing around for. I told him that I wanted to find a boarding-house, whereupon he told me to go with him and he would find me one."

" Well, did he find you one?"

" Yes."

" Oh, how kind he was!"

" Yes the bluecoats are very kind, it is a part of their duty you know to care for everything and everybody they think lost. Well, I stopped at that house over night, and the next morning went down to the wharf. I found that my ship had sailed and left me behind, so went back to the boarding-house, and met a young man there who took to me like a brother and I took to him, for, having no brother, I was glad to find one in him. There were a good many at the boarding-house who were going to California, and my friend was one of them. He wanted me to go; and as I had no money, he bought two tickets, and we came on to New York and came aboard this ship. Now comes the strangest part of my story. As I stood by the side of my berth, I saw a lady on the other side, and at the first glance thought I should faint. I thought that my mother had risen out of her grave to upbraid me because I did not go home and see my father and sister. I soon saw that it was no spirit, but real flesh and blood. Hearing her talking French, I knew that it was my sister, left at home a little girl."

"Bless my soul, wasn't it strange that you should get a berth so near to hers?"

"Yes, it was fate and nothing else. I soon saw her companion, and then I was sure that the other was my sister, for her companion was my old step-mother."

"The old lady whom I have seen with her?".

"Yes; when I recognized my sister, I wanted to fly into her arms; but after I saw my step-mother, I thought best not to reveal myself to them. Knowing neither would recognize me, I concluded to get acquainted with my sister, and then I would be a brother and protector until we reached San Francisco, where I would get an interpreter and make myself known to her. You see, I thought this plan the best, not wanting to make a scene on board, and she, poor thing, does not know that her brother is alive."

"Then the man with you is not your real brother, but simply a friend, that is all. Well, do you know that I have taken quite a fancy to him?"

"No, I did not know it."

"Yes, and I think he is quite handsome. Does he know that Polly is your real sister?"

"No, I will give him a grand surprise when we get to Frisco, and then when he finds that she is my real sister, he might think a good deal more of her." I saw Mary Jane's eyes flash fire in a moment as I said this. I went on: "Now, Miss Mary, do not say anything to my friend or brother, as I call him, because if you did it would be no surprise, you know, when I lifted the veil in San Francisco."

"No, I won't mention it," she said.

I knew she would not before she said it, for she showed her thoughts in her eyes plain enough.

Just at that moment I saw Polly's head rise above the hatchway. I wanted her to see me with Mary Jane without letting her know that I was aware she was observing us, so I pointed out over the water to some birds that sat on the water, and was trying to explain to her the difference between them and a goose. When getting as far as goose, I felt a light hand laid on my shoulder, and turning around said, --

"Why, here is Polly now."

I could see that I had kindled quite a brisk fire in Polly's eyes. I wanted to introduce them in such a way that each would think that I was the brother of the other girl, so jumped up and held out my hands to each and said, "Mary, Polly, my sister." They smiled, clasped hands and embraced each other. How I wished at that moment that I was Mary Jane instead of the lying cur that I was, dogging after two girls and deceiving both! Well, I left them to enjoy their blissful ignorance, and went below to my berth, where I found my brother poring over a paper that was a week old.

"Hulloa, Jim," said I, "what is there that is news? What are the latest quotations on Wall Sreet?"

"Well," said he, "I think that some of your late investments have sunk far below par, since I saw you not long ago trying to make a new deal."

I knew at once that he had seen me on deck with Mary Jane.

"Oh," said I, "I suppose you are alluding to Mary Jane as my new deal. Now, Jim, I don't care much about Mary Jane, because I am solid with Polly you know, although she is a deuced pretty girl, and I thought that, since you are a little bashful, I would just break the ice a little for you."

"Well, you need not trouble yourself about me."

"Well, Jim, you know it would be quite pleasant to have some one with whom you could pass away a few happy moments. Do you know, she told me she had taken quite a fancy to you."

"Did she say that though?"

"Yes, and that was not all she said either."

"Well, what else did she say about me?"

"Well, Jim, she said she thought you handsome."

He laid down his paper and got up and looked into a three-cent glass that hung on the wall and began to brush his hair a little, trying to make himself presentable. I began to think I was telling him too much, not knowing just how things would turn with Polly.

"There is but one thing," I went on to say, "that I do not like."

"What is that, pray, that you don't like about her?"

"Well, you know that she has a funny name."

"What of her name? I am sure that Mary is a pretty name, nothing the matter with that."

"But you have not got it all."

"Well, Mary Jane then; nothing wrong with that either, is there? Quite poetical."

" Well, yes," I replied, " but you know she has red hair, and you know that I always admired black."

" Well, who cares what you admire ? You are not every-body by any means ! "

" Then again," I went on, " she is very young."

He turned again to the little glass and pulled two or three gray hairs out of his flowing locks.

" And again," said I, " red-haired girls always want to ride behind a white horse, and you might not be able to get a white horse in San Francisco."

" Well," said he, " I would ten times rather have a white horse on my hands than a white elephant."

I found that my brother was paying me back with compound interest, so stopped at once.

We had now arrived at Aspinwall. We soon landed and boarded the steam cars, which were to take us to Obispo, a little hamlet about half-way across the Isthmus of Panama, that being as far as the railroad was finished. We arrived at the station late in the evening, and slept in our seats that night. I was on the watch that I might be ready to spring, at the first alarm, to Polly's side should anything occur, and suppose my brother did the same in behalf of Mary Jane. There were many bushrangers prowl-ing around at that time, on the watch for returning Califor-nians with their bags of gold. We got through the night without a surprise, and were up early and on the road for Panama. There were mules provided for the ladies, but we men had to go afoot, and some of us were glad to hang to the mules' tails before we got through; but we arrived in time to go aboard the boat that was to take us to the Golden Gate. When I had found my berth, we learned that we were separated from Polly and my amiable step-mother; but I soon hunted them up, finding them well cared for at a little distance from our berth. I helped Polly set up things a little, and then went on deck, meet-ing Mary Jane face to face.

" Hulloa, Mary Jane, how do you do ? "

" I am feeling splendid this morning. The air is so pure on this side that I think I shall spend most of the trip on deck. I have not seen much of you of late."

" No," I replied ; " I have been looking pretty closely after my sister."

"Well, how does she do?"

" Oh, she is all right."

She took hold of my hands and led me to a settee, where we were soon seated.

" I was observing you two the other day when you were at the table, and I should never take you to be brother and sister, as you do not look a bit alike."

"Well, I know that we don't look alike, but I will tell you how it is. When I landed in Australia I was very young, and living there so long, and growing up with a strange people, I lost my own identity, and took on the characteristics of the people that I was with."

" Yes, I have heard that there would be some changes in appearances, but I did not think that it would be so pronounced as in your case."

" Well, you see," I went on, " the climate has a good deal to do with it ; and again, Nature does her works in mysterious ways, and they are past finding out."

Just at that moment I saw my brother headed our way. I felt a little alarmed lest he might interfere, as he might think me a little too familiar with Mary Jane. I asked her not to say anything to my brother of what we had been talking.

" As you know, I want to see what he will say when I introduce her to him as my real sister, and not a mutual friend, as he now thinks she is.— Hulloa, Jim," said I, have you got well settled in our new quarters ? "

" Oh, yes, I think everything is all right now ; you had better go down yourself and see."

" Yes, Jim, I was just thinking that I would go down " ; and started at once below.

Things were lovely after that. I would flirt first with one and then with the other, as I found one on deck while the other was below ; but took care not to let my brother see me flirt with Mary Jane. I had concluded to let him have her the most of the time.

One day I saw my brother in close conversation with Mary Jane's uncle, and concluded that he was pumping the old man and trying to find out how many bonds the old fellow had. I thought by appearances that things were not to my brother's liking, since he left in rather an abrupt way and went below. I felt sorry for him, because I wanted to see him get an anchor to windward, since I thought that I had got one well to windward and my anchor grounded.

One fine morning we sighted the Golden Gate, and that was a signal for a stampede. Everybody was running hither and thither, while carpetbags and bundles began to appear on deck thick and fast. We soon ran into the harbor and up to the wharf.

As we made fast, I noticed among the crowd gathered on the wharf a large fellow with both hands raised above his head and singing out in some foreign tongue. As soon as Polly caught sight of him she began to wave her hands and yell at the top of her voice, starting at once for the plank, which had just been run in on deck. She reached the plank ahead of all others, and ran down to the wharf with her shawl flying in the air over her head. I followed in hot haste, knowing the critical moment had arrived. They were soon locked in each other's arms, while I stood there looking on, feeling very unimportant and sheepish. Presently, after their warm greeting, Polly's shawl fell to the ground, carrying a black and tangled mass with it. I looked up from the mass that lay in a heap at Polly's feet, and, horror of horrors! what did I see? That beautiful head of curly black hair become but a barren waste, with only a few gray hairs on a shining bare pate. I thought myself dreaming. but Polly quickly stooped down and gathered in the mass and drew the shawl over her head, saying something to her companion.

He turned to me and said in broken English,—

"I am much 'blige you for your 'tention to my sister. She you many t'anks."

The crowd began to laugh, and not wanting them to think me interested in the matter, I said,—

"Surely, sir, you have made a mistake. I never saw either of you before."

He took my late heroine by the hand and started up the wharf. Franky, coming along with a big bundle under each arm, started after them, and they were all soon lost to view in the dust that rolled up behind them.

Upon emerging from the cloud I looked for my brother. He stood on deck with both hands at his sides to keep from splitting with laughter. I sang out,—

"What in thunder are you standing there for grinning like a monkey in a fit?"

He came down with a carpetbag in each hand, but I was too blind just then to see either. I sang out,—

"Where is our baggage?"

"Well," said he, "I saw yours just now in the hands of a burly flunky going up the wharf leaving a big cloud behind them."

Determined to get one last shot at him, I sang out,—

"Well, since you have seen so much, did you see anything red in that cloud?"

"No," said he, "but I thought it looked black enough to be a thundercloud."

"Well," said I, "it was, and is full of red lightning, and will strike some one soon."

"I pointed up to a little white house and told him to go up there, as it was kept by a friend of mine, and I would soon follow. He proceeded, and going behind a pile of planks I kicked myself until black and blue. This over, I pulled myself out and went to my friend's house also.

My brother was standing in the doorway. He exclaimed,—

"Why, Jack, what is the matter with you? You look as if you had been chewed by dogs. Have you met that big brother whom I have heard you talking about, or has that lightning struck you?"

"No, Jim, neither."

"Well, then, do tell me how it happened."

"Well Jim, it was like this. You know that when I was in California before I got into a poker game with a big colored man. We had a jack pot of five dollars, and some one saw my hand and told the fellow that I had four aces, and he laid down four kings; and when he saw my hand and found out that my four aces were two deuces, he wanted me to divide the pot, and I would not, and then he told me that he would take it out of my hide when he got a good chance. I soon left the country and had forgotten all about it; and when I went behind that pile of planks, who should be sitting there but that colored man! When he saw me he got up and said, 'Ah, Jack, you are the very man I want to see'; and he quickly had me by the nape of the neck and mopped the wharf as long as he wanted to, and then gave me a kick and told me to get out or he would throw me overboard; so I got away, and here is what there is left of me."

My brother was not a bad fellow, and he would always take my part when he thought me overmatched. He pulled off his coat and said, —

"Where is the fellow? I will take the wind out of his sails in two minutes by the watch."

" Oh," said I, "he has gone up the wharf and is now out of sight."

" Well, if you are satisfied, then let him go."

We just then saw Mary Jane and her uncle go by. We mechanically turned our heads the other way as they passed. That was the last that we ever saw of Mary Jane or her friends.

Thus ended my fondest hopes of realizing on a large investment, not in smoke, but in dust, and I am sorry to say that it was not in gold dust.

Oh ! woman, woman, with all thy charms of art and grace,
Man knoweth not thy value by beauty of thy face ;
Though allied to him from earliest dawn of light on earth,
Whence may he then learn thy true worth?
Must he believe the story, weird and old,
That many say is true, so oft it has been told,
Thou art a single rib, from Adam taken at birth?
Then moulded wert thou, as a potter moulds his clay?
And art thou but a tinted, frail, and brittle vase,
Holding summer flowers, as changed from day to day,
Arranged with varying care to suit each time and taste?
Nay, loudly a voice resounding, disproves the ancient ban,
Thou art, indeed, the better half of man ;
Thou art not a wilted rose, nor yet a bric-a-brac,
But wast given unto man, as mother of the race.
Who then can tell thy value, on this broad earth,
Since time alone can reveal to man thy true worth?

CHAPTER X.

LEAVES FRISCO FOR THE GOLD MINES — CARSON CREEK MIN-
ING CAMP — THE VIGILANCE COMMITTEE OF CALI-
FORNIA AND THEIR METHODS — VARYING FORTUNES AT
MINING — TRIES NEW MINING CAMPS IN BRITISH COLUM-
BIA — TURNS TRADER — CONCILIATING THE INDIANS —
WINTERING IN THE MOUNTAINS — STARVING AND NAKED
INDIANS — ON SHORT RATIONS — PLENTY OF FOOD FOR
ONE MEAL AT LAST — THREE UNSUCCESSFUL ATTEMPTS TO
FIND THE GREAT SOURCE OF THE RIVER GOLD — GREAT
AMOUNT OF GOLD AFTERWARDS FOUND AT SOURCE OF
RIVER — DISCONTENT LEADS TO RETURN TO BOSTON —
FINALLY SETTLES DOWN TO LIVE IN CHARLESTOWN —
PLACER MINING — RETROSPECT — CONCLUSION.

WE started for Stockton on the day of our arrival at
Frisco, reaching there that night. The following morning we started for the mines, and the second night
brought us to my old friend the pirate captain. The
first mining camp that we reached was Angel's Camp.
We were without money; but finding my credit yet good,
I went to a man with whom I formerly traded when in
the country, and bought a kit of tools and started for
Carson's Creek, a distance of three miles. There I met
many of my old associates and renewed my acquaintance. We worked around Carson's Creek a month or
two, and made about twelve hundred dollars. About
that time the party for whom I formerly worked, building
the high fluming, hearing I was back in the country
again, sent for me to come up to Murphy's Camp and go
to work for them. They were then paying seventy-five
dollars a month, but offered me one hundred dollars and

board.   Mining had become rather dull, so my brother and I went to work for the company, and remained about two months, and then went back to mining again.

Finally my brother went south, believing that he could do better.   In a few days he returned and reported that he had found a better camp and better mining also, so we packed off for Coultersville, which was the name of the camp.

At that time the Vigilance Committee was organized at San Francisco; and it was none too soon, as the rougher element throughout the mining region was uncontrolled and going to great length in their unlawful acts.   The shooting of a Mr. King, the editor of one of the daily papers, by a man named Casey, was the immediate cause of the forming of the committee.   We received the San Francisco *Bulletin* daily, hence kept pretty well posted.

Much that this committee did has passed from my memory.   It was said that my old friend, Billy Mulligan, was banished, and Yankee Sullivan was jailed, but on the next morning was found dead, lying in a pool of blood with a case knife by his side, and a cut in one of his arms, having bled himself to death.

It was believed at that time that Yankee Sullivan had been a convict in Australia, but had run away and come to the United States and drifted to California.   The vigilants were intending to send him back.   He, learning of that fact, preferred death to further servitude in that far-off country, therefore committed suicide.   A number of the same class of men, from the same country, were hung.   On one occasion three or four were hung from one beam; and when the committee were ready to swing them off, one of the number sung out, "Here we go, gals," and they entered eternity, while those words were yet ringing in the ears of the spectators, of which there were many, both male and female.

At Coultersville the claim that my brother had staked out prospected pretty well, but water was scarce, and to work the claim profitably we needed to ground sluice about four feet of top dirt, therefore I built a reservoir that would overflow about one acre, it taking me two months alone in building the dam, while my brother worked in town at four dollars a day, which paid our expenses during the time. I dug a ditch to the claim, and when the water came we sluiced the claim down and went to work with sluice boxes, when, after a week's work, we found the claim would not pay expenses.

In prospecting we had hit the only pay dirt in the claim, and before abandoning it a freshet came and swept away my two months' work in less than two hours, although I had a three-foot floodgate, which proved not half large enough.

After that my brother got discouraged and soon left for home, I remaining a little longer in the country.

Going home one day from another camp I saw a tall man about three hundred yards from the road, and immediately recognized that well-remembered form, Long Jim, whom I had left a few years before at Hobartstown, Van Diemen's Land, dealing in firewood. Like the rest of mankind, he had taken the fever, sold out, and come to California. At this time he remained a few weeks with me before we parted. He was the last of my many shipmates that I met with, being the tenth one inside of ten years. All were many thousand miles from where I first met them, and all in a different business to that engaged in when I first met them.

At that time the excitement was at its height about the Fraser River mines, and, as a matter of course, I went there with the crowd. Notwithstanding all my experience, I had not got over the habit of running after all the new strikes, always having the idea that I would yet strike that bonanza looked forward to so long.

Returning to San Francisco, I there took passage to Victoria, British Columbia, which is on Vancouver Island, lying a few miles off the coast of British Columbia.

Miners at that time appeared to be as anxious to get out of the mines and to Frisco as they were in 1849 to get to them. Every stage returning was loaded, and looked like a swarm of bees; all wanted to get there first.

We arrived at Victoria in good time, and found every one alive with business. I bought an outfit and embarked on board of a little steamboat that plied between Victoria and Fort Hope, a landing about seventy miles up the river.

We soon landed, filled with hope, and began to prospect the sand bars. Before my first pan of dirt was all washed out, I thought I was about to realize my fondest hopes. When the water was washed over the dirt, it appeared to be half gold. I settled it to the bottom of the pan by shaking the pan a little, and then washed the dirt carefully off, while, as the sand grew gradually less, my hopes ran high, until finally, nearing the bottom, I shook the pan, which caused the gold to spread out, and the display added to my ardor. I thought that before washing the dirt all out there might be about three or four dollars; but when the lot was washed, fifty cents seemed nearer its worth, and even at that rate it would pay well to sluice; with plenty of water near at hand, perhaps one hundred dollars a day.

Taking my gold into camp, my mates eagerly flocked around to see the result of the prospecting; each making a guess what it would weigh, the guesses being as high as two dollars down to fifty cents.

The gold scales were adjusted, and we soon had the stuff in them. A two-dollar weight was put in, and down went that end of the beam, and down went our hopes with it; a one-dollar weight was tried, and yet that end hugged the table. Becoming desperate, I removed the weight and put in a one-cent weight, determined to end the suspense, and the end of the beam that had seemed to be frozen down flew up. When we got the thing to balance, we had four cents in pure gold.

Some of the boys began to look over their loose change to see if they had enough to take them back to San Francisco, while others began to talk about home and the dear ones left behind. Sick as we all were, by keeping quiet a few days we improved a little, and finally regained our strength and courage again. By examining the gold with a lens, I found that it had been beaten while travelling in the rivers until it was as thin as gold leaf, and concluded that it had travelled a long way and that the fountain head from whence it came must be near the head waters of the river. The banks of the river rose in terraces back from one hundred to five hundred yards, which were composed of sand and gravel deposited by the wash of the river. Gold could be found in about all of this mass of gravel to a greater or less degree. The gold would be little else than small atoms, and from these small atoms running down to particles only to be seen with a powerful glass.

The head man of that section of the country was a Mr. MacLane. He was agent for the Hudson Bay Trading Company, and had been in the Rocky Mountains about thirty years. I learned through him that he used to get considerable gold from the Indians up at a place near the head of Fraser River called Fort Alexander, the gold coming mostly from a creek called Williams Creek, which emptied into the river, and that the gold was coarse.

He said that in trading he would put the gold into a gun barrel, and then put in the rod and measure with his fingers the length of the rod above the barrel. He would then empty out the gold and fill with powder to the same height, and exchange the powder for the gold, even measure.

What MacLane said confirmed me regarding the fountain head being far off, and convinced me that it would require a long tramp to reach it.

Some eight or ten of us made arrangements with Mac-Lane to furnish us with horses to pack our kit, and an Indian as a guide to pilot us through the country up to Thompson's River, which formed a junction with Fraser River, about one hundred miles above Fort Hope. We took that route in preference to going up the river.

This river cuts through the Cascade range of mountains, which is a continuation of the chain which runs the entire length of this continent. In South America the Andes, in Mexico and Colorada the Rocky Mountains, in California the Sierra Nevada Mountains, and in British Columbia the Cascade, and how much farther they continue I know not. We arrived at our journey's end in about a week, and found a little gold on Thompson's River, but not enough to pay. We had struck Thompson's about ten miles above the junction of Fraser, and continued down to the forks, where the gold was about the same as at Fort Hope. After knocking around a week or two, eating horse flesh, and paying fifty cents a pound for it, I concluded to go down the river, prospecting on the way. Arrived at Fort Yale, which town is about ten miles above Fort Hope, I met a large number of miners going up the river with their kits on their backs, with some few canoes which they had got above the rapids by lifting them out of the water and carrying them half a mile or so around the rapids. Fort Hope was as high up the river as the steamboats could go, and Fort Yale as high as anything could get except a canoe, and it was with much difficulty that canoes got farther up the river. Many that made the attempt were lost.

Finally, I bought a few trinkets and a horse, and started up the river to trade with the Indians, and managed to peddle out my wares and mine a little at the same time; and as my bank account increased, I obtained a fresh supply, thus spending a part of that summer. At Fort Yale, where I had been stopping a few weeks, one day there was a large arrival of miners from up the river. They reported that the Indians were killing the miners, cutting off their heads and throwing them into the river. The miners kept coming into town, until we had several hundred added to the inhabitants. The week previous to this influx we had seen several headless trunks floating past the town, but did not know the cause until hearing the report of the miners.

No one appeared to know just what to do. I concluded that something ought to be done, because we could not afford to let a few Indians drive us all out of the country; so finding a man that could talk pretty well for spokesman, told him what ought to be done, which was to get all the miners together, form ourselves into a company, take a couple of weeks' supply of food and go up the river and treat with the Indians, and find out what caused the Indians to be so troublesome. Past experience with natives and Indians had taught me that, as a general rule, they will not trouble the whites if treated as well as you would do your dog, hence believed that the miners had, in some way, wronged them.

The man that I selected to take the stump harangued his audience about half an hour, and the miners concluded to form themselves into squads and go up the river, which we did in less than two hours after I made the motion. We marched over a long and rough trail, and the second day out came to an Indian camp. We found the Indians friendly, and willing to treat with us. They said that they did not want to be disturbed in their own haunts, and they wanted the whites to keep their word. They claimed that many of the miners had deceived them. They had packed heavy loads many miles up the river, and then the miners would only give them half what they had agreed to pay, and if they complained they would get a kick and be driven off, and in some cases without any pay at all. We assured them that kind of treatment would be stopped, and we gave them a little tobacco and a few small trinkets, after which they agreed to be at peace. We continued on up the river, and made similar arrangements with the rest of the little tribes on the river. We came to one bar that the miners had deserted, and I found, after prospecting, that it paid pretty well, so concluded to remain and let the others go on up the stream. An old log-cabin and a brush tent on the bar, which had been abandoned by the miners, became my domicile. The cabin was about ten feet square and the walls three feet high, with logs laid over the top, and boughs piled on top of them. It afforded a good shelter in dry weather, but was leaky in wet. A hole three feet square, cut in one side, answered for both door and window. I slept the first night in that pen, but found it cold, since I could get no fire near enough to keep me warm, so the next night took to the brush tent, the end of which was open, and by building a little fire at that end, found that I could keep myself warm at night.

The Indians used to come around at night when I was cooking my supper, and then, after I had finished, they would get into their canoes and cross the river to their own camp. They supplied me with salmon. A half-dozen matches would pay for a large fish that would last me two days, with a little flour. Back a few rods in the forest, while gathering dry wood, I found lots of flour and mining tools, which the miners had buried, but the flour was not fit to eat, so my find did not help me much.

In about a week the party that went up the river to make treaties with the Indians returned, having accomplished their work. They went on down, while I remained with my dusky neighbors another week, and then followed them. On my way down I passed through a canyon that could only be avoided by going several miles around. To get into the canyon I had to slide over a cliff down an almost perpendicular crevice, one hundred feet, and the exit from the place was about as hazardous. I arrived at the cliff about an hour before sundown. It would require at least two hours to pass through the canyon. I slid down the narrow crevice, not more than three feet wide and in some places less than two feet wide, and getting into the valley, concluded to camp for the night. I built a little fire by the side of the trail, ate my luncheon, and after dark spread my blankets for the night. About midnight I was awakened by voices, and sprang up, and before me stood three Indians. Stirring my fire and putting on some dry brush, it soon blazed up, and I discovered the Indians wore a very friendly look on their dusky faces. I soon filled my pipe and gave them a smoke all around. The Hudson Bay Company had introduced a jargon among the natives which was very easy to learn, and I had picked up a little of it. So after they had smoked and chatted awhile they went on again rejoicing, while I went to sleep and slept till daylight undisturbed. At daylight my tramp was again resumed, and the canyon left behind.

A few miles below the canyon I met half a dozen miners and two Indians going down to Fort Yale, and joined them. We soon came to where the river had cut its way through the mountain and had left walls on each side, nearly perpendicular, five hundred feet high. We could avoid that dangerous place only by going around about a mile. Part of the company went around, and two white men that remained with me sent their kits around, while I kept my kit with me, thinking that if I went over the cliff and down into the river my kit could go with me. I had a pick, pan, and shovel, seven dry salmon and two fresh ones, one pair of blankets, and a few cooking utensils. They were lashed to my back, and left my hands free for use. The two Indians remained with us, and carried only an old gun each. The two Indians started first, and had to hand their guns to each other in order to use their hands. The Indians went up all right, and one of my companions made the trip all right. The second miner started up, with myself directly after him. The height here was about fifty feet. We then ascended to a bench, and the trail that we travelled to get there had gradually risen until the spot where we began to climb the steep cliff was about five hundred feet above the river. It was so high that pine-trees on the narrow banks of the river looked like little shrubs. The river at that point had narrowed down to about a hundred feet wide, consequently was very rapid and appeared to be like a pot boiling. My man climbed slowly along, I bringing up the rear. We had about the same foot and hand hold that the Australian natives have when walking up a tree on the bark. We had got up about half-way when my friend turned his head and looked down the yawning abyss. The sight was so appalling that he lost his presence of mind and sang out, "I shall fall, I shall fall!"

I sang out, "Look at the rock, damn you!"

He turned his gaze toward the ledge, and finally got up, with me following him.

The situation was so desperate that desperate means were necessary to avoid the catastrophe which was impending. My head was level with his feet, and my large pack reached out behind; and with my pack and body hanging over the cliff, it will easily be seen that if he went I surely would have gone with him, flying through the air to our deaths. After all danger was passed, I looked back and viewed the situation, and determined, that if we came to another pass like that, to go around it if the distance was a thousand miles. We pushed on, finding no more very hard passes, and in due time reached Fort Yale.

It was getting toward fall by that time, nevertheless I decided to make a few trips up the river, carrying flour to sell to the miners, who were ready to pay a good price for it. Those intending to remain through the winter high up the river were laying in their winter supply of provisions. At Thompson's Forks, a distance of a hundred miles above Fort Yale, flour was worth eighty cents a pound. I began carrying flour up to that place on my back, taking two fifty-pound sacks at a load, with a small supply of grub to live on, and would make the trip in four days over that terrible rough trail, avoiding the worst places by going around. Selling my first load, I returned for another, but did not make many trips like this, for it was too hard work.

Frequently, when travelling up the river, entering a camp of Indians, I would stop awhile with them to rest, and as soon as my pack was laid down, the chief would untie all my bundles, overhaul my traps, hunting for powder, which I seldom carried, knowing too well what they wanted it for. Notwithstanding our treaties made with them, a miner would occasionally be missing, and we dared not sell them powder. On one occasion the little ones, seeing my budget of food, began to cry, and I gave them some bread and meat, which stopped their squalling. Ever after that, going into their camp, I would have to stop, eat salmon with them, and exchange food with them.

Many people would have been disgusted even to approach within five rods of their camps, since their fish and game were dressed near where cooked, and nothing was cleaned away. The accumulation would emit an odor rank enough to be recognized afar off. While many would shun such camps, it was not so with me. On meeting the Indians, I was an Indian for the time being. By adopting that method they readily took to me, and I have never been treated better by any white people than by the wild tribes in the many different parts of the world visited by me, and have found the old saying true, " When you are with the Romans, do as the Romans do."

As long ago as King George's time, the English and Americans were trading with the Indians on the north coast. The English dealt pretty fairly with the Indians, while the Americans used to play Yankee tricks on them; sometimes the Indians, finding out they were being cheated by the Americans, after that the natives disliked the Americans and liked the English, being particularly prejudiced against Boston men. When meeting a white man, they ask him, nearly the first question, if he is a Boston man or a King George man. If you tell him that you are a Boston man, they reply, " Wake close Boston man," meaning in their jargon that a Boston man is no good; but if you tell him that you are a King George man, he will say, " High as close King George man," which means, King George man very good. He is ready and willing to serve a King George man, but will have little to do with and rather avoids a Boston man.

An American myself, yet I have found that the name " Yankee " has a taint in many parts of the world, while the word " Englishman " has a bad reputation in many other parts of the world, more particularly so in the eastern hemisphere than in the western.

Mr. MacLane, of the Hudson Bay Company, certainly took advantage of the Indians when giving four fingers of powder for four fingers of gold; but there were no Yankees in that camp to run opposition to him, and the company had gained the confidence of their customers. The English were more crafty than the Americans, and by their craft saved their good name, while the Americans went in too rash at the beginning, and through that lost caste. I have learned that none of the savage people who inhabit this earth will be the first to dispute the approach of the white man. They rather invite him and treat him well if they are treated well, but they have manhood enough to resent abuse.

After extensive travel among savages, and carefully studying the habits of savage people, it seems to me that these children of the forest are the happiest people on earth and the most contented with their lot, whether it be cast in the tropics or in the Frigid Zone. The homes of the savages in the tropics are indeed cast in Paradise. Who that ever visited any of those islands in the Pacific denies this fact? From the earth springs forth spontaneously all that can tempt the palate, and all that is necessary is to stretch forth the hand and pluck and eat. What more do we get that is of any real value to man? The natives in the north do not fare as well as those of tropical countries, but the large rivers afford fish, and the forest, game and wild fruit. In winter, living in dugouts under ground, with a good supply of dry fish and fruit, they are happy, and only want to be let alone.

How ruthlessly they have been dealt with! The advance guard of civilization is upon them. The Indians' buffalo have vanished, the salmon has been cleaned out of their rivers and shipped to all parts of the world, while the game has been killed or driven off, and now little remains but wild berries for the Indian to live upon. Civilization means annihilation when applied to these people; and a climb to any elevated point once the landmark of some Indian nation, and gazing over the broad expanse, you will find these words force themselves unbidden to your lips, " Lo the poor Indian, oh where, oh where hast thou gone, thou once mighty race!"

After a few trips backing flour to the miners, I went to work at carpentering, in company with another. We built a log-hut which was used as a house to live and a shop to work in. We had plenty of work at fair pay.

Occasionally some one would come down the river and report a rich strike on some bar well up the river, but I kept on at work, paying little attention to the reports. Winter had fairly set in, and there was plenty of snow. In the first part of January, hearing that at a place called Bridge River, a small stream entering the Fraser River some hundred and fifty miles above Fort Yale, coarse gold and some nuggets had been struck worth as high as fifty dollars, I sold out to my partner, sacked up two weeks' supply of food, and on the twelfth day of January started up the river. Starting late in the afternoon I did not get many miles away, and camped at a cabin for the night, and next morning found about three feet of snow had fallen during the night, which, with what was on the ground before, gave me about four and one half feet to travel through.

After starting out and working my way through the snow about ten miles, I met a colored man.

" By golly, master," said he, " you make road for me and I make road for you."

It was a little easier travelling after our meeting. When I came to a cabin late in the afternoon, I remained with the owner over night; but when no friendly cabin was to be found, I would get under the low hanging boughs of some small tree, beneath which would be quite a space of open ground with a circular wall of snow some three feet high, which would make it a very comfortable place to camp in.

In this way I advanced up the river, with some very narrow escapes where the banks were steep and covered with ice. At those places had there been one misstep I would have been launched into holes in the river where the water was too rapid to freeze them over, and there would have been no chance for escape, as one would have been carried under the ice.

One afternoon approaching a cabin, and finding no one there and the door shut, I opened it and went in. Within was but a rudely constructed berth and a few smouldering embers in the fireplace, showing the place to have been recently occupied. I concluded to camp there for the night. The night before there had been about an inch of snow, and I noticed a track about two feet wide on the ground leading from the door down to the river and along over the ice to a water hole in the middle of the river. The strip showed something had been drawn from the cabin to the hole and then dumped in. A man's tracks were seen by the side of this strip to the hole and back again. I thought little about the matter until after lying down to sleep ; then while thinking over the day's tramp, remembered meeting a traveller not many miles below this cabin, who stopped and chatted with me, but who appeared to be excited and in a hurry to get to Fort Yale and from there out of the country as quickly as he could. When I had time to deliberate on the matter and the condition of things at and around the cabin, I came to the conclusion that murder had been committed in this cabin, and the victim thrown into the river, and the fellow whom I had met was the man who had committed the crime. In the morning I started early, wanting to get away from the place, since if found there by any one either going up or down the river, and it becoming known that murder had been committed at the cabin, how could it be proven that I was not the guilty one? After travelling about three miles and reaching a little camp, I told the miners what I had seen at the cabin. They said that two men had camped at that place, but took no steps to investigate the matter.

I once saw a man shot down where the sum at stake was but the price of a glass of whiskey. Being the only eyewitness to the crime, I reported it, but was not even called to testify, and the man who shot the victim was allowed to go scot-free, and this happened under the British flag.

The only man that I ever saw hung was hung for robbing a man of a petty sixpence. He was convicted of highway robbery and executed. This also took place under the British flag.

Continuing my journey, I pushed on, and after two weeks of hard tramping reached Bridge River. Going up this stream about three miles from where it empties into the Fraser River, I came to a cabin the occupant of which was one of my old California partners. He had caught the fever and was forced to start later after me, had taken another route across the country and struck the river near that point.

Renewing our friendship, I camped with him for a few days, during which he worked with me, and we soon had a cabin ready for me to move into. Finding a large bowlder which stood about ten feet high, with one side flat and perpendicular, we built the cabin against it, and the flat side answered the double purpose of end wall and fireplace. The walls were made about six feet high, and a few logs were placed on top and covered with boughs, making a very good winter house, which was necessary, as it was very cold at that time.

We tried to mine a little by building fires on the bars of the river, but could not do much, since it would soon freeze after our fires went out.

Some three miles above us was a camp of Indians. They were very short of food; the fish would not come that far up, since the miners had contaminated the water with their mining machines, and the game had also been scared off. All that was left the Indians for their winter supply of food were dry berries and a few horses, which they were killing and eating. They frequently came up to our camp and begged for something to eat, but we could not give them anything, since our supply was very limited, being on short allowance. Should I have eaten all my appetite craved at one meal, it would have been as much as I allowed myself for a week's supply. We did not know how long it would be before supplies would reach that locality, on account of the large amount of snow on the ground. This tribe of Indians wore no clothing except a little strip of blanket thrown over their shoulders and a part of their bodies; their legs, feet, and arms were all bare, men, women, and children. While I could not remain outside of my hut without freezing my fingers or ears, they did not appear to mind the cold. When they saw me wash my dishes they would drink the dishwater, to get the little grease that might be in it. Toward spring, wishing to learn how soon we might expect supplies, one day I started down Fraser River a few miles to a little camp, and finding a man who sold dinners at one dollar each, took dinner with him. He set before me a pan with about four quarts of boiled beans and two or three pounds of bacon boiled with the beans, and a large loaf of bread, telling me to help myself. It is needless to say what I ate, but the next customer that came along and wanted a plate of boiled bacon and beans had to wait until they were stewed. Having been about half starved all winter, I could not let such an opportunity to feast on golden beans pass, as I had let pass many golden opportunities when golden nuggets seemed of far less value than these rich brown, yellow beans, because beans could be eaten and gold could not.

Miners are sometimes so situated they would cheerfully exchange a pint of gold for a pint of flour. At a camp, where the miners were snowed in in one of the northern camps of California, and were without food, a man got to town with one sack of fifty pounds of flour, which was all the flour there was in camp. There was plenty of gold, but nothing to eat, and this man peddled his flour at his own price, it being said that one man paid three hundred dollars for one pint of flour. Five thousand dollars was realized on the sack of flour. Some of the miners protested against the high price, but the fellow replied that flour was the same price that it had been before the big snowfall that had shut out supplies, but that gold had declined in value, and as it was a matter of life and death, the miners had to submit.

When spring opened we found Bridge River was not the source from whence the large amount of gold came that was found scattered over so large a tract of country below. There was some gold of a coarse nature there, but I knew by indications there must be a very rich country somewhere above, so we started up Fraser River again with a couple of weeks' supply of rations on our backs. We pushed on past several miners who were getting a little coarse gold, which gave us courage to go on farther, and after a week's tramp we came to a camp of eight or ten men. They told us that four men with horses, belonging to the Hudson Bay Company, passed through their camp the day before we arrived, on their way to Fort Alexander, and that they wanted some of the miners to go along with them, but no one wanted to go.

We were sorry that we had not arrived sooner, as that was just what we wanted to do, we told them, as we wanted to get up as far as we could on the river.

They said that they were as far from home as they wanted to be, and that the Indians up there were bad.

My partner had not had the experience among the wild men that I had, and finally decided not to go any farther up, so I started alone. After two days' march, meeting a party returning who said they could do nothing farther up, they persuaded me to turn back, and I returned to my partner. After working a few days with him, but not being satisfied with what we were getting, one morning I told him I would make one more attempt to get farther up the river, and started again that day, travelling on in high spirits and very hopeful. After getting a little farther up that time than the first, I again met four or five men on horseback, who said they had been several miles above that point and could find no better prospects than below, and they were content to leave the country above to the Indians.

Again I returned to my late camp, and, after a day of consideration, replenished my stock of supplies, bought a rifle, thinking that if short of provisions I might shoot something to help me through, and started once more alone and pushed on over the trail which I had so repeatedly passed over within the last two weeks. I passed by all my previous marks and through a few Indian camps, whose inhabitants had nothing to say to me. I found that with now and then a little snow, and occasionally a hot day, the trail that the Hudson Bay Company's men had made was in some places quite obliterated. Below on the river I had found some bare ground, but now there was perpetual snow. I could not make much progress through the deep snow, and there were but few signs of the old trail, which seemed but a little depression in the large fields of snow.   After a couple of days of hard tramping, and camping where night overtook me, I concluded fate was against me, although I could see that golden glitter ahead in the distance which is so fascinating to all miners, and it was beckoning me on a little farther.   But my desire outlived my powers of endurance, and it was next to impossible for me to advance. I thought that if there was gold before me it was not for me, and would have to remain until time and coming generations should bring it to light of day.   I turned again for the third and last time, and slowly and sadly retraced my steps, arriving at the old camp and finding my late partner.

We then journeyed down the river a few miles, and got hold of an old rocker, and went to work on a little bar, where we worked one month and took out eight hundred dollars.   Then I told my partner that he might have the claim and tools if he chose to remain, as I was going home, thinking I had money enough to carry me; and he accepted my offer and remained.

Having no shoes that would do to tramp in over a rough country two or three hundred miles, I got an old saddle flap and the top of an old boot leg, and made myself a pair of boots, hewing out a last with an axe, and with a table fork and case knife completed the job in about half a day.   These shoes were worn three hundred miles and were then good for as much more wear, but I threw them away, being in a civilized country and ashamed of my big feet.

The day after completing the shoes I started down the stream with a limited supply of food, and after being a few days on the road found myself completely out, and a long way from where more could be procured.   One morning, after eating my last small sandwich, I pushed on at a rapid rate on a trail leading several

miles through a deep forest, which cut off bad canyons
on the banks of the river. Towards sundown arriving
at a camp which had been used the night before, there
still remaining a little fire and, scattered about, a lot of
dough that had been half boiled, I decided to occupy the
camp that night. The dough was soon gathered up and
in the ashes roasting. A ham bone was also found that
had a little meat on it and a large amount of gristle, and
when my bread was baked I sat down to my frugal re-

GNAWING A BONE UP IN BRITISH COLUMBIA.

past. I ate my bread and gnawed that bone as faithfully
as ever dog gnawed bone, laying it carefully aside, lest I
might feel like trying it again in the morning. Retiring
soon after, I rested well, and dreamt of the children of
Israel in the wilderness being fed with manna. In the
morning, early astir, there was nothing for breakfast but
the bone of the previous evening, so I gnawed it for half
an hour, then laid it where it could easily be seen by
any one who might come after me.

That day I arrived where there was plenty to eat, at a little store on the banks of the river. Having had nothing sweet for several months, I began to crave it, and, finding the storekeeper had a keg of molasses on tap, I bought a pint, paying three dollars for it, and sat down and ate the pint without potatoes or hard bread, as I used to dine on in Australia.

I once heard of a case similar to my own in this line. When our government had surveyors working across the Isthmus of Panama to ascertain if it was possible to build a canal, the men had cut their way through the brush and lived mostly on bitter nuts. When they got through down to a station, the first thing they wanted was molasses ; a bottle was given them and they emptied it, probably as quickly as I did the vessel which contained my pint.

After resting a few hours, I pushed on again, reaching Fort Yale in due time. From Fort Yale I went to Fort Hope, and there took the steamer for Victoria, and at the latter place booked for San Francisco, where we arrived in a few days.

After one week's stay in Frisco I took passage for New York, at which place we arrived in about four weeks without mishap. From New York I returned to Boston again, with about one hundred dollars in hand.

I visited around a little, and spent some money, not wanting my friends to know just how I stood financially. After buying a new outfit of store clothing, there was not much money left, so I began to look around for employment ; but being unsuccessful, I told my friends one day that I was going back to California again, ostensibly to look after some valuable mining claim left behind that was liable to be jumped if I did not return and look after it. The real object of my departure in such haste was to get to New York while there was money enough left to get there. I did not have money enough to get to California, but thought that if I could get to New York I might get a chance to work my way to California. On my arrival in New York I went direct to the steamers that plied between New York and Aspinwall, and applied for a chance to work my passage to Aspinwall, but found they had all the crew needed, and there was no chance for me without about one hundred dollars to pay over to the captain as hush money or passage money.

Roaming around the city the rest of the day, and having but little money left, I bought some bread and cheese and ate it on the street. About sundown finding myself in front of a hotel, without observing whether it was a palatial or modest structure, I entered it at once, not intending to beat the hotel, as in Lowell, for I had money enough to pay for my lodging. It has ever been my rule to pay as I went along when having money, but when without money to do the next best thing.

On entering this hotel I approached the clerk and asked for a bed for the night. He asked how high priced I wanted to go. I replied not very high, as my means were limited.

He started with me at once, and after we had arrived at our destination I thought he must have misunderstood me, believing I wanted to go very high, since he had taken me so painfully near heaven that the stars were plainly to be seen twinkling through the skylight. I did not complain however, thinking that if I was low in pocket, they had given me the highest berth in the establishment, from which I could look down on millionnaires, feeling myself elevated above them.

Early the following day I started for the steamer that would take me to Fall River, soon being on my way to the Hub again, where I arrived Sunday morning with but seventy-five cents in my wallet.

Not wishing to see any of my friends just then, I hunted for a sailors' boarding-house, and came across a building said to be the Sailors' Home. Entering I told the man in charge that I was comparatively a stranger in the city and wanted to stop there until the next morning.

He replied that they did not make a practice of taking people in that way, but as I was a stranger they would accommodate me.

I expected to renew my acquaintance at that place with that well-remembered ancient stew, but found the sailors who were domiciled at that institution had left that savory dish far behind.

On Monday morning I partook of a hasty breakfast of regular old-fashioned boarding-house hash, and paid my bill, which took my last cent.

I was now in Boston again, no better off financially than when leaving seventeen years before; all I had gained was a little knowledge of this wicked world. I had thrown away many fortunes or let them slip from my grasp, and now came regrets when too late. Realizing that it would not help matters to cry over spilt milk, and having gotten out of many a tight place before, I did not despair. Having an uncle at that time in Charlestown, I started out and had the good fortune of finding him, and stated my case to him. He directed me where he thought work could be found, and on going to the place I secured a job before noon that day at the munificent salary of one dollar a day.

I was as contented with my pay as when getting one hundred dollars a day, and worked for three weeks before letting my friends know of my return, and when informed my welfare appeared to be a matter of indifference to them. Perhaps, as I had been absent from home so much of my life, I appeared more like a stranger to them than a relative. I felt that they were strangers to me, and I was at work with strangers, but soon got acquainted, and worked at a dollar a day for about a year, when, getting better acquainted with my work, I got more wages, and so continued until I received four dollars a day. Soon after that I went into business for myself, succeeding well for a while. I met with a few quite heavy losses, but that did not discourage me; I worked the harder to make it up. By hard work and practising economy I have managed, after thirty years, to lay up enough which with care may carry me through.

A few years after my return from British Columbia I met a man who was there when I left, and he reported that two years after my leaving the country a party managed to get up to the head waters of Fraser River and struck on to Williams Creek. They found gold so rich that two men panned out sixty thousand dollars in one day. The place is now known all over the world as the Caribou Mines. I can but vainly imagine what might have been if I had reached that creek two years in advance of all others, as I tried to do on three successive occasions.

Had I discovered the gold, which undoubtedly would have made a large nugget, I could have used but a portion, and the balance would have been left for others to quarrel over after my death, therefore I think myself as well, if not better off than I would have been had I been successful in discovering the new mine.

Although my experience at mining is of no practical use to me now, it may be to others who may desire to seek fortunes at mining, as there is yet plenty of the yellow metal awaiting the miner's pick to bring it to view.

Of course I would not advise would-be miners to go to the rich parts that I visited, thinking to find them so still, since a great change has taken place. They would find the ground in a worse condition than it would be if ten thousand swine to the acre had been penned there, but there is plenty of unexplored ground as yet on this continent. If we can ever have the opportunity to explore Old Mexico, and from there on south, I believe we will find that what the people in those countries have found will prove but a drop in the bucket to what remains.

My experience having been in placer mining more than quartz mining, my remarks apply specially to that kind. It makes but little difference to the placer miner where the gold comes from; all that he needs to know is where to find it, and where to drive his stakes for the first choice, thereby saving much valuable time. Had I known where to drive my stakes when first going to mining in California, I would have soon been rich, had I kept at it.

It is this information I wish to give to others, since I believe there is yet plenty of virgin ground undiscovered, which will sooner or later be found and worked. It should be borne in mind that all placer gold is the deposit from quartz gold that has been disturbed by the action of the elements, and after the veins have been broken much of the gold is liberated, falling to the ground to be moved by the action of the water, while its own gravitation helps it along. It is the water and the gold's own weight that have all to do with the forming of placer mines. Therefore, in order to find gold liberated from the mother lode, we must study the nature of the ground and note the peculiar appearance of the water in different streams, also examine the bends and turns, the falls and long stretches of comparatively still water, and places where it moves slowly. All these should be carefully looked over, since they all tend to form either eddies or bars, thereby giving the gold a chance to settle. On the inner side of an elbow in the river will be found a bar which may show an eddy; and if gravel and pebbles have settled at that point, gold may also have settled there. A stretch of still water is oftentimes proof that heavy bodies settle along the banks and river bed; and also where the country rock is slate the same tendency is shown. This rock will often run across streams making rifts in which gold will lodge and remain until removed by some force of the elements, or dug out by the miners. Where clay is found in the beds of streams there gold is likely to be found, since clay holds the gold. The miner should look for all eddies and all other places where, in his judgment, the water would lose its force on any material which it was carrying along, and should drive his stake covering all such places.

Experience teaches me that nine times in ten the miner will strike the richest spots in the stream, let it be river, creek, or gulch, if experienced in the business. Gold moves a good deal faster when there is a freshet, as it is carried by the force of the current. In such cases the streams are swollen much over their banks, and much gold is carried high up out of reach of the current and soon becomes buried several inches under the sand. The force of the water being less high up than in the middle of the stream, much gold is found quite high on the banks. Again, streams are constantly wearing down and the rivers frequently change their courses on account of being blocked by landslides, which often occur in countries where there is a large fall of rain in winter instead of snow. The tenderfoot, as beginners are called, needs to be very careful when sinking his shaft, and upon nearing the bottom should try his dirt often with his washpan. He can always tell when near bed rock, finding considerable clay mixed with the gravel, a good many pebbles and much stain of different colors. If in the vicinity of gold he will almost invariably find black sand, which is little else than magnetic iron, which appears to be closely associated with gold found in placers. In both California and Australia I have seen large amounts of gold thrown out of a shaft and not discovered until after a rain, which would wash the gold out of the dirt, when it would be seen in plenty. When one gets a shaft down to bed rock, if it is found hard and quite smooth, not much gold will be found if any. But if the bed is soft and rotten, as it often is, gold is likely to be found, from the fact that there is something to hold it. It will thus be seen that all of the gold found in placers is dependent on chance whether it remains at rest at any one place for any length of time. If the miner happens to strike it when at rest, he gets it ; if not, it will take up its line of march again, with occasionally a rest which may in some cases continue for many ages before the conditions are favorable for it to move again. Gold will wear away quite fast when travelling, and is often beaten as with a hammer by the stones that are tumbled around by the water. It continues to wear, travel, and rest until reduced to particles, and finally passes into the ocean unless reclaimed by man snatching it from the destroying grasp of the elements.

Undoubtedly there are many places in the bed of the ocean that would pay well in gold if it were known where they were located; the sands and gravel could be dredged and brought to the surface.

Miners have been known to make good pay at washing the sand on the sea beach between California and Oregon. The gold, shifting with every tide, would be found at some new locality on the beach at the next tide. If the miner or the man who is hunting for gold in the placers will bear in mind the fact that water and specific gravity are the forces that make all gold deposits in the placer regions, he will succeed in finding the yellow metal without much trouble.

In conclusion, it has been one of the hardest tasks of my life to recount my gold experience, since it has carried me back to those old haunts, and vividly restored many familiar marks known so long ago. I have seemed to see the rich gold claims yet before me. It has caused me to wish to fly back to that time, so full of opportunities, again, as I can now better appreciate them than when they were within my very grasp. But I then held riches lightly, casting aside many rare chances, passing them by only to mourn their loss at this late day, when they should have long been forgotten. Had I received an early education I would have properly valued these opportunities. While the results of my experience can be endured, no period of time can be long enough for me to forget what might have been.

THE END.